THE GODS OF FALL:

The Immortali

Shawn-Paul Allison

iUniverse, Inc.
New York Bloomington

iUniverse books may be ordered through booksellers or by contacting:

iUniverse
1663 Liberty Drive
Bloomington, IN 47403
www.iuniverse.com
1-800-Authors (1-800-288-4677)

ISBN: 978-1-4502-1599-2 (sc)
ISBN: 978-1-4502-1600-5 (ebook)

Printed in the United States of America

iUniverse rev. date: 04/05/2010

This book is dedicated to the

Brotherhood

and to its

Ideals.

The Cabin will always be open
every Friday night at 10:30.

A special thanks goes to:

My technical assistants:

Dante Macreno
Josh Steadman
Alex Urquhart

PROLOGUE

New Orleans, Louisiana
December 1880

At the beginning of times, when the earth was fresh, the sons of Life, blessèd be they, took unto themselves choice wives, the daughters of the kings, the daughters of the rulers; choice they were these daughters of the rulers and kings. At that time and afterwards, their progeny was blessed with longevity, with life in abundance. Their sons were called the Immortali, the great ones of the age. Unlike the Nephilim of old, those giants whose age was set at one hundred and twenty years, the Immortali comforted and healed. Their touch assuaged the pain of others. Their look gave hope to the downtrodden and to the poor ones of the kingdom, the anawim *of the kingdom* (Book of Pisho from the *Kuhduush*).

Inside the main hall of the *Mansion,* as it was known, the *Maestro* was playing "Silent Night" softly on the concert grand piano. A fire blazed up and spread its warmth from the fireplace below the mantle festooned with candles and pine. An ornately decorated Christmas tree stood in front of the dining room window, warmly inviting the winter's eve to come close but blocking out the vision of fraternal preparation to those passing by on the quiet street.

In the kitchen, several cooks busied themselves with preparing the dressing, a concoction of chunky dried bread, sage, apples, celery, oysters, a dash of onion, and some zesty stock to accent various fowl and other delicious Yule treats. One chef in particular worked intensely over his oyster sauce making sure it was not too runny. The color had to be just right, not too clear, and the taste was not to overpower the dressing itself. Like musicians finely tuning their instruments, the kitchen staff worked in perfect synchronized harmony, creating the steamy notes to their scrumptiously edible symphony that would please the eyes, nose, and palate.

In the foyer, nine of the *lesser brothers*, the newly initiated, dressed in white tunics with gold trim, assembled for the introductory rite. Most stood around awaiting some type of organization from the *Confirmandi*. The First Guard tapped his staff on the hardwood floor three times. The sound ricocheted from the hall through the foyer and back again.

First Guard: *What is the hour?*
Second Guard: *It is the hour to convene.*
First Guard: *What is our duty?*
Second Guard: *To uphold sacred honor.*
First Guard: *How are we to do that?*
Second Guard: *By the sign of trust.*
First Guard: *Do all here know the sign of trust?*
Second Guard: *All have been previously prepared.*

The group formed a large triangle with the brothers who were present. The lesser brothers had trouble at first making a triangle with three people in each line for some reason. The First Guard placed each upon his correct place, verifying that the lesser one was where he was supposed to be by a simple nod of the head. The Confirmandi, those well-established, entered from the foyer and made a triangle outside the one made by the lesser brothers. Their wall symbolically protected the younger ones from worldly harm. A minimum of twelve constituted the quorum for the opening exercises. The First Guard walked to the very center of the triangles.

First Guard:	*Shake the hand from left to right and left again to make it right.*

The handshake was given; the second guard stepped to the center of the inner triangle.

Second Guard:	*Done it is and done it was.*

He turned slowly in a circle before finally pointing to one of the brethren assembled.

Second Guard:	*What is your name?*
Brother:	*My name is honesty.*
Second Guard:	*What is the brother to your left called?*
Brother:	*He is known as openness.*
Second Guard:	*What is the brother to your right called?*
Brother:	*He is known as obedience.*
Second Guard:	*And what drives you to seek fulfillment?*
Brother:	*Determination.*
First Guard:	*It is well and true. Sign to one and sign to all; give your rank in secret grasp; detect the false one in your midst.*

The brothers "broke the triangles" and quietly offered an embrace and handshake that showed rank and status. One brother, the *Lone Wolf,* had been selected by the members of the *Grand Guard* beforehand to try to pass himself off as a real brother, pretending he knew not how to give the symbol of rank; by doing such, he tried to pass as far as he could without being detected. Tonight, however, he did not go any further than the Brother-of-the-Lance near the fireplace.

Brother-of-the-Lance:	*Form your lines and guard your rank! An imposter here among us goes!*
Brother-of-the-Code:	*Hold him firm; present him here!*
First Guard:	*Let us call the roll to see if any are tarrying away from us this eve. Whose place has he taken? Wherein lies his deceit?*

(A call of names is performed by the Knight-of-the-Registry standing at the podium.)

Knight-of-the-Registry:	*All are present name for name. He can't be the Lone Wolf who creeps at night.*
Lone Wolf:	*I have given the pass in error; my rank escaped me for a moment.*
First Guard:	*It is well that you admit your error. Pass your rank grip to me slowly, so that no more confusion can come herein to our den.*

The *Lone Wolf* gave the grip and rank satisfactorily; the brothers retired to ornate sofas and handsomely-carved chairs; the allegory was finished; the First Guard awaited the entrance of the Alpha.

The ceremony had opened that way for years. Some of the brethren hadn't even been born yet when the first group of initiates had passed through the ritual that was, in the beginning, much more ornate. The current Alpha had streamlined all the rites and practices years ago, at least by 1875, after some of the older members had tried to take things into their own hands once they were outside the den. But that was of no interest to anyone tonight. More important things were on the agenda.

Two of the guards held up a large piece of wolf skin between them, behind which the Alpha processed from another chamber unseen, until he reached his seat at the head of the room in front of the blazing hearth. The guards passed the skin over his head and draped the silver-grey fur over the chair where he was to be seated. All rose to their feet, and placing their hands on the shoulder of the brother to the left, they recited the sacred pledge and sang the "Song of the Bond":

Behold the Brotherhood gathered!
In splendor has gathered!
To each and from each member, a pledge and sign of our trust.
Long before the break of dawn, when darkness sat on creation's rim,
A new and glorious day was planned when all would be gathered in.

"First, the *lesser brothers* are dismissed to go with the Fraternal Master for more instruction. You, the *Confirmandi,* may be seated, brothers," the Alpha began. "Your enthusiasm and dedication are to be admired and treasured. It is Christmas time, and I know you have much to do as you prepare to spend the season with your family and friends, but I would ask you not to forget your brothers. Your honor to them is paramount. They form the nucleus of your existence. It is for them that you sacrifice because they, in turn, will give their all for you."

Several nodded in agreement to his statement. Others reclined and closed their eyes in meditation. Some lightly drummed their fingers on the ornate leather chairs, while others waited to sip the elixir.

"I know that this is difficult for you to fathom, but someone broke the vow of silence and showed the secret sign. Brothers, the Crewe has been violated from within. The secret of the Immortali has possibly been revealed."

CHAPTER 1

21 October 2009

October had been wet. The leaves from the maple trees surrounding Trinity Academy's athletic complex stuck to the pavement in the parking lot. Tardy commuter students in careening cars skidded slightly on the asphalt that separated the massive fieldhouse and athletic complex from Osolin and Wetzel-Cestaro Halls. The trees began to shed their foliage a little behind schedule. October's frost finally short-circuited nature's rhythm, and the cold nights, drenched with storms and battered by wind, began to accelerate the autumnal process.

Steep slate roofs on the Gothic revival buildings on the East Campus of the private college cast off the rain as quickly as possible. Stone gargoyles spewed the overflow into gutters and drains always athirst for more. But when the sun did shine, and it often did, the remaining resilient leaves along Maplehurst Drive were particularly stunning. Flaming orange and vibrant deep-red foliage drew the eyes upward to meet the brilliant oceanic blue of the sky that massive, fast-moving clouds teasingly obscured for brief moments.

On the particular morning in question, the twenty-first, the rain, falling from swiftly passing charcoal and gray clouds in the pre-dawn hours, shrouded shards of lightning until the last minute, seconds before the thunder rolled its mournful dirge over the school and down into the valley. Mothers at home in town were quickly laying out rainwear for their elementary school children. Older children, still asleep, later had to debate using umbrellas or not. The Academy's students, however, were oblivious to the rain, for the most part, and would later dash and scatter between buildings, or they'd stroll along as though they were in the middle of a drought on a sunny afternoon. The rain couldn't touch them, or so they thought. But when they entered the classrooms, they soon discovered that they were truly wet all the way through, and then came the realization that they would be uncomfortable for the next fifty minutes.

Such mornings might be foreboding to some; others, however, found rainy days comforting. There was no way to read what the weather would bring that October morn anymore than one could have read tea leaves at the Café du Bois on East Bickett Drive in order to predict who would win the approaching homecoming game.

The football game, of course, would never be washed out or frozen out or snowed out; Trinity always played its games in adverse conditions. And although the chance of freezing rain and snow was minimal at that time of year, some old timers often jawed about the big game back in the last century. The mud and field rapidly froze over after a rare arctic downpour and temperature drop, so it was said, and ice skates were strapped on to complete the plays. How the skates suddenly materialized was anybody's guess. No one today believed such stretches of the imagination. The date when that game supposedly happened still remains elusive, but the story showed that the team never capitulated to the forces of nature.

Coach Jared Hominy was tenacious, his players fiercely loyal. But tenacity and loyalty were sometimes trumped by other events that even Coach Hominy couldn't directly control. He was confident when the season began, but by the time it had run its course, even he couldn't explain how things could have gone wrong so quickly.

Steve Gruder, the team's only talented quarterback in years, a star athlete, the golden boy of the gridiron, was out for his morning jog a good two hours before the school day began. His energy level always seemed to peak before mid-morn, then it would spike again in the evenings, especially on Friday nights during the season. Steve was disciplined, and he always set realistic goals for himself, but it was his dogged determination that kept him always pushing onward to some unseen goal, to some inflexible ideal that even he couldn't articulate. He didn't feed off the energy of others; he had his own supply of internal power, an almost unending force that drove him to success. Even in the weight room, he focused on what he alone was doing. The clanking of weights and the sounds of others grunting as they strained to complete the final rep or set fell upon his deaf ears. He heard only himself.

Buck McDougal, the assistant coach and science instructor, who had been observing Gruder run his laps, had just jumped out of his Dodge Ram and slammed the door when Steve, dodging some mud puddles along the slick asphalt, loped up to him.

"You could set your watch by the time we arrive!" Steve panted. He shook his head and cocked it to the left. He squinted at Buck as the rain hit their faces.

Steve tried to mentally decide if Buck was just rugged or if he was a redneck. A fine, blurred line stopped the classification in his mind. It was a dumb thought anyway, but in speech class the day before, the instructor had asked his students to look at a person and make certain judgments or classifications based on body language, clothing, and looks.

"When there's work to be done, we gots to get it done, muh man," Buck McDougal answered, slapping Steve on the back before putting up the collar on his lumberjack-plaid shirt to stop the rain from dripping down the back of his neck. *Rugged,* Steve thought.

"Uh, listen, Coach. I was wonderin' if we could get together sometime."

"Sure. How about now?" Buck asked. "Actually, I've got some time before I have to set up the lab."

"Can't. Still have a few more laps to do before the rain *really* slows me down. They say it's gonna pour down terrible hard before school...worse than it is now. I don't have time after school. We have drills, remember?"

"Meet me in the fieldhouse before drills after school. I can excuse you for a few minutes."

"Naw. Coach Hominy don't like it if we try to ditch. It can wait, I guess. It's just that...there's something strange going on around here. There's something really strange going on."

"Strange?" Buck wondered aloud in response to Steve's comment.

"Nothin', Coach. It can wait. We'll talk later."

Steve bent over and tied one of his shoe laces and checked the other...more out of habit than necessity. Both parted with a nod and a handshake. Buck watched him sprint through the gate onto the track around the football field and disappear into the blinding rain that had just begun. *That boy's gonna make it to the pro's,* Buck thought to himself.

Steve's run that morning through the driving rain and wind was exhilarating for him. He flew around the track trying to break imaginary school records that had never been officially recorded.

He felt the rain stinging his face. The cutting volley of water picked up its intensity; the deluge had hit. His lungs began to burn, and he knew he had reached the pinnacle of his workout. His final lap, the one he always forced himself to do, left him winded and gasping. He checked his watch.

He was stressed out with school; he was stressed out with himself. He was afraid of what he had discovered. . .if, indeed, he had discovered anything. *What one sees is often not what one sees,* someone had told him once in a philosophy class where the professor was trying to prove the error of sense testimony.

On a regular day, he would have continued on with another half hour of sprints and steady jogging, but this particular morning was different. He had pushed himself hard; he had pushed himself to the point of exhaustion. It was the only way to take care of the stress and anxiety. Work at home was just not going to happen. He could barely concentrate on his school requirements. He was ready to snap; he had had enough of the world around him.

His only solace was that the Crewe of Adelphos, a most ancient order that encouraged fraternal bonding, had tapped him the previous school year in April and planned on using him to formally induct the Neophytes after the homecoming dance. He learned the sacred Secrets of the Perseids in August, and he was ready to help others discover their true identity. Homecoming was the night the Neophytes, the Confirmandi, and the Inner Circle came together for the first time in public after the tapping. While others danced and dreamed of lazy fall nights and sunny, yet cool, crisp days, the Crewe knew that the dance was for them alone. Behind the scenes they planned it, and they executed every moment between the dinner, the dance, and the dismissal into the night at the cabin.

Although the fieldhouse had already opened its doors to welcome him in, it was musty, stagnant, when he entered. In front of his locker, he bent over slightly, his hands resting on his knees, and continually tried to fill his lungs with air. The slower he breathed in through his nostrils, the harder it was to fill up his lungs. It was a struggle to reach that level of contentment, that level of satisfaction, whereby he knew that he was on his way to relaxing his body after a grueling workout.

He quickly stripped down and tossed his clothes onto the floor by the benches, grabbed a towel and some soap from his locker, and flipped on the light switch to the open shower complex. The air chilled his body and he gave a slight shiver. He touched the side of his neck for a moment. His pulse skipped a beat. His nostrils flared, but he dismissed his sense of fear as coming from his own frustrations that he had to work out as quickly as possible.

Twelve nozzles were his for the choosing, but he always selected the third one from the right near the corner. Because he was somewhat superstitious, and although he never revealed why, this particular shower was his.

A leg cramp began to develop in his right thigh causing him to limp up to his favorite spot not far from the corner. He twisted on a gush of hot, steamy water that seemed to clear his lungs and soothe his cramped leg. Turning around slowly under the powerful jet, the stinging pellets massaged away his tension.

Resting his hands up against the slippery tile wall and bending his head prayer-like under the spraying nozzle, he let the water surge over his neck and shoulders and cascade in rivulets down his back. Raising his head for just a moment, he sucked in some water and swished it around in his mouth, making gurgling sounds before spitting it out.

Like a great sheepdog after a summer bath, he shook his head, splashing and splattering water up into the air and onto the tile wall. He bowed his head once again, almost reverently, concentrating on the water as it washed away his fear and doubts. Flowing water can be a meditative rite of purification, surging over the body and cleansing the soul.

Keeping his eyes closed, he focused on the rhythm of the forceful torrent. All his cares and frustrations flowed down the drain, deep into the earth where he could bury everything.

His neck had another slight spasm. He rubbed it for a second before continuing on with his rite of purification.

He couldn't see the shadow fall across his back, and he didn't have time to react when a muscular, well-defined arm grabbed his throat from behind, dragging him away from the nozzle's wet, calming warmth. A well-executed upward *snap* caused his body to go limp. The next gurgle he made was when he found himself floating into a pit of open darkness from which he would never return.

* * * * * *

"We'll have to wait for a definite autopsy report. Could take weeks. Broken neck it appears," Coroner Code Schaffer stated with no emotion as he pushed his glasses back up the bridge of his nose. "Hate these glasses. Never did fit right. If I hadn't read so damn much in med school, I wouldn't need these blasted things at all! Should have become an accountant like my mother wanted. Yeah, broken neck. Whojasay found the boy?"

"Kid named Billy Tanker or Hanker or something like that," Dr. LaCause, the coroner's assistant, answered. "Came in to use the steam room and heard the water running full force in the shower. When he went to investigate as to who would be here that early, this is what he found. What a way to start off your day. Sucks, don't it?"

Inspector Milo Vasilovich had just arrived after a ten minute drive from Culver City with sirens blaring and all lights flashing. That was a rush in itself to him. He should have retired a few years ago, but he didn't want to turn over his post to men thirty years his junior. *Today's training is far too soft and incomplete,* he often thought. He should know.

Before police academy at Clarksburg Hill Barracks, he spent time teaching in the Soviet Union before the Cold War ended. He was all protocol and no nonsense. Some speculated that he had been trained by the CIA in ferreting out information from international criminals. Others believed he worked secretly for the KGB as a double agent, and they weren't noted for their ability to respect the civil rights of anyone in their claws. He always denied affiliation with both groups, but he often made a recalcitrant suspect sing like the fat lady at La Scala, the famous opera house in Milan.

Vasilovich began to mentally lay out the situation and the scene. He picked up on the conversation between the coroner and his assistant before he interrupted. "We'll need to question Billy-boy some more. Any reason to suspect his story isn't right?" Inspector Vasilovich asked.

"I've seen him play ball. Kid seems to be honest. Smiles a lot. I don't think he is hiding anything. Built like a stainless steel freezer," Schaffer stated.

"But just what are we supposed to tell the school community?" Sterrett Hamilton, the Academy's president, interrupted by asking anyone within earshot who had authority. He didn't really care how much the coroner had read in med school or if the glasses didn't fit right. And he certainly didn't care if a witness was built like a stainless steel anything. "The news media got here almost before the ambulance did. They're licking their chops for a story as we speak. They won't buy the *no comment* line."

Normally, Sterrett was a model of calm and comfort in tense situations, but there's a world of difference between two girls dragging each other kicking, screaming, and scratching to the ground during a chick fight in the cafeteria over some boy they both thought they owned and having a dead star football player sprawled out face up on a wet shower floor for everyone to see.

Some of the men on the local police force were cordoning off the area with yellow tape that was redundant with *CAUTION* and *CUIDADO.* Vasilovich eyed the tape, smirked, and wondered why they hadn't added Russian in bold black letters, too. At least in Russia there was no need for such tape back in the 70s. According to *Pravda,* no crime existed at all in the Soviet Union, yet the *militsia* always seemed to have enough to do.

Jared Hominy, the football coach noted for his gruff manner and no-nonsense approach to life, whom most people called *Grits,* was pacing behind the easy chair in his office in the corner of the fieldhouse. He wanted so much to interject his thoughts to the others, but the interjection just wouldn't come.

His crew cut, accented by a slight touch of gray on the sides and washed-out blond on the top, bristled at his fingers when he rubbed his muscular right hand absent-mindedly over his scalp. He kept some bourbon and vodka in the bottom desk drawer, and just the thought made his mouth water uncontrollably until he came back to reality. No one in his office that day paid any attention to him.

"Mr. Hamilton, is it?" Inspector Milo Vasilovich asked in a raspy voice after forcing himself to re-focus on the situation at hand. Too much action and too many people vying for attention had caused him to lose track of his thoughts. "You might want to try the truth. At approximately 6:15 this morning, give or take, and with all murders there is a give or take period, this Gruder kid succumbed in the shower area to an unknown assailant. More details will be released later. For now the police are handling the investigation. Then you're finished. You can't tell what you don't know, now can yuh?"

"That's right, Mr. Hamilton. Listen to the law and stop worrying about the ramifications!" Coroner Schaffer exclaimed. He was not the type to mince words. Most of his clients, for obvious reasons, didn't ask questions. He never had to deal with a school, his own alma mater, that was about to come unglued for the first time in its history. And he was still angry that he had to leave his apartment so quickly that he didn't have a chance to call his current fiancée the morning after they had just got engaged at Schiller's Tavern over a meal of pulled-pork and cheap Chablis.

The faculty, staff, and student body, notified by e-mail and emergency text messages, retired in muffled silence to the ivy-covered assembly hall to offer their respect and to comfort one another. The students and faculty were briefed about the situation, and after a few moments of silence, Mr. Hamilton dismissed classes for the rest of the day at 9:30 AM. Most of the resident students retired to the dormitory area. The commuters spent some time talking in the parking lot before driving home.

"But I've been planning a test for *two* weeks," Mavis complained to Mr. Hamilton after he announced that the Academy was being closed down for the day. Mavis would kvetch about anything. She was an equal-opportunity-whiner, and that, perhaps, was her strong point. But every objection she made was like a long, chipped fingernail scraping on a blackboard, a sound that today's youth will probably never hear because SMART Boards™ have seen to that. One person on the faculty joked once that if Mavis had won two hundred million dollars in the lottery, she would have complained that she hadn't won it the week before when it was twice as much. "I have to give a review *today* because we've lost so much time because of late night bonfires that delay the next morning's classes by two hours and by food drives and by retreats and by. . .you know. . .all those goody-goody things that take away from the academics here. Sometimes I think this is more of a high school than a college! The rate we're going, we won't have that test until Thanksgiving!"

"No one gives a flyin' fig about your tests or your plans at the moment, Mavis!" And those were Mr. Hamilton's final words about academia that day.

She turned on her heels, shrugged her shoulders, and muttered something under her breath that could bring down a banshee's curse, assuming they curse in the first place. At least Sterrett Hamilton had released his pent-up anger on someone he didn't care for.

The media filmed the grieving students leaving the various buildings. By late afternoon, satellite dishes had sprung up above news vans parked near the front gate. One camera caught Mavis with a scowl on her face when she exited the administration building after running off a batch of tests that might never be given on time. A lone figure, slowly sipping some warm cider, stood at the library window watching the police arrive and depart. *Why here? Why now?* played over and over again in his mind.

* * * * * *

By late afternoon the coroner had finally completed the unpleasant task of writing up his preliminary report at the county health office. The cause of death, unless it could be otherwise determined, was *facilitated,* as he put it, by a broken neck. Neither the head itself nor the torso had received any noticeable trauma. In fact, it looked as though the perpetrator had gently laid Steve down on his back, positioning him with his legs and arms slightly spread. A small equilateral triangle had been carved by a sharp instrument onto the left side of the chest in the pectoral region after death had occurred.

"Probably cut into the skin within ten or fifteen minutes, give or take, after death. Can't be sure. Not deep as far as I can tell. What do you make of it?" Coroner Schaffer wondered.

Dr. LaCause, his assistant, said, "The same thing you make of it, and you know what I mean, but let's take some detailed pictures of it from different angles. It's odd, though.

The vertex is pointing down, isn't it?" He then set up the camera directly above the pectoral region. "And we need tissue samples taken and preserved one more time. Nothin' under his fingernails. I checked. No sign of a struggle. Let me review a few things later. No slip ups, right?"

"Got that right, Jack!" said Schaffer. He called everyone *Jack*. "And the less said about the mark, the better. Get my drift?" LaCause agreed to the enigmatic warning. Code washed his hands with mounds of lather after putting Gruder feet first into the cooler. He slapped LaCause on the back and made plans for dinner. There was another pulled-pork special at Schiller's Tavern, but there was always a pulled-pork special at Schiller's (except for Saturday night when they often push a chili and corn-dog combo, grated cheese extra).

* * * * * *

Inspector Vasilovich began the intensive interview process in the accountant's annex shortly after the funeral. The only "person of interest" was Buck McDougal, and that was certainly because he was the last person, other than the perpetrator, who had seen the Gruder boy alive. Buck's earlier statement to the police, shortly after the body had been removed, was the only evidence that something was wrong with Steve. But Buck never had the chance to find out what that "factor x" was. The equation could neither be balanced nor be solved.

"What was your relationship with the deceased?" Inspector Vasilovich asked after he had poured himself a cup of coffee from his own thermos. The escaping steam clouded his vision for a moment, and he had to fish for a handkerchief to wipe off his reading glasses so he could follow his prepared script.

"He is, was, a student of mine. Earth science. I am also an assistant coach, and I worked with him on what we call his *skills technique.*"

"Had you planned on meeting him at the fieldhouse?"

"No. We often run. . .ran, into each other in the mornings, though. We both arrive at the same time." It seemed odd referring to Gruder in the past tense.

"What do you know about his social life?" Vasilovich asked, looking Buck directly into his eyes. "Who did he *hang with,* as you would say? How did he spend his time? Kids always confess to their coaches what's going on. What's the scoop?"

"No scoop. Never talked to him about his personal life. I'm his coach, not his confidant," Buck replied, looking directly at Vasilovich, observing his own reflection in the inspector's glasses.

The inspector created an intentionally uncomfortable pause, a pregnant pause. "Well, then, what's a crewe?" Inspector Vasilovich asked Mr. McDougal, the four year science veteran. The question appeared to come out of nowhere and caught him off guard.

"A crew? Like in a bunch of rowers?" Buck asked.

Inspector Vasilovich replied, "No. It's spelled c-r-e-w-e around here."

"Oh," Buck responded. He gave a nervous little cough before continuing. "Well, Tyler Pettigrew and the Rev. LeBoeuf, the school's founders, came from New Orleans in the middle of the 1890s." He sounded like some kind of tour guide. One thing about Buck, he rarely talked in more than one or two sentences, and even those sentences were often limited to one or two words, but once someone engaged him about a topic he had a passion for, it was hard to stop him, and the history of the school's early days was his passion. His rendition was so vivid; it was almost as though he had been there when it all happened. "During Mardi Gras, each group of citizens down in *Nawlins,* as they pronounce it, who were in a *krewe* had a float in the parade down there, see. They transplanted the idea here. Each crewe, now spelled with a *c,* had a name, a faculty sponsor, rituals, mottos, colors, and so forth. They were something like fraternities today."

"My, you are a virtual wealth of historical information!" Vasilovich responded with his attempt to mock a "Looziana" accent. "And was Gruder a member of a crewe?"

"I really can't say. With all due respect, Inspector Vasilovich, crewes were something of importance in the first decades of the 1900s. I can barely scare up enough interest for a rocket team. A homecoming dance that always happens at mid-term is almost impossible to stage like back in the day. Forget about groups with some kind of secretive, complicated rituals! These kids today can't remember a locker combination. That's why the good Lord invented the Blackberry! They now have a place to store their memories.

"Is membership in these crewes confidential?"

"Like I said, 'I can't say.' People don't talk much about the past. They seldom discuss the present! I come here, do my job, and leave." It was obvious to Vasilovich that Buck was side-stepping the issue.

"But you do seem to know the history of the crewes. Don't some have symbols like squares or triangles or circles?"

"I dunno," Buck answered with a strange inflection.

"And, by the way, how do *you* know the rituals were complicated if the crewes were so secretive? I went here, too, don't forget. Crewe of Atlantis." That was the inspector's last salvo. Buck shrugged his shoulders, shook hands with Vasilovich, and walked away to the Commons.

CHAPTER 2

New Orleans, Louisiana
June 1885

Tyler Pettigrew, son of Beauregard Pettigrew and grandson of Harland Pettigrew, had just walked down the gangplank of the steamer arriving in the Crescent City, New Orleans, from St. Louis, where he connected after his arduous rail journey from Boston. He wasn't used to the unusually oppressive air and the relentless dock noise. Young Mr. Pettigrew removed a handkerchief from his jacket pocket, snapped it at the air a few times, and then mopped his drenched brow. His right hand shading his eyes from the brilliant sun, he scanned the dockside to see if his father awaited him, but it was possible that his father had not received the telegram announcing his arrival.

In the clatter and chatter surrounding and distracting him, he reflected for a moment about his new life up North. The hustle and bustle of the dock in New Orleans was transformed into Boston for a moment in Tyler's mind. Summer in Boston had a different kind of heat, he recollected. It could be muggy, of course; it could be veiled within a steady breeze from the bay. New Orleans just squeezed its heat out of the floors of the bayous and sucked it up from the verdant acres lollygagging along the delta.

Tyler preferred Boston, at least its educational institutions, because they accepted him for who he was and not for who his parents were. He fit in up there, and although he had been born *post-bellum,* shortly after the Civil War, 1866 to be exact, he found that Bostonians didn't dwell on about the war so much or about its aftermath. Life moved on, and so had he. His college didn't care who his "people" were. In New Orleans, who your "people" were often determined your academic success in institutions of higher learning.

His English literature instructor and advisor, Hanley Collins, was from New Orleans also. They didn't sit around and wish for the glory days of the South, nor did they talk about how much better the food in the Cajun quarter was. They talked about literature; they talked about life. Sometimes they would walk along the Charles River and watch people watching people. A teacher wasn't just an instructor there; he was a mentor, a guide, a beacon.

What impressed Tyler most about Prof. Collins was that they weren't separated that much in age. Collins had an accomplished air about him, but he was a typical southern boy who still was a rough stone that needed some grind and polish.

"Mr. Pettigrew," Prof. Collins would always address him formally, trying to be polite, his smile still that of a youth from the bayous, "see those people over there sitting on that bench?"

"Yes, sir, I do," Tyler answered softly.

"Then write me a story telling how they got there. How did they get to this moment in time?"

"How they got there?" Tyler asked. "I suppose they walked there."

"That's not what I meant, son. You can start forty years back if you'd like! But I don't think you have the time to write it, and I'm not sure you'd master the point of the exercise." Prof. Collins watched the surprised look on Tyler's face. "When you think about it, everything they have ever done and everyone they have ever met and everywhere they have ever traveled have led them to this one moment."

"You're a deep thinker, sir," Tyler pointed out.

"Obliged. Much obliged." Southerners were always *obliged* about something or other, and Prof. Collins fit the mold of the perpetually obliged gentleman.

"Now how far back do you really want me to start?" the young lad asked.

"It's your story," Prof. Collins began. "Surprise me!"

Several days later Tyler wrote. He created a story that no one had ever written before, and Prof. Collins read it through quickly and then tossed it into the trash in front of the boy's eyes.

"Now write me a *real* story about those people on the bench we saw the other day. I want to hear the wood creak beneath them. I want to feel their conversations stir my mind as you paint pictures of what their hearts reveal. I want to know why they paused at that point in their history! I don't want mediocrity. And I surely don't want to waste my time on it again. Do you understand me, boy?"

"My characters are somewhat cliché, as you'd call it, eh?"

"Abysmal! And abandon the *eh*. You sound like you come from Canada or northern Minnesota!"

The boat whistle of an arriving packet steamer on the east side of the wharf brought his mind back to the dock in New Orleans where he stood so far away from his mental image of Boston at that moment.

His luggage was being pushed on a handcart toward no place in particular. "Sir! Sir! That's *my* luggage!" Tyler yelled.

"Ain't gonna steal it none," the old man wearing a moth-eaten cap muttered.

"I didn't mean...I wasn't questioning your honesty."

Tyler handed the impoverished, stooped-over man fifteen cents and motioned for him to leave the baggage cart where it was. The wrinkles in his face hid a smile of gratitude if there was one.

"Tyler! Tyler Pettigrew!" a young man in his mid-twenties shouted above all the din.

"I'm afraid you have the advantage, sir," Tyler replied.

"Tyler Pettigrew. It is you, isn't it?" he persisted.

"Why, yes. I suppose it is," Tyler answered; an ever-present drawl stretched out the word *is*. He studied the man's face without being too rude. The young stranger's smile was somewhere between being friendly and being cautious at the same time. Tyler was sure they had never met before.

"Then may I introduce myself to you? I am a mailman and I have a letter for you. Will you accept it?"

Tyler looked at the young man's hands, but he saw no letter. The polite stranger wasn't even carrying a delivery pouch about his neck. Perhaps it was a letter from his father explaining why he hadn't met the boat that sweltering afternoon.

"Of course. I'll accept it. Who's it from?"

The man looked around to see if anyone was paying attention, and with all the comings and goings, it was clear that the mailman wanted no one to be privy to the conversation. He stepped in closer and gave Tyler a letter of the alphabet and told him what that secret letter stood for.

"You are not to tell anyone about the letter I just gave you, and you may not pass it on. There will be other mailmen and other letters. Hold all of these letters close to you. Good day, Tyler. Until another place and time."

"Much obliged," answered Tyler, "But sir, who are…" It was too late. The man had disappeared into the crowd that began to mill around the gangplank as the famous opera star, Hannah Morgan, descended, holding her parasol high enough to shade her alabaster face and her shimmering white gown from the broiling sun. Tyler watched mesmerized as she moved along so gracefully, nodding to man and woman and child alike.

"Tyler!" his father called out, startling him a bit. "I thought I was not going to make it. The horse got a slight limp, and I had to stop at a livery on the way down and change off. You look good, son. Real good," his father said before patting him on the back and putting his wooden steamer trunk into the carriage for the trip home.

CHAPTER 3

26 Oct 2009

Paul Docket, the English teacher with the most tenure, sat at his office desk at school catching up on academics and hoping to put the past week behind him. A pall of gloom and confusion veiled the campus. The joy at the beginning of a new school year had vanished, and paranoia had dug its talons into the hearts of the faculty and staff. Paul reflected on what the chances were that he knew who had killed Steve Gruder. After his short contemplation that offered no insight, he saved his grades on the computer just before Joel Garret knocked on the door.

"Got a few minutes?" Joel asked.

"Just wrappin' some things up. Come in. Take a seat." Paul Docket motioned to a chair near the desk.

"I've been working on that family history writing assignment and trying to jump-start the project," Joel said. "I think it will work out, but I've got a question."

"Glad you decided to take the course on writing family history with me," Paul acknowledged with a nod.

"Wouldn't have it any other way. I'm much obliged, Mr. Docket. Much obliged. Anyhow, I've gone back a few generations on my direct line, but I've come across something that puzzles me."

Paul took the pedigree chart and began to scrutinize the information that lay before him. Joel had decided to progress backwards on his paternal lineage to see if he could push aside time's veil for at least one hundred years, his personal goal, then he would select an individual to bring back to life on paper through various primary and secondary documents.

"Let's see," Mr. Docket began. "You were born in 1990. Uh, huh. Your father was born in 1960. You need to find the county of his birth. Uh, huh. Your paternal grandfather was born in 1935. Do you know when he died?"

"Not sure. I got some of this on the phone from mom. Dad has some of this at home. I think I can find out more next time I call," Joel replied.

"You've made some good progress with this." Mr. Docket studied the pedigree chart, pretended to be interested, but his attention was not on pedigree charts or family history research. He just wanted to get outside and get a breath of fresh air. He felt trapped. Gruder had been in the family history class, and Paul realized that he had lost a student, who, in time, might be researched by future generations. What would the future discover about Gruder that no one in the present knows? "Now, you said you had a question."

"Yeah. Well, I think it might be more of an observation than a question. Look here. My great-great-grandfather was born, according to this, in 1886 in Boston. His mother was Sarah Garret."

"I see that on your chart," Paul Docket said.

Joel explained, "Whoever did this research a long time ago noted that Sarah's son was illegitimate, a bastard son, who took *her* name, not his father's. She and her kid were living up in Boston and then they headed south to New Orleans at some point. That's according to one article I read by a second cousin twice removed. I wonder if Sarah's child, Barley, ever knew he was illegitimate."

"So that's why you are a Garret and not a Culpepper, I assume!" Paul interrupted Joel, joking about Joel's southern heritage or lack thereof.

"Exactly, sir, exactly," Joel said with a pronounced drawl.

"Then see if you can get a copy of Sarah's son's birth record from Boston," Paul pointed out.

"Been there; done that," Joel stated. He reached into his backpack and took out an envelope that he had folded in half twice. "Feast your eyes on this, Mr. Docket. Got this in the mail a couple of days ago."

Paul opened its contents and perused the document carefully. Sarah Garret claimed that the father of her son, Barley Garret, was Tyler Pettigrew, son of Beauregard Pettigrew, son of Harland Pettigrew. Whoever had entered the information about the father into the birth register had been sure to put the exact lineage.

"Tyler Pettigrew! Does that seem possible? I'm the great-great-great grandson of the founder of Trinity Academy?" Joel asked.

"For your sake, Joel, I hope you're not! Somebody might want you to take over someday!"

* * * * * *

30 October 2009

Coroner Schaffer had spent several hours in the laboratory trying to find more reasons or causes for Steve's death, but nothing had been conclusive, other than a broken neck. No drugs had been found in the system; no alcohol was present; no sexual trauma. Although some forensic tests could still take several weeks before being returned from the central lab, pathological exams showed no abnormalities. This was simply a case of murder, if murder ever was a simple case, and Coroner Schaffer felt that all had been resolved except for who the perpetrator was.

The burning question that he couldn't answer was about the motive. He knew that if nothing came forth in the first few days, then the case could go cold. Greenlawn and Culver City were limited, and even though the government would often poke their heads in to see how things were going, it was just a matter of time until the local police would have to move on to other things.

He remembered how the county voters had elected him coroner five years ago, the youngest coroner on record in Chevron County at age thirty, and the greater portion of his career had been dedicated to seeking out the truth. His job wasn't pleasant by anybody's standards. He enjoyed trying to solve the puzzle that surrounded some deaths. Often he became too involved with the cases, and when he had to deal with the demise of young people, he was often frustrated about why some never had the chance to live out their lives into their seventh or eighth decade. It wasn't fair, but his mother had always told him that life wasn't fair. Someday, he hoped to find the document that said it was.

* * * * * *

Although the fieldhouse had been unsealed within a week after the murder, students, out of their own volition, never arrived before seven, and none stayed on after football practice concluded or a game ended. Most of the guys found an excuse not to take a shower, and Coach Hominy pretended to understand. He figured, however, that this whole mess had turned the team into a bunch of weak women who were afraid of their own shadows and, possibly, of each other. They would rather whistle while walking past a cemetery than pass through with confidence and without superstition.

The team lost the homecoming game, and the alumni were afraid that this could herald a losing streak. Trinity had never lost a homecoming game. The benefactors in their fogged vision seemed to forget that the school was in one of its worst seasons ever, and the lost homecoming game wasn't going to herald much of anything.

Roger Honeycutt, the new sophomore quarterback replacement, barely twenty-one years old, who suddenly shot up through the ranks at the last minute in an attempt to save not only the day but the entire season, worked as well as could be expected. Coach Hominy liked the boy. He trusted the boy.

Roger never cared about trust. And he didn't worry about whether people liked him or not. He did know football. He knew how to showboat at the season's final games, but he was like an eagle "trooping with crows."

The crowds were often brought to their feet by his sudden forward pass that could sail and curve like a glider before finding its target in the end zone just short of the goal line. He had never been sacked, at least on the field, and he inherently knew how to dodge, sidestep, leap over, and twist away from any aggressive attacker. On some plays, his own teammates would often just stand and watch his maneuvers for the sheer enjoyment of his movements, a gazelle in motion. Many were oblivious at times that they were in an actual game themselves, so captivating were his moves on the field.

One night in particular stands out to his fans as being truly remarkable. The ball was snapped to him. As he stepped into his dropback, he started to roll out to the right side of the field. Scanning his receivers, he hawk-eyed two possibilities. He got the pass off for a moderate gain, though, just as his tight end blindsided the outside linebacker, hitting him into unconscious submission. The referee blew the whistle; the cheerleaders went silent with faces that mirrored fear. Gawking at what had just happened on the field, the fans in the stands rose slowly to their feet. The entire stadium was silent.

Roger hurried over to the opposing team's outside linebacker, observed how still he was lying there, almost communing with another world that only the linebacker could see. Out of the corner of his eye, Honeycutt could see the trainers running towards him, but before they got there, he knelt down and cradled the boy's head that seemed to flop around with no muscular support. He bent over and whispered into the injured boy's ear, "Kuhduush sem d'chaimu. Eloth ram hannel." The team's medical assistants stood watching the injured linebacker raise his head, stand up, and shout, "Let's go, men. We got a game to play here!"

"What the hell just happened here?" Coach Hominy asked one of his assistants. "Does anybody know what's going on?"

"Nothing, I guess," Roger answered back. "He wasn't hurt at all. Just stunned it appears." Roger took off in a sprint to get ready for the next play, and by the time the referee blew the whistle announcing a penalty, the fans had forgotten about the strange incident on the forty yard line.

Roger may have become the new rising star, but the team itself was just an old piece of battered bronze. It didn't matter how impressive his plays were or how forceful his plays were or how high he jumped to execute a pass because the team without Gruder was lost.

Roger couldn't play down at their level, and they couldn't raise themselves up to his. Gruder and the team were one, not always successful, but they were one. They inherently knew what unity was all about. But on Friday nights now, there was Roger, and there was the team. People paid to watch the quarterback, and win or lose, Roger delivered what they wanted. He had come of age.

To most of the players, Roger was smug, and to prove that he was as cocky as hell, he'd strut into the shower area alone after every practice with his self-assured swagger, stand under "Gruder's" shower, and crank up the water. Even if the team had lost or if the coach had just verbally harangued them, he'd sing his lungs out as if to prove that collective fear had no hold on him.

He knew he had what it took to be a great athlete on the field, and he had even more chutzpah in the locker-room. He didn't care what others thought of him; he had his own future to look out for. At one time, he wanted to play at Baylor or Auburn on a full ride. But presently, he was going to be content just where he was, and Trinity was where he wanted to be. It was his home, and nothing was going to lure him from what he believed to be rightfully his.

Roger used that feeling of being at home at Trinity to attract those who needed him. Women loved the bad boy image and the lethal smile. He had a slightly crooked grin, but his teeth flashed each time he laughed; his eyes mesmerized as much as his richly tanned skin attracted. But women were disposable commodities to him, much like the BIC® razors he'd use and toss after a well-earned shower and shave.

He was far from being ready to settle down, and there was no reason to be serious because any new relationship never went past three encounters. That was a rule he said he had established long ago. "Boys, it's all about the pleasure," he said to the team once when they were waiting for practice to start one afternoon. "It's all about the pleasure." Most of the guys on the bench never had an idea as to what he was really referring to, and most would never catch a glimpse as to who Roger Honeycutt really was, but life was a pleasure to live. It was a pleasure to share; it was a pleasure to take pride in who you are.

Guys were eager, naturally, to be seen with him in public---especially where the girls were concerned. They thought it gave their own image a boost, but they were often intimidated by his ability to sidle up to teachers, to other adults, and to those who had the power and the money when it came to funding the team. He knew how to work any crowd he was in. And he was the type of man's man no one could really dislike.

Roger, however, was a paradox. Where he was haughty and arrogant to some, he came off as being sensitive and vulnerable to others. It was that susceptibility that Paul Docket found to be so interesting. Gruder had projected the same type of vulnerability in the classroom and on the field, but most, including Coach Hominy, either didn't see it, or they simply chose to ignore it because being vulnerable was not a trait of strength and athletic prowess.

For example, Roger thought Gruder had been an excellent quarterback-in-embryo whose moment hadn't yet come, and he challenged others to wear small black ribbons on their uniforms to keep Steve close to all concerned. Grits thought it was a good idea to show team support and didn't view Honeycutt's caring about the deceased Gruder as a sign of weakness. The coach thought it would make good press, and positive publicity was what he wanted above all.

The more playing time Roger had and the better the local news portrayed him, the more the benefactors couldn't do enough to make sure that he was happy and that he wanted to stay on for the following year. He played the political game quite well. The entire athletic scene was always a little unethical, but big money bought big things, and he believed that he had a right to success as much as the next guy. One group of alums wanted to help him move up to the next level as a returning on-staff coach after he graduated. It was a win-win for him, and he knew where every string on the alumni puppet was placed.

Honeycutt often lived on the edge when observing the proper social mores. His Mazda coupe wasn't something he was able to pay for by working weekends at the campus pizza shop for free soda and minimum wage. Cars and weekend getaways were often scrutinized by the athletic office and by some of the alumni who wanted to see more money go to the arts, but where and how some of the team members got their "rides" or spent some R&R off campus was officially kept under cover.

Never stir up the athletic hornets' nest unless you are prepared to be stung with cover-ups and prevarications. Trinity was no different than most institutions. Many male grads felt that what you learned in calculus was secondary or tertiary to what you learned at a bonfire before a game where you guzzled down moonshine fresh from the still. Others believed that tidbits of manliness could be transferred in a game huddle on the field just before the home team stomped the visitors' brains into the turf.

Roger didn't want any part of that "stomping someone's brains into the turf" philosophy. He just wanted to play well, become physically fit, and stay mentally alert. Athletics was planning; athletics was executing skill; athletics was moving faster and being in more control than the opponents. Athletics was mind over matter and mind moving matter.

Let the fifty-yard-line-Friday-night-quarterbacks up in the stands go home pretending they are eighteen again; give them the illusion of being transported back in time to a place and an age that really weren't as they imagined. But they'll still wake up on Saturday morning knowing they're fifty-eight and the big game was a hypnotic illusion as to who they once were. He was a god of fall; they were often the autumn of his discontent.

* * * * * *

The Academy wanted to make sure that it survived, of course, and so, various edicts were issued to the faculty and staff during the rest of October warning them that they were to keep away from the press. Sterrett Hamilton also reminded them to avoid making speculative theories to friends and relatives and to keep a good professional distance between their private lives and their professional ones. Like most institutions, however, when something goes awry, they always try to close the barn door long after the horse has escaped. At Trinity, however, no one informed the administration that the last barn on campus had disappeared in 1908.

In a private memo, Coroner Schaffer even suggested to Sterrett Hamilton that Coach Hominy was ultimately responsible for Gruder's death because someone should have been in the fieldhouse supervising that morning. Issuing keys willy-nilly to anyone was an invitation to a lawsuit regarding irresponsibility and negligence. Many former graduates still had their own keys long after graduation, and they came and went whenever they felt like it. Even Itch Schutte, a rooky on the police force in Culver City, still stopped in for a quick steam bath before heading off to work a couple of times a week. If the door to the fieldhouse was locked, he used his key, the key he had had since his junior year many years prior.

Dr. LaCause began a petition to have the coach dismissed without pay until the case was completely resolved. The athletic department protested that idea. The school was already receiving enough negative press, and printing reports about the possible negligence of the coaching staff would only add more fuel to the well-stoked bonfire.

With Hominy's job on the chopping block, the only thing the coach could do was to make sure he crossed the *t*'s and dotted the *i*'s. After every game and practice, Coach Hominy made sure no one remained in the locker area. His "last one out shuts off the lights" policy was no longer permitted, and the Academy's president showed approval that Jared Hominy had taken it upon himself to institute a new policy without being asked.

Many a night before the tragedy struck, Grits would sit back and enjoy a big guzzle of hooch from his private stock after the last jock slammed the locker shut. On occasion, he invited some of the team to join him. Unethical, yes, but that assumes he may have had ethics to begin with.

CHAPTER 4

Boston
September 1885

Boston was fairly temperate that September after Tyler's sweltering summer in New Orleans had run its course. He remembered that on the dock when he had first arrived home, at a haberdasher's shop in the city, where he always purchased kid gloves and talcum, and on the return train trip from St. Louis to Boston, he met mailmen with special letters for him. As requested, he accepted the letters and kept their meanings to himself. No one was privy to what appeared to be a mystery. He was a man of his word.

Tyler reflected back to the time when he was about ten or eleven. He and his father had gone into the city to watch the parades and listen to the music. For a young boy, he had never seen so many feathers and costumes and insanity, even in the early evening hours. The carousing and insanity, however, which took place later at night, were not part of his childhood memories. His father had shielded him from such decadence. He would have been at a loss for words to explain how such flagrant debauchery could even remotely be connected to religion.

Tyler had heard about the krewes from his father and grandfather, and he even knew the history of some of the ones that made their appearance on or before Shrove Tuesday each year at Mardi Gras time. His father had enjoyed membership once, but after marriage and after a family had become a reality, he gave up the frivolity of the pre-Lenten season to focus on making a good living for his wife and child. Life was penance enough.

In Boston that September 1885, Tyler decided to attend church one Sunday morning at St. Mark's, a high Episcopalian church not far from his college, where the provost always sponsored the autumnal convocation ceremony. It wasn't unusual, however, for many of the boys, linked together by sport, subject major, or common interest, to attend together, but this time, Tyler went alone to contemplate about his future, sitting in the back, well away from the others who were renewing friendships once again.

The opening hymn, "Immortal, Invisible, God Only Wise," swelled with each verse until the pipe organ almost burst with celestial power when the organist rushed headlong into a crescendo at the end of the fourth verse. The young men's singing matched the enthusiasm of the organist, whose feet danced systematically over the pedals, a seated ballet of sorts, while his upper torso swayed to the cadence of the last lines. The silence after the final swelled note was so profound that some of the boys produced a few fake coughs to pierce the stillness.

The rector, Rev. Entwhistle, D. Div., standing at the ornately-carved oaken pulpit, his robes flowing and his hands gesturing, reminded the boys that they were, indeed, the gods of fall, in a manner of speaking. They were young. They were strong. They had control of life and were creating their place in society. The were creating and re-creating themselves according to their age and understanding of what society expected from them as they matured. Others looked up to them because of their enthusiasm and vigor. They were the gods of fall because they shaped and formed their own destinies, with the help of Divinity, to be sure. They were the gods of fall because this was their season, the season of new beginnings where academics and sports mingled and merged once again. "You are the great *immortali,*" he preached, "those immortal ones who absorb life during youth and live upon those memories year after precious year. This place and this time will always remain in your minds as it is now, never growing older and never fading as you pass through all of life's changes."

Sports, academics, and a well-rounded, pure life created the ideal, and the young men reflected through those attributes what the Divine had created in them from the very beginning. "Rise up, oh youth! Meet the standard that has been set! Nothing, save greed and over-zealous ambition, will curtail the vocations for which you have been selected by a wise and benevolent Heavenly Father!" he concluded. Had Tyler only understood all the nuances of that sermon!

After the Rev. Entwhistle had left the pulpit and the applause ceased, the students began to drift out of the chapel and congregate on the great lawn that spread out to the lake beyond. The grass was so lush that particular late summer; it invited one and all to linger about, curtailing any plans of returning to the *Cloisters,* the student quarters during the academic year.

"Tyler! I thought I'd find you here on the lawn," Prof. Collins shouted above the dozens of conversations going on around the two of them.

"Good to see you, sir," Tyler stated before giving a slight bow to show that he still exhibited southern manners. His drawl had become more pronounced over the summer.

"I trust your holiday was a good one, boy."

"As good as can be expected, sir. I hope yours was just as refreshing."

"I must admit that it was quiet, refreshing. There's something that you should know," Prof. Collins began. "I'm a mailman, and I have a letter for you. You have received mail before, haven't you?"

"Yes, sir. Three times before."

"Will you accept this time also?" Prof. Collins asked.

"Yes, sir, I shall." Prof. Collins gave Tyler the fourth letter and word as they walked away from the crowd and strolled slowly toward the lake. "I'm afraid I still don't understand," Tyler commented. He brushed a gnat away from his hair. A dragonfly chased another around some flowers that nestled on the shore.

"You will, in time. You'll come to learn there's always time.

CHAPTER 5

19 November 2009

One week before Thanksgiving break, the local police issued a brief statement delivered by Inspector Vasilovich, who posted it in the various faculty lounges around the campus: *After evaluating the murder scene and reviewing the completed autopsy reports, we can confidently state that Steven J. Gruder, 19 years old, a Caucasian male, was killed by an unknown assailant, and the motive was, according to preliminary reports, robbery. Further comments from this department will not be forthcoming until new evidence has emerged. We thank you for your patience during the on-going investigation.*

A month had passed since the death, and the police report was not only a disappointment, it was almost an insult to the faculty's intelligence.

"Robbery!" exclaimed Paul Docket in the English and foreign language faculty lounge while he was reading the report the police left for the faculty to view. "That's the dumbest thing I've ever heard. Steve was in the showers when he died. Anything of value would have been in his locker, and the guys never lock their lockers! How many college boys carry money into the shower!? It's all a bunch of hooey! Talk about creating a spin-job on all of this!" he yelled to no one in particular. Only Mrs. Racine Woodburn, the research librarian who spent her free time in the lounge, paid any attention to him.

"That's what they say," she added as she sipped her tea and gulped down some hot oatmeal and read the local paper, flipping from one page to the other trying to follow a story that had caught her attention. "Ah, no! Got another tear in my panty-hose. Dang stockings cost an arm and a leg. If men had to wear these blasted things, the death knell for panty hose would sound before they all took off for a power lunch! I'm gonna fire off an e-mail to Sterrett Hamilton. We shouldn't have to wear these things, and if he insists, he can just buy them for us himself!"

"It just doesn't make sense, does it?" he continued.

"The murder, Hamilton's draconic dress code, or the demise of the panty-hose?" she responded before jumping up to see why her toast was burning. Her heels clicked and clacked on the tile floor. She wasn't a great conversationalist in the morning until the caffeine kicked in shortly before opening the research stacks. Paul didn't reply but left to prepare his room for the first class of the day.

* * * * * *

Inspector Vasilovich was re-filing some of his notes. He still had teachers and students to contact before the end of the day, but everything he studied led him in circles. So far, no fewer than three teachers told him that Steve had wanted to talk to them about something important, yet when they pressed him to set up a time and a place, he seemed to balk at the idea.

Vasilovich was truly frustrated. This case should have been solved, and if not solved, there should have been more leads. Life at the school just went on as though nothing had happened at all. He felt stonewalled, but he couldn't prove it. This was turning into a cold case before it had boiled over with possibilities.

He began to wonder if those who might know things were leading him in circles...big, loopy, concentric circles. He kept coming back to the Crewe of Adelphos, and no one within that group, it seemed, had any desire to talk or see the case move forward.

He understood loyalty. He understood secrecy. He understood pride. He couldn't understand, though, how a group could be so loyal to each other in the face of such a horrific crime. Some were clearly devastated and wanted to help as much as they could. They didn't have any information, but they at least promised to keep their eyes and ears open. Others simply moved on with their lives as if nothing of consequence had transpired that rainy morn. Vasilovich thought they were backpedaling. No one knew anything, and he couldn't find a list of the Crewe members anywhere. A subpoena would do no good because you can't subpoena what you can't find.

Chapter 6

Boston
09 November 1885

Tyler Pettigrew, his tweed coat buttoned tightly at the neck, walked quickly up the sidewalk that joined the *Cloisters,* his dormitory, with Old Main, one of four buildings on campus that survived a catastrophic fire in 1856. He was fifteen minutes late for his Renaissance Literature class, and he knew that Prof. Collins detested tardiness.

The wind off the river had picked up, and he felt it sailing around him. The chill of autumn's bite had become a reality. One hardy tree near the botanical gardens, however, still held a few leaves on the odd branch or two; the sparse, withered foliage begged for release.

Several birds landed on the wrought iron fence that surrounded Old Main, and Tyler, even though he was in a hurry, stopped to watch them twitter and flap their wings as they moved up and down the gate. *Why don't they all leave? Don't they know that the others have left because they were supposed to?* He often wondered if he should head back home for the winter, far away from the predictable onslaught of nor'easters and stinging rain.

He tip-toed into the classroom and sat in the last row, hoping Prof. Collins hadn't seen his late arrival, but when Prof. Collins lowered his head and looked up over his glasses, Tyler knew that he had been caught.

"Perhaps Mr. Pettigrew could give us three symbolic metaphors used in Dante's *Inferno*," Prof. Collins said. Tyler shifted in his seat and opened his book trying to find the magic answers. He flipped through pages that all looked the same. Actually, they all looked blank to him. He had no idea where the answers were. "Well, Mr. Pettigrew. Your peers are waiting, not to mention your instructor." The class turned and watched Tyler give a lame, crooked grin.

"I'm sorry. I can't seem to find the answer," he said.

"That's because the answer isn't in the text, Mr. Pettigrew. It's in the notes I gave the rest of the class a few moments ago. Now may we proceed?"

"Yes, sir. Sorry, sir," Tyler answered, obviously very embarrassed. He knew he had been rebuked, and he deserved that reproach. He knew Prof. Collins had his best interest at heart, and Tyler always tried so hard to impress all his teachers.

His essays were coming along better than when he first tried to write about the people on the bench. For his next essay, he thought about writing about the birds on the fence and why they had decided to spend the winter in Boston instead of Florida or South America. That could prove to be a challenging topic were he to pursue it. Professor Collins dismissed class, and Tyler ducked out the side door as quickly as he could.

A few days later, on the thirteenth of November, Prof. Collins began to explain to him about the letters and the mailmen. Tyler didn't know why the professor had waited so long to inform him about some of the mysteries, but he knew not to ask unless he was told. His father had instilled that in him at an early age. Tyler was polite and courteous, a well-bred young gentleman.

According to Prof. Collins, who continued on with Tyler's instructions, the Krewe of Adelphos, as it was first called, and, as far as he knew, had its origins in the early days of the 1850s in New Orleans. Some say it went farther back into antiquity. At one time it was known as the Brotherhood of the Delphic Oracle. Later, it was know as the Fraternity of the Three Points.

No one knows why the name was changed back and forth. Perhaps other organizations had the same name, too, but most likely emphasis was placed on some ritual or symbol that best expressed the fraternity, and that ritual or symbol came to the forefront as time progressed. By the middle of the 1870s, however, the name reverted back to the Crewe of Adelphos, spelled with a *c* this time.

The Greek word *adelphos* refers to *brother*. It was odd, Tyler thought, that the word was singular. Professor Collins didn't know why it was in the singular either, unless the individual was being emphasized. Prof. Collins was quick to explain that if you change the spelling to *adelphus*, you have the word for *womb*, at least in some Greek dictionaries. The professor pointed out that if one pronounces *adelphos* and *adelphus* the way that Americans would pronounce those two words, they are pronounced the same, blurring the difference between *brother* and *womb*.

"In a way, Tyler, the brothers form a womb of sorts, protecting each other from the outside."

"The outside? The outside of what?" Tyler asked.

"That's for you to contemplate, son."

"Yes, sir. I shall contemplate," Tyler responded. He closed his eyes and leaned back in the chair in Prof. Collins' office. One thing about Tyler, he was obedient to a fault.

"Well, not now!" Prof. Collins playfully shouted. "Contemplate when you have time on your hands. Now, just one final thing and your instruction for the evening will be complete. *Adelphos* and *adelphus* have the three letters *d-e-l* embedded within. That reminds us of the fourth Greek letter, *delta,* and the letter *delta* looks like a triangle. Also, Tyler, *down on the Delta* is a term you've heard referring to New Orleans. We use a yellow triangle to represent *delta.*"

"Why is the fourth letter so important? Is that why we have four letters from the mailmen? What about *alpha, beta,* and *gamma*? Why yellow?"

"Calm down, son. I don't have all the answers. It appears you've been given more than you can mentally masticate tonight!"

He left the professor's office thinking about allegories and symbolism, and he wondered if the Crewe of Adelphos was an ancient order or if it was something that Professor Collins had made up to have make a fool out of a Louisiana boy.

Along the walkway leading up to the east door of the *Cloisters,* Dean Stephens, out of breath from walking against the wind, approached Tyler, who stopped and smiled.

"A little windy, eh, Dean Stephens!"

"Tyler, this just arrived from the telegraph office for you. I wanted to make sure you got it quickly. I hope it's not bad news for you." He pressed the sealed envelop into Tyler's hand, bowed his head, and turned on his heel and walked off in the direction of his office on the second floor of Old Main.

Tyler watched the dean ascend the steps and disappear through the oaken doors into Old Main's lobby. The telegram began to feel heavier the tighter he clasped it, and Tyler didn't know if he should read it out there in the open or not. He looked around and saw no one else. The young lad was alone. He tucked the envelope into his coat pocket and briskly walked to the *Cloisters. Perhaps it is good news* played in his thoughts as he took two steps at a time up to his third floor residence. His room provided the necessary privacy that such a worrisome moment required.

Sitting on the edge of his bed, he ran his fingers around the envelope trying to discern what was inside, but that was only postponing the inevitable. He removed the letter opener from the nightstand, to be proper, of course, and slowly slit the envelope open across the top.

TYLER STOP YOUR DADDY IS ILL STOP COME SOON STOP MOTHER

At first, the telegram confused him, but he remembered that telegrams had no punctuation marks and the word *stop* had to be used to show where a period or other mark of punctuation should go. He sat on the bed for a while; he then went to the wardrobe and began to pack up a small bag for the trip home.

* * * * * *

Leaving Boston as soon as he could on Sunday, he had to deal with inclement weather for part of his journey by rail, breaking off his trip for hours until the rail lines could be cleared of debris. He missed the fastest steamer on the

Mississippi by a few hours and had to settle for a regular paddle wheeler that seemed to load and unload goods far too often.

By the time Tyler arrived on Thursday, the nineteenth, he only had enough time to spend one pensive Thursday evening at home in New Orleans with his father, Beauregard Pettigrew, son of Harland Pettigrew. He instinctively knew that his father didn't have much time left, and when he pulled up a chair to hold vigil at his father's bedside, his father took the boy's hand. Beauregard tried to say something, but Tyler, his ear close to his father's mouth, couldn't make out what was being whispered. His father's breath smelled rancid from the elixir that the doctor had prescribed. And try as he might, he couldn't hold his father's hand still. Beauregard kept trying to turn it over or to grasp the boy's hand awkwardly. He didn't want Tyler to hold it quietly.

"What's he doing?" the boy asked the doctor.

"Could be a nervous reaction, you know. A spasm of sorts, perhaps," Doctor Buford Knight replied. He stood watch on the other side of the bed. From time to time, he took out his pocket watch, noted the minute hand slipping slowly by, drew in a few puffs from his crooked cigar, and nodded to Tyler by the bed and to Mrs. Hettie Pettigrew seated near the bureau.

"Tyler, you keep your daddy calm now, y'hear," his mother said. "Don't be fussin' about with his hands if the doctor thinks you're agitatin' him."

"Things are fine, Mrs. Pettigrew, just fine. Sometimes people don't have control...at the end. He sorta comes and goes," Dr. Knight explained as delicately as he could. Tyler and the rest watched patiently. They observed the ill man drift between being lucid and being, for a lack of a better word, comatose. Tyler's father appeared to be on a coaster ride of sorts. Beauregard slumbered, but suddenly, he was awake once again though it was obvious that the man was weak and in great discomfort.

"Leave me alone with my boy," Beauregard whispered after summoning up some strength. He coughed hard when he looked at his wife and at the doctor. They nodded and retired to the antechamber, closing the tall French baroque doors behind them.

"I wrote a letter. On its way to Boston now. There's not much time…," Beauregard began in a barely audible whisper.

"Don't talk much, papa. Save your strength," Tyler said.

"Save it? For what, boy? The transformation is hard. Mighty hard. I'm looking forward to it, though," Beauregard sighed. "Come here, son. Let me hold you."

Tyler sat on the bed and let his father, already weak and in decline, hold him for the first time since the diphtheria outbreak back in 1873 when it looked as though the child would depart the world long before his time. Beauregard feebly embraced his son; he kissed his boy on the side of the neck, and almost immediately, Tyler's skin felt irritated. A burning feeling began to spread out where the kiss had been, and when he touched his neck, it felt as though there was a small abrasion. Tyler shivered. His father saw a slight bruise appear.

"It's all right, boy. You're supposed to shiver. You'll find out soon what it's about." Beauregard propped himself up on his right elbow. "Open up the drawer on the stand. Take out the book. Keep it to yourself. Give it to no one. It will explain things now unknown to you." He obeyed his father.

He sat on the bed and quickly thumbed through the small leather book. His father's furrowed brow was a signal that now wasn't the time to explain or to explore its contents. "Now go out. Fetch your momma and the doctor. Have them take up their watch once again." He fell back onto his plump pillow filled with eider down, coughed heavily, and resigned himself to rest.

Tyler took a quick, final glance down at the book, noticing its pages tattered and worn on the edges, before he placed it into his topcoat pocket that was draped across the chair with the embroidered fleur-de-lis. His neck still smarted, and the burning sensation spread through the upper muscles of his back and around his shoulder blade, but he complained not; he was too concerned that his father wouldn't live to see the dawn.

He summoned his mother and the doctor to take up their places. Silence gave comfort; hope waned.

Beauregard Pettigrew, son of Harland Pettigrew, passed away quietly the next afternoon lying under the fringed canopy above his bed. He was alone. It had to be that way. The transformation wasn't as hard as he expected, but he had to have his privacy at that final moment. It only took a second.

His stately bedroom held solemn watch as friends and neighbors came to pay their respects as the news spread around the parish, and Tyler nodded to and shook hands with each person in a communion of quiet southern solitude.

On the following day, Saturday, the mortician and his assistant lifted the deceased from his repose on the canopied bed and gently laid him into a casket of fine silk and polished mahogany. The pallbearers carried the precious cargo down the main staircase carved from rich rosewood. Somberly, they placed Tyler's beloved father into a beautiful hearse adorned with cut glass windows and black Victorian bunting that six powerful horses pulled in solemn procession to the church for the final obsequies.

The small pump organ droned out the traditional hymns, and the reverend spoke words of comfort to ears that really didn't hear what he had to say. People filled up the small nave, and some younger men waited outside reminiscing about what a good man Beauregard had been, and between fond memories, they imbibed of southern whiskey hidden from the lady folk in small silver flasks. Beauregard was known to tip a few in his day, too.

During the final verse of "Rock of Ages," Tyler took his mother by the arm and escorted her to say her final farewell. She stopped, raised her Chantilly veil and looked upon the only man she had ever loved. Reverently, she opened her black leather purse with the silver snap, withdrew a small yellow silken triangle, and placed it above her spouse's heart.

"What's that for?" Tyler whispered.

"He asked me to do it. Must have something to do with one of his groups. You know how your daddy liked his groups." She pulled her veil back down and began to return to her pew. The minister acknowledged her action with a slight bow of the head and closed the coffin's lid with a dull thud.

Tyler smiled and understood. The restless hand was no longer a mystery. His father was trying to give the sign of the Crewe of Adelphos, and Tyler's only regret was that he didn't return the favor because he didn't understand his father's intentions.

When he arrived back at campus a week later after helping his mother begin to settle some of his father's estate, he noticed that the obstinate leaves on the tree by the botanical garden had disappeared, exposing the branches to a blustery New England storm that drenched the campus in freezing drizzle.

Tyler visited the small post office in the basement of Old Main to see if there was any mail from home. A letter from New Orleans would often take a little over a week, sometimes two or more, depending on whether a packet was sailing north on the Mississippi at the right moment. Often the missive would go overland by train from St. Louis or Cincinnati. That November morning, Tyler asked politely for his mail, and Beverly Weltzer, the postmistress, scampered between the various bins looking for a letter that she knew had arrived the evening before.

"Imagine. Coming all the way from Louisiana," she said before she handed him the letter.

"Yes, ma'am, just like me," he replied.

She looked at him and laughed at his cleverness. "We don't get many letters from so far away from here, you know. Now take this, young man. I hope it's good news for you!"

Tyler wanted to talk a little longer because Mrs. Weltzer was always interested in him. She apparently didn't know that his father had died.

Tyler studied the envelope and took in the bold curves of his father's script. The black ink was still confident, yet there was a slight variation from his normal self-assured crossing of the *t's* and his ostentatious scroll of the *P* in *Pettigrew*. His father certainly had written the letter to him; Tyler didn't doubt that. But he did perceive a slight change in his father's cursive expression.

In the lobby of the *Cloisters*, he seated himself on the soft leather couch, kicked off his shoes, crossed his legs and read the letter his father had posted to him shortly before his untimely death.

New Orleans
Ninth of November
A.D. 1885

My dear son,

It is quite possible that by the time you receive this from me, I shall no longer be part of this mortal life. Already, I can write only a few lines at a sitting, but today I seem to have my strength once again. Time is a very strange thing. It seems to be endless, but I have come to realize that it does, indeed, run out in its own way. I am not as weak as I shall become, but the signs of my demise are encroaching, and I am quite helpless, son, to stop that horrid intrusion.

I have been informed that the fourth mailman visited you, and I am extremely happy. I am only saddened that we may never give each other the signs and oaths of the Crewe, but those signs and oaths that bind us in life shall keep you strong long after my passing.

There are those who want our secrets. There are those who try to imitate us. Be careful and divulge nothing you are about to learn through your post-initiatory instruction which has just begun and is far from being finished.

Our particular Crewe was born out in the bayous one misty night when we vowed to counteract those who sought to destroy our secrets, who sought to destroy our bonds. We had to break away from the Krewe of Orestus, a most ancient Order. Evil had infiltrated them. They took our knowledge and perverted it.

We redefined ourselves and went further into hiding. Our sacred text was removed and sequestered. Keep clear of the Krewe of Orestus. Often, they try to hide within our dens, sometimes with success. They'll suck the life directly out of you. They cause misery beyond your feeble understandings.

Not long ago, an errant brother was reprimanded for betrayal, a betrayal he denied. He was taken to the cabin where he could meditate, realize his delinquent behavior, and seek a new communion with his brothers.

He imbibed heavily, walked along the dock, and fell into the water during the night of the new moon, fracturing his skull on a submerged rock. It has been said that he cursed me and my posterity before he passed on. To him, I had caused him, in his own mind, to drink and then fall into the murky waters of the swamp that moonless night. It was his own misuse of free agency, however, that caused his death.

I have been growing a little weaker each day. Whether it is because of his curse, I know not. The doctor says I have the fever, whatever that means. At midnight, I grow stronger, feel well, and sleep through the night. The following morning, however, I am worse off than the day before. Tyler, you are my only child. I shall no longer be here to help you, but it is only right, son, to tell you what you must know. You will make a change soon, I believe. Accept the challenge if you want. We shall meet again.

Guard yourself. Protect yourself.
In deepest respect,
Father

Tyler uncrossed his legs, picked up his shoes, and returned to his room on the third floor where he tucked the letter securely away for another time. He fetched the book given to him by his father, studied the title page of the *Kuhduush*, and opened the book randomly to the first chapter of Jezreél: *In the twinkling of an eye, thou shalt change from eternity to eternity.* In the First Book of Nashrám, he read: *As the father supports his son by love, the body supports the neck, and the neck supports the head. So it is that all things work in unity to sustain our eternal nature.* Finally, he studied the words underlined in the Second Book of Nashrám: *An embrace, a kiss or a touch, and a shiver seal one's life to the other, unending and immortal as it was, is, and shall be through the ages of the ages until the Eternal One, blessèd be He, gathers His creation unto Himself and bestows the final Crown of worthiness.*

He placed the *Kuhduush* back into the dresser under his winter scarves and thought about what an odd book his father had given him. He touched his neck where his father had kissed him and remembered the shiver that had coursed through him. It reminded him of what he had just read in Second Nashrám.

He felt a slight fever come upon him, and for the first time in years, he felt utterly alone. That night, far from the edge of campus, Tyler found comfort with Sarah Garret.

* * * * * *

New Orleans and Points North
June 1886

Tyler Pettigrew completed his second year of college education in early May, the first in his family to have such a lofty ambition. Although Boston had become his home, he felt alone and sequestered for most of the time. Sarah Garret avoided him, and she stopped answering his letters to her and refused to answer the door when he came calling in the spring. Her friends and acquaintances weren't able to contact her. Some said, without supporting evidence, that she had gone to live with an aunt in Wilmington, Delaware.

He longed to return to the place of his birth to continue his schooling. He wanted to honor his father's memory, but Boston was where he decided he would finish up his education. For some reason, Boston permitted him to focus more on the present, and New Orleans kept him anchored to the past.

The first thing he did when he returned to his family's estate was to take out his guitar, restring it, tune it, and strum soft, sentimental chords up in his room. The soft strains echoed his internal melancholy. He always heard melodies that others could never hear. Many of the songs he played were tunes his father had taught him. Some didn't have words that he knew of. He often improvised, changing lyrics that were too old to reflect his present-day emotions, but he knew that he sang the songs to overcome his grief of losing a father, Sarah Garret, and his own youth. He now stood at the brink of maturity, and it scared him more than any single thing or any person. The unknown future was waiting to swallow him up like some bloated whale a fisherman might find off the coast of Nantucket.

About two weeks after he arrived home, much to his dismay, his mother suddenly departed to Natchez to visit a girlfriend, Martha Ellington, she had attended elementary school with. Martha's husband was suffering with consumption and was doing poorly.

Having been left alone so abruptly, almost callously, his mind wandered back, for some unknown reason, to the beginning of the previous summer when he was standing on the dock in New Orleans awaiting his father, but this time, of course, his father didn't arrive to fetch him; the coachman did. No mailmen were in sight. He wondered where Hannah Morgan was at that very moment, but he had to laugh at the thought that he had been infatuated with an opera singer, albeit for only a few seconds, a year ago.

His mother, now known as the *Widow* Pettigrew, draped in an almost a regal title, had sent a letter to him only once since his arrival, quickly explaining that she didn't know exactly when she would be returning. She assured him that the servants would take good care of him, but he didn't want people fawning over him. Each boring, uneventful day was the same, but all boring, uneventful days are always the same.

The heat was oppressive, harsh. And before he had become accustomed to the humid inferno and to the servants and to the cyclical life on the estate, he boarded a steamer and sailed down around the Florida coast, heading north to New York City after a two day binge in Miami where he found consolation in a bottle of bootleg bourbon, Sarah Garret being too far away to be even a pleasant memory.

He watched New York City appear when they steamed into the harbor, and he realized that New York and Boston were nothing alike. New York was so busy, so stuffed with humanity, or at least that is what it looked like as they approached the pier. Hundreds of stevedores milled around keeping the docks running smoothly. It was well-orchestrated mayhem, if there is such a thing, but he came up with no other description in his mind for what he observed while waiting to descend to the dock. His pocket watch, the one engraved with his father's name, let him know that he had about two hours until the train would begin its leisurely, chugging journey to Maine.

Tyler had never been to Maine, but one of the young men at the *Cloisters* always spent his summers up there somewhere with the family, perhaps in Portland, and just the name itself conjured up images of cool winds from the ocean with its rocky beaches and rugged cliffs and mysterious, foggy bluffs. That image was more consoling to him than the reality of violent summer storms and hurricanes in New Orleans. He was ready to launch out on his own. He desired to vacate the nest for mysterious places. And if he had to go somewhere, then Maine was just as good a choice as any. New people, novel places, a fresh life unknown to him at the moment, silently beckoned him into the unfamiliar, and Kennepointe, Maine, a small village he found on a map, was as unfamiliar to him as was Shanghai or Bombay.

His father had left him with a goodly inheritance, at least by the standards of 1886, and he enjoyed flapping his wings of independence in order to circumnavigate his own world, the world he was so desperately creating.

After a slow overnight train ride that snaked through hidden, unnamed valleys and miles of timbered land in Connecticut, Massachusetts, and New Hampshire, he arrived at Kennepointe, a quaint village of brilliantly painted rowboats and fishing trawlers that basked more in the sun of the past than in the realities of the present. A white church glistened in the rising sun. A few shopkeepers were opening their doors and setting up their produce on the sidewalk as he walked along with his suitcase in hand. He tipped his hat to the gawking townsmen and greeted them with a *Good day;* the shopkeepers nodded and responded with *eh-yuh.* He now knew he was in Maine for certain.

At Mrs. Murphy's tourist home, he spied a *Room to Let* sign nailed to a post on the front porch, and after a short interview, he took up residence for a month, payable in advance. The room itself was sparse, but a single bed, washstand, and writing desk were all he required to be comfortable. The bay window opened to a vista of the Atlantic, its waters already churning hours before the afternoon storm hit with fury.

"And over here's your wardrobe closet. Feel free to hang up your clothes. If anything needs ironing, I iron on Tuesday. Monday's the day I do my worsh."

"Does it cost extra?" he asked.

"You paid for a month in advance; the ironin' and the worshin' are free to you."

Tyler nodded, was much obliged as usual, and hung up his clothing before turning down his bed for a short nap.

The wind began to howl around four o'clock, and soon the rain hammered against the windowpanes, but he just turned slightly and fell deeper into sleep. The thunder echoing through the tempest and the bolts of lightning dancing off the cliffs could not move him.

During the early evening, he dined on a supper of soup and roasted bread. Exploring the area after eating, he noticed that the wind had snapped some tree limbs and damaged several roofs along Bloom Street where it crossed Delbert Alley. His small leather bag in hand, Tyler removed the journal he had been keeping and made a few entries down by the ocean. The rocks were still soaked from the afternoon storm.

A gentle breeze was blowing and he smelled the salt in the air. He inhaled deeply; he felt exhilarated. This is where he was supposed to be. He fished around in his little bag and withdrew the *Kuhduush,* opening it to the Book of Khalief. He thumbed through the pages. Many of the passages were taking on special meaning to him. *Go thy ways into the north country and await the setting of the sun. There the power and the presence of the Holy One, blessèd be He, awaits.* In another verse, he found solace in *Hail, the Immortali. Many shall never see the Great Translator of men. They shall never fear his sting for their necks are strong in the embrace of their fathers and of their brothers.*

He touched his neck and remembered his father's embrace. He remembered the shiver once again. He asked himself why his father had underlined this particular passage. His eyes were drawn out to sea. A large ship was steaming up the coast; perhaps it was going to Canada or England. The smoke poured out the main funnel. The bell atop the lighthouse on shore rang out a warning for those on the vessel not to drift too closely to shore where the rocky coast was exposed at low tide, or that's what he thought the bell meant. . .perhaps it was a warning to the small lobster boats bobbing on the waves about something else.

He briefly watched a young man up on the cliffs painting the sea. Tyler stretched out his tired legs for a while, observed the time, packed up his bag, and began the long ascent to the top of the precipice from which he had come. The force of the sea had given him energy, and his long climb back up would sap him of that strength. He laughed at how everything had its own price.

CHAPTER 7

01 Dec 2009

Joel Garret had papers strewn all over his room. Papers obscured his bed, hid his desk, and covered the floor. Papers taped to the lamps (he had seen that once in a movie and never believed that people actually taped things to lamps, but he decided to imitate art), taped to chairs, and taped to the door showed nothing but clutter and confusion to the untrained eye.

In all that disarray, however, the irony was that he was organizing his material. At first, much of what he possessed came to him via his father's files from back home in southern Louisiana. The newer material came from other researchers he had met on line while trying to find some more primary sources for Mr. Docket's project. Unfortunately, most of the sources he was able to acquire were secondary at best, and he knew that he couldn't trust secondary sources as much for their authenticity.

The latest batch of material, however, had been under his nose most of the time. Paul Docket suggested that Joel get permission from Mrs. Woodburn to access the private collections in the library's archives. Tyler Pettigrew had left behind several large boxes of bulky material upon his demise in 1896, one year after he opened the Academy.

Over time, various librarians had attempted to sort through it all, but there were always other projects that railroaded them, and the works and thoughts of one Tyler Pettigrew were left to father dust on the forgotten shelves in the basement.

Joel had made copies of as much as he felt relevant, but even he didn't know how it all fit together. Racine Woodburn even let him sign out a box of material for twenty-four hours with the stipulation that he try to categorize some of the material before returning it. Tyler hadn't left things in a tidy order for anyone to find. Why should he? He hadn't planned on going to his grave at thirty years of age.

Paul Docket stopped by to survey the chaos and to offer a helping hand if needed after Joel e-mailed him for assistance.

"My! I suppose you have all this under control!" Paul said.

"It's taken on a life of its own at the moment. Why don't y'all take a. . .well, I wanted you to take a seat, but I'm afraid I can't even offer that hospitality at the moment."

Paul meandered around the room and looked at the various documents that appeared to be in no particular order. From time to time, he would pick one up, study it, and put it back where he had found it.

Joel said, "On this small slip of paper, you can see that Tyler Pettigrew sent off some money to Sarah Garret for 'supplies.' That was in 1887. Over there is a letter from her to him talking about the baby and being happy that both are being taken care of in 1888. But nowhere in his documents have I found a paper where she actually says *'you' are the father, Tyler.* It's implied but not specified."

"I'm sure you'll find something somewhere. There's so much to search through, but you do have the birth certificate. And that's a primary source. The answers always don't come so easily," Paul explained. "Family history is a puzzle, and at times most of the pieces have been misplaced."

"Is that supposed to lift my spirits or deflate all I've done?" Joel asked.

"Well..."

"Well, peruse this, Mr. Docket. It's from something called the Book of Pisho. Someone wrote it on what looks like parchment. Doubt if it's the real stuff. *At the beginning of times, when the earth was fresh, the sons of Life, blessèd be they, took unto themselves choice wives, the daughters of the kings, the daughters of the rulers; choice they were these daughters of the rulers and kings. At that time and afterwards, their progeny was blessed with longevity, with life in abundance. Their sons were called the Immortali, the great ones of the age. Unlike the Nephilim of old, those giants whose age was set at one hundred and twenty years, the Immortali comforted and healed. Their touch assuaged the pain of others. Their look gave hope to the downtrodden and to the poor ones, the* anawim, *of the kingdom.* I wonder what it means.

"Maybe it meant something to him. People save all kinds of things, don't they?"

"Any idea about the Nephilim?" Joel asked.

"Supposedly a race of giants that came from somewhere. It's mentioned in Genesis," Paul replied. "What's that little book over there?"

"Don't know exactly. It's a little leather bound book called the *Kuhduush,*" Joel explained. "Looks like some kind of bible or something by the way it's laid out. No date of publication and no printer's name."

"Some of the early Crewes used to have compilations of sacred sayings from many sources. I sometimes think that someone just made them up to sound holy or philosophical. Toss it over here," Paul said. He caught the book, thumbed through the text, and noticed that some of the passages had been underlined. One in particular caught his attention: *Upon the body, devoid of spirit, the three-angles* Δ *with the vertex pointed up toward the heavens shall mark the worthy servant. There shall it hold its vigil until the Day of Days. But with its vertex pointed down, the evil ones have shown their power. They have sapped the worthy servant of his strength.* "I'd like to explore this a little more."

"Sorry, but you know Mrs. Woodburn. She entrusted it all to me. It's due back tomorrow morning. She said I could take it back out after exams and Christmas if I need to snoop around some more. Just stick the book in that box over there," Joel said.

"She wouldn't even know it was missing, but I'll lay it to rest for the moment. Until another time. Make sure you return it all to the archives as she requested."

Joel nodded, and Paul started for the door, feeling the *Kuhduush* tucked secretly away in his jacket pocket. He knew no one would find it missing.

"Wait!" Joel said. Paul stopped. He was sure he'd been caught pilfering the *Kuhduush*. "Look at this," Joel said, pointing to an old picture he had laid on the table. "Who do you think this is?"

Paul took it, turned it over, and made his pronouncement saying, "It's Tyler Pettigrew. At least that's what it says on the back. 1886. Kennepointe, Maine. If he's your 3G grandfather, you don't look much like him!"

"You're faster than I am! I didn't turn it over. I've never seen a picture of him before. You'd think there would be some big oil painting of him hanging above a fireplace somewhere on campus. It looks like someone I know, but I can't place him at the moment."

Paul Docket studied the young man in the picture carefully. "If you change the hair style a bit, it looks like Roger Honeycutt, right down to the slightly crooked smile. Look at the round chin, the sunken eyes. Could be Honeycutt's twin from over a century ago. It's downright spooky, isn't it?" Paul stated.

Joel continued to work well into the night after Paul left. His project became easier because there was a wealth of material for him to sift through. At least he had information. Others still weren't sure where they were going to find their ancestral treasure trove. He wondered if anyone in his family knew the connection involving him, Trinity, and Tyler Pettigrew. No one had ever mentioned it to him before.

The Crewe of Adelphos was having a short meeting later that night to discuss plans for the Christmas program and about how they could help some of the poor residents of Greenlawn who had lost jobs in recent months, but Joel couldn't attend because of his work load at the moment.

The Crewe had given him confidence, and it seemed to him that the fraternal attention had helped him with his grades. He was learning discipline and how to schedule his time, and the Crewe was always there to support him. He felt comfortable with Mr. Docket, but he felt closer to Roger for some reason. Joel wasn't a jock by any stretch of the imagination, but as of late, Roger had taken him under his wing especially after Paul Docket had told Roger about Joel's link to Tyler Pettigrew.

That night, Joel turned over in his sleep and felt a hand slightly touch his head. He stirred and shifted over onto his side. He recognized the outline of someone standing by his bed, but he didn't feel fear, and he didn't come to complete consciousness. His breathing became deep. He sensed an island of calm surrounding him. A slight touch caused his neck to burn; he didn't wake up. He shivered and pulled the covers up before sleeping deeper than he had in years.

* * * * * *

02 December 2009

Paul was walking along the side of A. Boarman Hall going toward the Woodburn Library, named after Racine's husband's great-great grandfather, Willis B. Woodburn, who had donated the first ten thousand books to make the Academy the best in the state for that time.

The football season had finished the first week in November, and most of the alums were glad it was over. *That Gruder thing* was blamed for the poor playing record, but others were certain that Coach Hominy had passed the zenith of his career years ago.

Paul had been thinking about Hominy and the hold he had on the players. Can a coach get winning results through intimidation, or do the players have to have the proper respect to produce victory after victory? Does a team lose because it plays better teams, or does it lose because the coach and his players are no longer in harmony? And what happens after a cataclysmic event? Shouldn't the coach and team form a new unity and perform even better than before, or does such an event devastate everyone to the point of becoming lethargic?

Paul looked down at the ground and noticed a shadow approaching him from behind. He kept his pace. The shadow was about to overtake him.

"Mr. D! Out for a stroll?" the Coyote, a literature student, asked.

"You should put a bell around your neck. You gave me a little fright!"

"Yeah. Everyone's still touchy about things, huh?"

"I've been meaning to ask you something. You play football, right?" Paul asked, knowing that he did in a mediocre way.

"If you want to call 'hoggin' the bench' playing football!"

"Explain something to me, will you? I've been thinking, and it isn't always good when I've been thinking! After every football game, several of the junior and senior varsity players sprint over to the chapel where the band and other supporters have already gathered. It doesn't matter if the team wins or loses; the obligatory trek has to take place. It isn't because the players are particularly pious. They aren't. Most of the boys are in involved in things that would *schreck* even *low* Episcopalians! They go to the chapel because tradition dictates it!" Paul shouted out the last sentence and raised his hand mimicking an eloquent speaker.

"Hey, Mr. D, you're pretty good at that!"

"Thanks, I've been known to teach speech from time to time. But I digress. Before I moved to my new house, I didn't live too far from the school," Paul began. "One night after the game, I heard the band playing some peppy ditty while they marched over to the chapel, so I decided to stroll over to the campus from my apartment and see what all the noise was about. Someone in the band told me to stop and stay where I was. The team's upperclassmen were going through some kind of private ceremony inside. Well, I wanted to go in and see."

"I know the ritual," the Coyote answered softly, almost whispering.

"One of the underclassmen players was standing porter at the door. He quickly pointed out to me that I couldn't enter. That lack of tact unnerved me greatly," Paul responded.

There was no reason to bar a faculty member from entering the chapel and taking part in the post-game prayer. But Paul wasn't to be outdone. Not for one minute. The following week, he entered the church long before the game was over, stealing along the wall and stairwell, hiding himself up in the choir loft away from probing eyes.

Although the team had lost by over twenty points that particular night, he could hear the approaching band playing some unrecognizable fight song or a "hootie-hootie" march, the name he gave to any song where the clarinets squeaked and the trumpets blared so loudly that a bystander couldn't tell if they were playing "God Bless America" or "We are Family."

Raising himself up in the dark to observe the proceedings from his secret perch, Paul witnessed the private ritual. Although he couldn't hear the words clearly enough to understand them, the senior captain lay prostrate up the altar steps by the communion rail and said some type of prayer. A prayer wasn't unusual, although the captain lying prostrate seemed to be a little dramatic. After the prayer, another senior joined him, stretched himself out over the three steps leading up to the altar, and began to tell God how sorry he was for losing the game.

Coach Hominy approached him and yelled, "Tell Him *WHY* you lost the game, boy! Tell Him so we can *ALL* hear!"

The tight end began to confess the sins that he had committed since the last game, one by one.

"There has to be more reasons than that as to why we lost the game tonight! My grandmother's committed bigger sins while playing canasta! That's a card game, boys. A freakin' card game!" the coach yelled again.

A junior cornerback fell across the steps and began acknowledging his sins, much more serious than what the senior had confessed. Soon he was joined by others. Before it was over, every junior and senior who comprised the coach's Lion's Pride had confessed aloud all their transgressions.

"And that's why you lost!! Do YOU hear me?? That's why YOU lost!" the coach continued in an intimidating voice. "I'm not perfect, boys, but you have to keep it clean before game day! UNDERSTOOD!!!"

"Yes, sir, SIR, yes, sir!" they answered in unison, a string of *s*'s echoing off the vaulted walls.

Each time he remonstrated them, they all repeated the *Yes, sir, SIR, yes, sir!* It almost began to sound like a litany. The harassing continued for several minutes, and many of the players lying prostrate up the steps began to cry, and each promised to eschew sin at any cost.

"If you really are straight about what you've confessed, no one here will go to the homecoming dance this year just to prove your sincerity, UNDERSTOOD!!!"

"Yes, sir, SIR, yes, sir!" they thundered back. And that year, two years ago, none of the Pride went to the dance.

"Now get the hell outa here and hustle back to your showers at the fieldhouse. I want it done in double time! And this time, keep the hot water turned off. If I see any steam, you'll pay for it later," he threatened.

"Yes, sir, SIR, yes, sir!" the Pride thundered back in unison.

Paul and the Coyote had paused by the old oak tree where it was believed that Tyler Pettigrew had carved his initials when he first purchased the land, but as the tree grew, the letters, if they were ever there in the first place, had blurred and were illegible. The Coyote began to explain to Paul as they approached the library that only the coach's chosen were permitted to attend the post-game rite. "That's how he controlled everyone. That was his Lion's Pride. Everyone was elite in their own way. I used to be part of it, but after I got hurt, I was no use to them. I had to sit on the bench trying to heal, and I wasn't healing fast enough. The weak are cast out. Isn't that the law of the jungle?

"That's rough. Really rough. I'm sorry you were hurt... physically and mentally. But doesn't that tradition of going to the chapel go back for generations?" Paul asked.

"The tradition does, but not *his* tradition. He changed it all the year he came here."

"Didn't he attend Trinity as a boy?" Paul continued.

"Yeah. He took so many things and turned them into what would serve him. But I don't think he made them all up. He once told us that even when he went here, there was *the Pride,* but it was very much underground," the Coyote explained. "Besides, I'm a coyote, not a cat!" He thought about what he had said and laughed out loud.

"Is the Pride one of the crewes?"

"Not sure, Mr. D." The Coyote didn't want to continue on about the Pride.

"There are other things that are better than his old Pride around here," Paul began to explain. The Coyote just stared down at the sidewalk. He didn't want to interact any longer. "Your people have been around here for a long time. Your father attended this school, and so did your grandfather," Paul stated as a prelude to something else.

"Sure did. I'm third generation."

"Long tradition of good men. Dr. LaCause and the coroner, Code Schaffer, graduated from here. They were all part of a great tradition that didn't involve cats! Someday we'll talk."

* * * * * *

07 Dec 2009

Sterrett Hamilton, the president, sat in his office that overlooked the parking lot that stretched down to the fieldhouse. The sun was just about ready to plunge down behind Barker's Hill. The first major snow of the season had already made the numbers on the parking spaces invisible, and unless the snow plow arrived early in the morning to push the heavy white slop aside, half the faculty would be complaining that they couldn't find their parking spaces. People were dying throughout the world of starvation and war, and he had to hear about how someone couldn't find a piece of asphalt!

He thumped his yellow Ticonderoga pencil on his desk blotter like an absent-minded drummer focusing on a distant beat that only he could hear. The phone ringing in the next office brought him back for the moment from his private thoughts.

He had been trying to keep the lid on the boiling kettle, but the longer the Gruder case went on, the more he felt frustrated with the entire campus. Whether he was dealing with Tommy the local cop, the coroner, or Inspector Vasilovich, all he ever got was a series of *we're trying* and *we're still working*. The Board of Directors was afraid of the financial problems that could hit the Academy if a solution to the *Gruder problem* wasn't forthcoming. It was always about the money. No one cared about the lost life. No one cared about the grieving family. How the Academy's coffers would fare was all that mattered in the end.

* * * * * *

08 December 2009

Paul Docket scraped the snow off the Jeep's windshield in the parking lot that night after giving a short tutorial in the library annex. The wind began to whip the white powder into his face, stinging it like a fistful of needles. The gusts were blasting out of the north across the valley like the volleys of cannon that often shot in waves across a meadow of attack. Nights like this made him curse himself for not taking a teaching position in Florida.

"Have a good evening!" Rains yelled as he passed Mr. Docket's car.

"I can barely see you," Paul shouted back as the wind picked up again. "Who's with you?"

"Just me, Lindsay, and Sarah. I'm taking them back to their campus."

Trinity had once been co-ed, but that stopped in the 1950s when the sister school, Maple Woods, was created to prepare young women for leadership. Although Maple

Woods had taken the lead in the liberation of young women, the schools remained close over the years.

Ivy covered the major buildings on each campus; Tudor or Gothic revival, and deep woods and lakes surrounded and protected both institutions. Trinity still had dormitories for most of the young men, as did Maple Woods for the women, and there was always a hearty debate about whether or not living on campus for weeks at a time was too exclusive or even conducive to avoiding modern elitism. Younger professors thought that living off campus would teach the students responsibility. Parents, however, wanted their progeny on campus where others could monitor their social progress.

Paul Docket observed the three in the darkness; the white-out ripped off Rains's blue hood and exposed his brown hair which, under normal circumstances, usually fell across his eyes, but he had had it all shorn off last week because Lindsay liked it that way, and what Lindsey liked, Lindsay usually got. Paul wondered how a downtown boy had actually hooked up with such an uptown girl. Rains had bitten off more than he could chew, but he would have to learn that lesson on his own after Lindsey saw another uncut diamond like Rains and decided to do some further cutting and polishing of her own. Lindsay was high maintenance in a low maintenance town. And Rains? He was just a boy infatuated with the glitz and glamour of someone out of his league.

In class, Paul often wondered how Rains could see to take notes with all that hair hanging in front of his face, but at least the boy had shocks of hair that *could* fall over his forehead! With his locks shorn off, Rains would now be able to *see* the exam that Paul had prepared for the class. Paul smiled at the thought of when his own hair had once been much longer and thicker than that, but that was a different generation decades ago.

As Paul scraped the ice off his rear window, he kept his eyes on the three figures walking forward and backward depending on the direction of the gale. They arrived at Rains's car, and he would soon have them safely returned to Maple Woods.

Water, Steam, Snap, Darkness.
Steam, Snap, Darkness.
Snap, Darkness.
Water.

Paul had been plagued by visions and premonitions most of his life. He had *the gift.* When he tried to explain to his mother about seeing things or knowing things that he wasn't supposed to know, she told him it was about his special talent. But he was too young to really understand what she was talking about.

The visions had started, as far as he could remember, in sixth grade when Mrs. McNally was killing time by asking the students about current events. Paul raised his hand and told the class about a plane crash in the Everglades.

"Some of its four propellers were conking out and it went down. No one survived," he explained.

"How awful, Paul," Mrs. McNally commented. "Imagine how horrible such a thing is!"

"I know, Mrs. McNally," Paul continued. "It blew up when it hit the swamp."

Later that day when Paul went home for lunch, he turned on the TV to the local news in Pittsburgh to see if they had any more information about the disaster, but after the normal run of international highlights and local commentary, he was disappointed that they hadn't broadcast the story again.

Two days later in class, Mrs. McNally looked Paul straight in the face and said quietly, so that others couldn't hear the conversation, "Paul, remember that story about the plane crash in the Everglades?"

"Yes, ma'am," Paul answered after sitting up in his seat.

"When you told us about that, Paul, it hadn't happened yet. It happened yesterday evening, according to the news this morning. How did you know about it?" she whispered.

"I guess I saw it on the news or something," he answered with a bit of confusion in his voice.

"Don't you understand? You couldn't have. It hadn't happened," she said sternly, accompanied with a smile so the others nearby couldn't read her true thoughts.

"Musta been on the news," he responded because he still didn't understand her point.

That was his introduction to a world of feelings and senses and scenes that he simply couldn't explain to himself, and he had to learn to hide his *gift* early in life lest others ridicule him for not being the same.

That quick flash of water and steam and snap he experienced in the parking lot lasted for only a few seconds, but it had taken his breath away because of the energy that was forced upon him. He doubled over for a moment and slowly righted himself as he tried to regain his balance. He had just seen Steve Gruder's demise in his mind, but he didn't recognize the killer from behind. He only knew that the perpetrator wore blue and had a strong build.

When he opened the driver's door to his Jeep, a downburst of snow and frigid air caused him to falter as it ripped the door out of his grasp, swinging it all the way open. A gloved hand grabbed his shoulder from behind. He turned with a start, coming face to face with a hooded figure.

"You OK, Mr. Docket?" the voice spoke out of the scarf wound around the neck and face.

"You just scared me to death, that's all. Who is it?"

"It's Jackson. Jax Forester. Don't you recognize me?"

"Recognize you! I can barely see you. What are you doin' here this time of night, boy? It's honkin' nasty out!"

"Some of us had to stay and work on some science projects that we have to present at the university up at Tyson Grove next weekend. Thought you'd be long gone by now," he shouted in direct competition with the wind.

"Had to take care of a few loose ends. Would like to chat but have to get home. Send me an e-mail sometime and let me know how things are going! You never stop by the classroom anymore." Jackson just nodded and walked away into the darkness.

That was the most that Paul had ever heard Jax say at once. Usually, he just grunted and nodded. They had their own language, it seemed, but even a Neanderthaler, Jax's former girlfriend said once, had a larger vocabulary. But out of all his students, Jackson and Rains were the most trustworthy. Paul laughed out loud at the thought that he and Jax could have an entire conversation with just a few *umms* and *ughs* and *huhs*. Paul knew that words often got in the way of communication.

He turned the ignition on, backed up into the dark before turning on the headlights and headed out to the open gates at the south-east end of the lot. As he gunned the engine to make the long, snow-packed hill, he had a mental flash of a human torso clad in a bloody undershirt and suit pants, which seemed to have jumped suddenly in front of his

Wrangler as the Jeep sped through the gates into the blinding sheets of snow and freezing rain.

He slammed the brake pedal to the floor out of reflex. The Jeep slid sharply to the right, then to the left, and came to a stop blocking the hill horizontally. Slowly, he maneuvered the vehicle to the left to face downhill to survey just who had jumped in front of him. His headlights, as he had suspected, revealed no one on the road. He eyes searched the open emptiness of the lot, the fieldhouse immediately to his right.

Is it what shall be? he thought to himself driving back through the parking area, exiting from a different gate this time. His headache was a sign that all that he had endured in the past was about to be repeat itself at Trinity.

Chapter 8

Kennepointe, Maine
July 1886

Mrs. Murphy's lobster bisque and her vegetable soup with roasted bread tempted Tyler to stay on through the month of July. His mother returned to Natchez after Martha Ellington's husband succumbed to consumption a few days after Tyler had left for Maine. He was happy to receive her letter, but he was more enthralled with the coast and the Atlantic. The warm, dry days that year, sprinkled from time to time with long, leisurely showers, were more refreshing than the searing afternoons along the bayous that his mother had written him about.

He had made one friend during his sojourn in Maine, Lucas Granville, of English-French extraction, whose passion for painting the sea was second only to his infatuation with sailing upon it up and down the coast, often to the Canadian border. Tyler quietly observed Lucas creating his art down on the beach in the morning light, and then, in the evening session shortly before sunset, Lucas hurried in the failing light to capture the richness and the darkness of the billowing waves and swells that crashed into the rocks near the shore.

One day, when Tyler was sitting on Mrs. Murphy's porch, Lucas came along with his supplies and asked her if he could paint a canvas from the bay window that he had observed from out at sea. His skin was tanned from his hours in the sun. He was brawny; his arm muscles stretched the white cotton sleeves taut when he reached up to scratch his face or to run his hands nervously through his light brown hair, already streaked by the rays of the sun. He knew that his strength impressed women of any age, and his physique helped those women to agree to whatever he was asking of them.

Mrs. Murphy, blushing at how handsome he was, had no trouble with the request of turning her home into a summer studio if Tyler permitted his room to be used for such artistic purposes. Tyler had no objections, and he soon watched Lucas create something that had never existed before, much like the creation story in Genesis, he thought. A few strokes of color, and depth soon began to solidify and separate as ocean and landscape and sky. Tyler's neck twitched slightly and he swatted it. Perhaps a bug had lighted there to rest on its way to find food. Perhaps Tyler was the cuisine.

"Mosquito?" Lucas asked. He let out a slight chuckle.

"I don't know."

"They don't come out this early in the day," Lucas said matter-of-factly. He studied Tyler for a moment.

On a cloudy afternoon that awaited a sunny reprieve, the two engaged in a detailed conversation for the first time. Tyler didn't want to intrude on the inspired artist who held constant communion with his canvas, but he was fascinated by the creative process.

Tyler discovered that Lucas Granville attended the same college in Boston and had Professor Collins as his advisor, too. Furthermore, Lucas used to live on the first floor of the *Cloisters* until he moved into a small rooming house where he came and went as he pleased, often with his painting supplies tucked away in large a canvas bag.

One afternoon, Lucas and Tyler went out on a picnic with two young ladies on holiday from New York, chaperoned, of course. But after a light repast on the imposing bluffs, the girls changed their minds about spending the rest of the afternoon with the young gentlemen when Lucas told them that he had been unable to hire the sailboat he had promised. Unfortunately, they all would have to play lawn croquet near Greissing Park. The young ladies had dreams of adventures at sea; Lucas wanted an afternoon adventure somewhere else other than on the water. Lying under a tree in the dense shade being read to by a soft-spoken woman would be more romantic and comforting than having to hop around on deck trying to make sure the ropes were secure and the sails were properly trimmed so they wouldn't luff or flap in the wind.

The girls, realizing that their day upon the wind-swept surf was not going to transpire, decided that returning back to their rented summer domicile would be preferable. After all, they only went out for the picnic to gain the open sea as dessert.

Disappointed that the afternoon would wax and wane without their lady friends, the boys were true gentlemen, though, and escorted the demure beauties back to the boarding house not too far from Mrs. Murphy's. Their chaperone, Miss Twyla Langtree, much older and wiser, followed at a respectable distance, giving them some privacy, but she intimidated nonetheless.

"Maybe another time," Lucas said. He took the more attractive one's hand and bowed far too deeply to have been serious. He knew what their ploy had been. Tyler didn't.

"Maybe," Miss Ginger answered and took her cousin by the arm and walked away; her head downcast, she gave a slight chuckle. . .perhaps a giggle.

Lucas didn't want to waste the afternoon light, and Tyler was looking forward to a summer's nap. They walked along Conroy Street, a quaint street with one story homes and small porches on the front. The larger sitting porches were attached to the rear overlooking the ocean. Geraniums filled flower boxes and morning glories twined up the porch posts just as they did in decades past. Fishermen still went to sea and their wives often busied themselves with beautifying the homestead until their husbands came back, their fishing boats filled with the catch of the day or of the week.

Lucas asked, "How late is it?"

"It's two o'clock by my watch," Tyler replied after checking the time.

Lucas noticed the ornate pocket watch, and Tyler let him carefully examine it. He held it in his hand and felt its weight in his palm. The watch showed excellent craftsmanship although the brass had tarnished a little and showed some wear. It was a magnificent timepiece by anybody's standards. The engraving caught his attention. "Is Beauregard your father? And what's the little triangle below his name for?"

"Beauregard was my father, the son of Harland. Died last November at the estate. The triangle was part of one of his groups, as my mama used to say."

"Then Tyler, I should ask you, What is the hour?"

Tyler thought for a second about the difference between asking for the time and asking for the hour. He felt strange in his gut. Lucas's look and demeanor had become serious, but his eyes showed a little humor and sent out a non-verbal message that it was all right to answer the question.

"It is the hour to convene," Tyler answered with a smile. His neck twitched again. It was more of a skipped pulse, perhaps, than a twitch, but he rubbed it for a second. Lucas, who had been very observant, watched him and said nothing. Now the truth would be revealed.

Both laughed. They gave a firm handshake, slapped each other on the shoulder, and, following Lucas's lead, headed down to the remote cove that Lucas had discovered during an afternoon of exploring along the coast.

"You can't see this cove from up on the bluffs. I found it by sailing around in a skiff one morning," Lucas explained.

"It's so cut off from everything. Hard to believe that this inlet can be so calm with the sea foaming and frothing about the way it does," Tyler observed.

"This is where I come to read and to write," Lucas said. "I don't mean to imply that I'm a recluse...far from it, but I enjoy being away from most of the holiday makers."

Tyler said, "I write down along the coast below the bluffs when I find some time, journals mostly. Nothing that is of importance. But I bet that Prof. Collins put the love of writing into you."

"Maybe the fear of writing! I think I write something good, er, *well,* and he tears it to pieces, almost to the point where I wish I hadn't taken the time to write it out in the first place!"

Both laughed about the professor's writing assignments and how he had taken so many under his wing to encourage excellence.

Tyler asked, "Are there any others from the Crewe in the area?"

"There's Jonathan Adamson from Connecticut. He's taken out a room down on Bay Street. He's an upperclassman at college. I bet you've seen him. He's a good athlete. Member of the organization, too."

"I wonder if the mailmen have ever been here to Kennepointe," Tyler said.

"I think they've been everywhere. It seems *we're* everywhere!"

Although Tyler did most of the talking, the conversation turned to such things as the letters, the symbols, and the rituals, and both became aware that neither knew too much about them at all. Lucas believed that the Crewe originated in ancient Greece. Tyler insisted that it all began in Louisiana. They talked about the rituals, but even the rituals were veiled in mystery. The enigma of the entire thing was certainly food for thought, more food than they had enjoyed at the picnic with the young ladies, Tyler observed.

CHAPTER 9

12 December 2009

The leafless oaks and maples, sentinels to the past and to the present, lined the circular drive from Wetzel Road all the way to the imposing portico at Osolin Hall, hiding the façade of the main building until the last minute. The sprawling structure appeared regal on such a night. The weathered brown bricks and Italianate windows were awash in well-hidden lighting. Electric candles on the inside sills beckoned.

The architecture was imposing; however, at one point, back in the 1940s, a member of the Board of Trustees wanted the windows changed because they clashed with Tudor revival style, but the alumni quickly put the kibosh on that idea. The original architect had misunderstood what the academy's founder, Tyler Pettigrew, really had in mind, and once everything was completed, it was too late.

Tyler had spent some of the early years of the 1890s sketching abroad and had to hurry back for the dedication that had to be completed before the academy opened for business in 1895. Mr. Pettigrew was used to seeing so many architectural styles, he didn't even notice the fenêtre-faux-pas until someone pointed it out to him. He shrugged his shoulders, so the story goes, and assured the purists that this style might just catch on in Boston someday. In Greenlawn, by the way, people didn't know the differences between Italianate and Gothic revival back then and still don't.

Clumps of snow rested lazily upon the dried-out bushes. Brown, brittle leaves that had avoided last autumn's rakes still hunkered down around the roots, protecting the plants from winter's assault. A few walnut shells that the squirrels had snacked on before carrying the rest back to the trees littered some nooks and crannies along the drive where automobiles and limousines crept along, each stopping in turn to let the underclassmen valets open the doors for the upperclassmen arriving in style.

The formal Christmas concert and dance gave the campus residents, known as the *dormers*, and the *commuters*, their counterparts from town, a chance to fraternize one last time before the long holiday break right after semester exams.

The theme was "Ivy and Holly", an obvious reference to the ivy-covered Osolin Hall, or to just about any building on campus for that matter, and to the holly bushes and trees planted in the little park between the hall and Laury Road. The live band could be heard from the portico, and several students began to catch the beat as they ascended the steps leading to the massive carved doors.

Inside the foyer of the grand hall, the quids (what Trinity freshmen were called) acted as hatcheck boys in a makeshift cloakroom. Topcoats and wraps were tagged and placed on movable coat racks donated by Kropf's Flowers and Memorials from nearby Jamestown. On such a blustery night, it didn't take the checkers long to realize that they were a few racks short. Inez Prattler-Helms, who had appointed herself advisor to the hatcheck boys over thirty years ago, began to fidget with the lace handkerchief she had perfumed with lavender and vanilla before leaving her room at the boarding house.

"David, please start putting coats on top of coats, but make sure you have the correct tag attached to the correct coat. Understand?" she asked with an inflection that sounded as though she had just addressed a second grader.

"Yes, ma'am. Correct tags, correct coats, coats on top of coats."

"That's a good boy, David," she fawned. "That's what I call a good boy."

The grand hall itself was decorated with a twelve foot Christmas tree in Victorian style, a large angel with flowing robes and ribbons kept guard over the celebration. The festive boards were spread with punch, cookies, cheese trays and crackers. A formal dinner had been served at the residence halls for those who had reservations, but others had preferred Don Luigi's over on the cliffs outside of town. All was quite cozy that winter's eve within the imposing structure that was Osolin Hall.

Buck McDougal was sloshing down a bit of the red punch, but he wanted what he had squirreled away in his hip-flask even more. Paul Docket came up and elbowed him in the ribs.

"Having a good time, Buck?"

"Yeah."

"Man of many words," Paul chided.

"Yep." A conversation with Buck was often as enlightening as a conversation with Jackson. And that was about all that Buck was going to say until he had his fill of the cheese and crackers. To him, that was haute cuisine! He planned to guzzle down a healthy slug o' hooch in the boys' room when he pretended to go in to check if *they* were drinking or smoking at a social event where such frivolities were frowned upon. He already had a can of dip for his "Kodiak snack" stashed in his back pocket, the contraband hidden by his suit coat. From time to time, he reached back and tapped the can with his fingers just to make sure it was there waiting. That was enough to make his green eyes glaze over.

The fireplace was ablaze with a Yule log that sparked and hissed; a blue flame licked its way up along the wood into the gold and amber fire in the middle. Two students, discussing the physics final exam, stood in front of the flames. After finishing their ginger ale, they tossed the plastic goblets into the fireplace and watched the melting plastic disappear into a puff of smoke. They laughed.

Around the perimeter of the room, tall leather chairs invited others to sit and watch those on the dance floor. The leather creaked whenever an occupant changed position. Tiffany lamps added to the ambiance, providing just enough light. The students dancing in the center of the Grand Hall didn't have the feeling they were in the spotlight. The subdued lighting encouraged quiet, mature behavior, except when the band began to agitate the crowd with "Y.M.C.A."

Adam, who was one of Mr. Docket's composition and research students, and the Coyote revved up the group, even if the Coyote kept confusing the letters. No one was even sure if he knew he was supposed to be making letters at all! It didn't matter. The girls were singing along louder than the guys, and even some of the stodgier faculty members were soon taking part in the uninhibited gyrations. Sterrett Hamilton was sitting at a table in the red salon and couldn't see that the faculty was having just as much fun as the students, but it wouldn't have bothered him in the least.

Tim, the team's rock-solid linebacker, had just tossed his tuxedo jacket onto a chair. He raised his arms to spell out *M* when Alexis, who was trying to squeeze through the dance floor and drink some cherry soda at the same time, tipped her glass and splashed the red liquid down the front of his shirt before he had time to complete the *C*.

"Watch what yer doin'!" he shouted above the din.

"Sorry, man," she said, patting him on his sweaty shoulder before she disappeared into the lounge area.

Buck and Paul both saw the accident at the same time. They waved for Tim to come over, but he motioned back that things were just fine. After the song, he met Paul at the cheese table.

"Nasty spill, eh?" Paul commented.

"Yeah. The tux company will go ballistic over this!" Tim complained.

"You may end up having to pay for that," Paul said.

"Naw, it was an accident. Accidents happen!" Tim hadn't really processed what Paul had said.

Buck, wolfing down some crackers he had wrapped his paws around, followed Paul and Tim along the side of the buffet table. "Go downstairs to the custodian's area and toss it in the wash. They have some stuff there that will take that out before it sets," Buck explained, licking his lips and using his index finger to remove the cheese residue from his teeth all at the same time.

Paul added, "That's a good idea. Wash your shirt and your undershirt, too. It won't take long."

"It's OK. Really. Not wearing an undershirt," Tim said.

"I'd do something before you end up having to buy a new shirt. That can cost you a plenty," Buck admonished. "Let's go and see what we can do."

"Naw. Stay here," Tim said. "You have to be on the lookout for unruly drunks! I think I can tame a shirt all by myself. Besides, I have some Crewe business to take care of downstairs anyway." He flexed his left muscle and gave it a smooch before laughing out loud. Before Paul had a chance to ask about the Crewe business Tim had mentioned, a couple of the teachers dragged Paul and Buck out onto the dance floor when "Brown Eyed Girl" blared through the trumpets. The crowd felt the beat once again.

By 10:00, the DJ, who had taken over when the band went on break for half an hour, decided that the crowd needed to be whipped back into a frantic frenzy, so he unleashed heavy metal that blasted forth from every tweeter and woofer surrounding the makeshift stage. Paul could feel the percussion and bass vibrating off the bones in his chest, and this rhythmic thumping caused some of the senior football players to slam dance, colliding against each other like moose in a territorial fight. The dean of students had banned such activity years ago, and soon Paul and Buck jumped into the melee to break it up before someone came flying through the air with or without the greatest of ease.

"Jax, Rains, Billy!" Paul shouted, but the music was so loud they couldn't hear his words; they could see the expression on his face that usually spoke sermons in one glance, so with some back slaps going around, they split up and tried to figure out some other way they could have some excitement while still straddling the border line between fun and trouble.

"Hey, buddy, 't's up?" the Coyote asked, coming out of the center of the "mosh pit" somewhat bedraggled. He wiped his forehead with his sleeve.

"Not much. Same old, same old," Paul replied, handing him a tissue. "Works better than your cuff!"

"Huh? Oh...yeah," the Coyote responded with a perplexed look at first.

"Who did you come with?" Paul asked to be polite.

"Me, myself, and me. Missy's sick with the crud," he explained, although that wasn't stopping him from having a good time even if he didn't dance with anyone in particular.

The disk jockey dimmed the lights when the Righteous Brothers began to softly sing their 60's version of "Unchained Melody" into the ears of the student dancers who, by the way, had been joined on the dance floor by some of the faculty chaperones trying to re-live their high school or college days of slow dances and stolen romantic moments. Even Sterrett made a cameo appearance, nodding to students and faculty alike as he took some crackers back to his table until it was time for him to come out and chaperone the final dance before saying goodnight to each couple personally at the door.

Mr. Docket entered through the double doors of the main salon at a quick clip, letting them slam shut behind him. He was eyeing the dance floor as though he was on one of his *I think you have been drinking before the dance* raids.

Holding his hand up high, like he was trying to wave down a taxi in New York City, Paul motioned for Jax and Rains to come over. They stood back a few feet in case this was some type of new breath test that he had devised to catch them even if they hadn't been imbibing.

"You boys see Tim?" Paul asked out of breath. "He never came back up from the laundry area. Muttered something about Crewe business. Got away before I had a chance to ask him what he meant. I just went down, but he wasn't there. I don't know anything about Crewe business tonight. Do you?"

"Nope. Can't help you there. Haven't seen him," Jackson explained somewhat relieved that he wasn't under suspicion for something.

Adam's date, Meghan, noticed something was going on. She always had a good sense for knowing when a good dose of drama was about to happen.

"Over there. There's somethin' goin' on around here tonight. Mr. Docket is talking to the security guys in the corner. See? Just a minute ago he came running into the hall looking bewildered. Nabbed Jax and Rains," she explained.

"He's probably talkin' to 'em because he knows 'em. He knows everyone. Now be quiet, will ya?"

"What's he got in his hand?" she asked

"Dunno. Looks like a rolled up cloth or something. Let it be," he sighed.

She put her head back onto his shoulder, positioning herself so she could watch whatever was being played out near the punch bowl. The Righteous Brothers could certainly stage the right mood even if Meghan couldn't.

Paul took the security guards into the stairwell that led down to the laundry area and to one of the academic sections of the building. "He went downstairs to wash his shirt. Someone spilled some punch on it. I found this in the dryer," Paul said. He untwisted the dry shirt. Someone had cut out a large triangle on the back of the shirt; the vertex pointed down.

"You need to see if you can find him downstairs. I'll go back to the dance to see if I can turn something up," Paul said.

Mr. Docket was talking to one of the parent volunteers when he suddenly had a flash of a cup of dark liquid being drunk and a candle being extinguished. He suddenly fell to the floor on his knees.

Two ladies rushed over to see what had happened, but he stood up slowly, grabbing one lady's arm, and explained that the heat had suddenly caused him to be a little dizzy. The ladies, doing what ladies seem to do best when a sudden emergency strikes, assisted him to a chair and brought him a cool sip of punch and a moist paper towel although they offered no explanation as to the purpose of the wet towel.

Sipping the drink slowly, Paul noticed the security guards approaching at an almost open trot. Bringing up the rear, Buck McDougal quickly joined in the procession.

"Come with us to your room, sir" the senior security guard said to Mr. Docket.

"To *my* room? Yes. What's wrong?" Paul asked, but he knew the news was not good.

"Mr. McDougal, you call 911. We found Tim," the guard said.

CHAPTER 10

Kennepointe, Maine
First Week of August 1886

Tyler felt guilty that he had not returned to New Orleans in July as he had promised his mother. In her letters, she hinted that it was time for him to find his way in the world, but she was having difficulty letting him go. He was all that was left, except for the estate, but she knew the day would come when he would either leave her and put down his roots elsewhere or return to begin where his father had left off. He was still young. He had room to make decisions.

Tyler was drawn to Maine more than he was to New Orleans that summer. He reinforced his love for his new home over and over to himself every time he looked out to sea. The coast was wild, untamed, and the churning surf held his attention when he meditated on the way his life was going. The cool shoreline breezes kept the humidity at bay through their welcomed embrace during that first week of the month. This was the first time he had ever experienced a summer that didn't drain him of his vitality.

He could tell the way the sun would lazily cast its rays in the late afternoon that the season was changing. The sun wasn't as bright, as vibrant, as it normally was in early July, and although it was still certainly warm, it was obvious to him that nature was sapping the sun's strength with each passing day; its rays were slightly more diffused.

The ocean, however, appeared placid to Tyler as he stared out to sea one morning from his bed chamber. He observed the *Nora,* Lucas's sailing boat that he had hired from a friend at Graydon's Cove, gliding over the calmest of calm, effortlessly, as though the ocean were made of polished glass. The wind caught the mainsail, stretching the billowing canvas and making it taut, yet the sea was unusually peaceful for a change. The prow cut through the ocean, splashing water up the sides with each turn. Lucas made the *Nora* appear to be a lithe figure skater cutting her way around the sea.

Mrs. Murphy had just placed a tray of bread, butter, mixed fruit and juice outside Tyler's door after her gentle knock. Breakfast was always tastier near the ocean, he had come to realize, and it was his favorite meal of the day.

He finished shaving and washing up in the corner at the washstand. His black hair, according to the reflection in the mirror, had become curlier during that summer, and his tanned skin from walking along the beach and the cliffs in the late morning, more than anything else, would have made his mother think that he had turned into a common laborer. There was something to say about a life of leisure.

He had spent much of July and early August sitting in the shade of Greissing Park during the early afternoon hours when the sun was at its warmest. Often, Miss Ginger would pass by, nod, and play some croquet on the lawn nearby with a myriad of friends. She made sure to catch Tyler's eye by making squeals of delight when she won a point, or she would stomp her foot and pout when someone made her lose. He thought her, at first, to be awkward for a young woman of her breeding, but over the summer, she had become as graceful as Hannah Morgan the day she descended the gangplank in New Orleans.

Tyler always looked over at Miss Ginger, smiled, and continued on with reading or writing or doing whatever his fancy was for that day. They had never shared a word since the day of the picnic, but they noticed each other. She thought, however, about Tom, her fiancé, working at his father's finance firm in Connecticut for the summer, and he thought of Sarah Garret.

* * * * * *

Kennepointe, Maine
11 August 1886

Lucas stopped over for supper about twice a week, not because he was invited, but because Mrs. Murphy's cooking was especially tempting after a day out on the ocean. Most of his meals were taken at the local inn where variety wasn't a concept. The menu rarely changed, and when it did, there was always some dish that he didn't find appealing.

He was quiet. Perhaps he was contemplating something, but he didn't make small dinner conversation as he was wont to do when he stopped over after docking the *Nora* at the pier. He pushed the boiled potatoes, topped with a dollop of butter, around the smoked ham on his plate. From time to time, he cut the ham and potatoes with a knife and fork, eating only a morsel. He looked out the window toward the sea, his eyes squinting at past memories. Something about him made him look weak, almost exhausted.

"Tyler." He paused collecting his thoughts. He took a small bite of food and waited until he swallowed. "Tyler, have you ever heard of the Immortali?"

Tyler thought the question to be strange. He almost answered in the negative, but he remembered passages from the *Kuhduush* where that word was mentioned. "The Rev. Entwhistle said it in a sermon when he was encouraging us to become 'the gods of fall.' I have seen it in print in a book my father gave me, but I don't know what it means. Are you feeling well? You've barely touched your food. Mrs. Murphy will be hurt if you don't."

"I'm fine, really. From time to time I get worn out. Then I have to replenish myself. Where was I? Yes. In the Crewe of Adelphos, there's a legend that some of the members are the Immortali, people who never experience death as others do," Lucas said. He went on to explain that as far back as ancient times, some people have been spared from passing over from this life to the next. He made reference to Enoch and Elijah in the Old Testament, to the three Nephites in the Book of Mormon, and alluded to other sacred scriptures. "All cultures tell of people who are immortal. They are heroes set apart from the others." He clarified that in the Crewe, it was done in stages and shrouded in the mystical teachings of those who have gone before.

"I'm afraid the Crewe of Adelphos isn't shrouded in much, my dear fellow. We've conversed about this before," Tyler responded before he served himself some more potatoes and washed them down with a swig of lemonade. "Let me reiterate one more time. It began in Louisiana. I ought to know. My father was one of the founders. It appears we broke away from another faction, the Krewe of Orestus. Now, I don't know where or when *that* group had its beginnings, but if it came from the bayous of Louisiana, I can assure you that the only mysticism involved was probably a good healthy gulp of bourbon spirits on a hot summer's night up on a wooden veranda overlookin' the back forty!"

"And I suppose your father wrote the *Kuhduush* while sitting up on some veranda sipping on a mint julep," Lucas asked.

"I don't know who wrote that. He gave it to me and told me to show it to no one, and I haven't. I have read many parts of it, but I'm not certain that I understand it." Tyler touched the right side of his neck with his index finger. It felt as though a mosquito had just bitten him again. A burning sensation made him lose focus.

Lucas comforted him by saying, "Don't touch it. It will pass. You've been touched by the embrace, haven't you? Did your father ever explain about the meteor showers? He must have given you some veiled instruction about the meteors."

Tyler shook his head in the negative; he knew, at least internally, that something was different. He had had that burning sensation before, after his father's kiss, at the funeral, when he first met Lucas, and at previous times when he was emotionally distraught. During the first two weeks of August, his neck would hurt more when the sun was setting. Often a cool cloth soaked in water and vinegar brought relief.

"Do you have your copy of the *Kuhduush* with you?" Lucas asked.

"I promised not to give it to anyone. It's put away for safe-keeping at the moment." Tyler had that strange gut feeling again about not letting anyone know where the sacred text was located…not even Lucas.

"I respect your being careful. Your father, Tyler, gave you the only gift he had. Do you believe he is still with us? Do you still believe he lives somewhere in the world?"

Tyler arose from the table, placed his napkin beside his plate, and walked away after he said, "My father is dead. When it's over, there is no more. Maybe the soul drifts off somewhere like some ethereal vapor. That's what immortality is, living in some heaven way out there beyond the stars. I'd like to believe that anyway, but does he still live? Not in our sense. I watched them place him into the ground." He did not turn to catch Lucas's look, and he did not excuse himself when he bumped into Mrs. Murphy bringing in some freshly baked dessert.

Back in his room, Tyler sat on the edge of his bed, poured himself a drink of whiskey he kept hidden away from Mrs. Murphy's eyes, and watched the amber liquid slosh around in the glass. He poured himself a second. After his third, he fell into slumber sprawled out on his bed.

* * * * * *

Mrs. Murphy hadn't seen Tyler since dinner, and in case he was out taking a stroll before retiring, she wanted to make sure his bed was turned down. She always turned her guests' covers back because her mother had done the same for her when she was a girl. There was something comforting about it.

When she entered his chamber after lightly knocking, she saw him lying face down on the bed, the empty glass still grasped by his left hand. So he wouldn't wake up in total darkness, she lit the oil lamp at low wick, and in doing such, she inadvertently kicked over the whiskey bottle on the floor that had escaped her attention. The cork kept the liquid from spilling.

"Mercy! What's that boy gone and done now?" she blurted out. Tyler stirred, turned on his side for a second, and became aware that someone else was in the room.

"What time is it?" he asked.

"Time to get under the covers, young man and stay put until dawn. That's what time it is!"

"I'm fine. Just drifted off. Was resting my eyes after dinner," he explained.

"You don't have to turn the truth. Now, you know that I don't allow alcohol in my rooms, except a glass of wine on New Year's Eve, but that's several months away. What were you thinking?"

"Is Lucas still here?" he asked. "I'm afraid I was most rude."

"He stood on the porch for a while after dinner and kept checking his watch and puffing on an obnoxious cigar. Why do men enjoy such abominations? I think he said something about the cove. When he did, his eyes were as big as saucers."

After she left his chamber and quietly closed the door, Tyler shuffled over to the washstand, splashed water on his face, and rinsed his mouth out. His tongue was coated, and the taste of whiskey still hung on his breath. His clothes were wrinkled and his hair was disheveled. At least the mirror reflected him in the soft light of the oil lamp with some compassion. He sat on his bed and fought the sleep he so desperately needed. Finally, he picked up his father's pocket watch from the desk, noted that it was 11:05, an hour later than he expected. His mind told him to go to the cove. There he would find what was missing from his life's puzzle.

The moon wouldn't be full for another three days, but its soft, diffused light guided him along the bluffs to the winding trail that led downward toward the cove before the clouds set in. He paused from time to time and wanted to return to the safety of his room, but something instinctual had taken over, and he pursued those inklings on this night when nothing would ever remain the same again.

He followed the path to the inlet, not Graydon's Cove, but the small cove that Lucas showed him that one afternoon when they discovered they shared the bond of brotherhood that had been passed on to them from previous generations.

Lucas greeted him during the final descent by saying, "I almost didn't think you were coming. There are only a few times during the year when we can partake in the ritual that gives us what our fathers wanted. What your father wanted. What my father wanted. You do feel it, don't you?"

"Yes." The answer escaped him. He was still groggy; the burning feeling had become more intense. He was where he wanted to be, yet he didn't quite fathom why he was standing at this particular cove on an August night.

"Go on down and join the others. I have to wait here," Lucas said.

In the shadows by the rocks, he saw others gathered. He tried to make out their forms but could neither determine if they were well-dressed or poor, old or young. They seemed to be clad in robes of different colors; gold and silver reflected in the light of a single torch. Soon, twelve torches formed a blazing triangle in the center of the cove.

The moon's soft glow, often obscured by the rolling clouds, great curtains covering the moon and the darkness above, didn't reach down into the cove's narrow gorge that night. The rock-strewn shore provided a barrier between the sand and the cool water. The surrounding landscape looked like how Tyler imagined the moon looked on its surface.

The clouds parted from time to time before dissipating shortly before midnight, revealing the light of the moon cascading down into the water far out over the Atlantic.

"What is the hour?" someone asked.

"It is the hour to convene," a voice near a cave answered.

The men began to move toward Tyler, forming a double triangle around him. The ritual began its rhythm, and Tyler began to sway slightly as the ceremony picked up momentum.

From time to time, he touched his neck; he was aware of his pulse, the force of life that coursed through his body. This was nothing like the friendly arrival of the mailmen or explanations given by the erudite Prof. Collins in his paneled study on campus. Something primal had taken over, and Tyler felt the comfort of the warm evening surround him, encircle him, and embrace him with humid arms and sultry breezes. He felt lazy and at peace. He looked up toward the heavens and watched the stars become brighter as the final vestige of the clouds moved off and away to reveal a spectacular view of the night in all its secrecy and majesty.

"The *Kuhduush* states, '*The cave, a symbol of what gave Elijah protection, standeth as the womb, the* adelphus, *to give thee birth. Before thy birth, thou wast blind to all around thee in the spiritual and in the physical womb, but now thou shalt see things, not as in a clouded mirror enigmatically, but as they truly are.*'"

Tyler removed his shoes, and, assisted by Potentates of the Inner Circle, walked over to the small cave interiorly illumined by two freshly-lighted torches, where he entered, removed his clothing, vested himself first with loose white pantaloons, and then put on a white tunic with gold trim.

The Watchman of the Night blindfolded him with a large, red folded cloth, and he and the Watchman rejoined the brothers on the shore. The blindfold was removed only after he approached the inlet's water, his feet and ankles cooled by the gentle splashes of moribund waves. All the brethren were looking toward the heavens, and Tyler followed their gaze upwards toward the infinity of space. He was so transfixed by the meteor showers that had just begun that he never once looked down to admire the fine garment he was wearing.

Time was no longer a concept. He became aware of the infinite *Now.* No past to chide him about bygone youthful follies; no future to force him to become what he was not. The ghosts of yesteryear had vanished; the time for the gods of fall had begun to arrive as the days of August prepared to herald the way for September and its new seasonal beginnings. The present, however, was where he was centered. The present resonated within the depths of his soul.

"The *Kuhduush* states that '*Tonight the planet slips into the earliest twinkling of autumn. Long before the earth, the dwelling place for all living things, turns on its axis to proclaim the beginning of a new season, the heavens announce the arrival of change. The falling stars summon the conclusion of summer's short lease. The earth pauses to observe the celestial splendour. The water cools and stills the passions of the flesh,*'" the Watchman solemnly stated.

The Purificator, leading Tyler into the peaceful waters away from the shore and, keeping his own eyes focused on the heavens, immersed the son of Beauregard, the grandson of Harland, each time the meteors shot through the heavens.

Three times he was placed under the water. Three times he arose.

Tyler had unquenchable thirst. His body became hot and uncomfortable. His skin was prickly and sensitive, and the tunic began to feel oppressive to him. Even the air that had cooled his skin felt stifling. He drew in some deep breaths, but he wasn't satisfied. His lungs began to burn.

He ripped the tunic from his body, tossing it out toward the ocean, toward the waves and the tide. It floated for a while but soon disappeared into the inky depths of the churning current. Except for the pair of pantaloons, he stood half-naked in the water. His chest heaved, and his muscles became taut. He shrieked a primordial scream with his head and hands raised to the heavens, then his head hung limp toward the water. Profound silence surrounded him. Only the flickering of the twelve torches caught his eye for a moment, but they were soon hurled into the water, one by one, each succumbing to the watery grave with a slight hiss, much like the meteors that streaked through the heavens only to die in the blackness above.

The Mariner said, "It is written that '*in the darkness of the womb, thou wast given life. Through the light of the twelve torches, thou wast raised into light. In the darkness that now surrounds thee, thou wilt be given the promise of the Ancients. Thou wilt commune with the descendants of those Heroes of Old.*'"

The Purificator led him back to the shore where the water was not too deep. Tyler touched his own neck, knelt down into the cool water that now covered him up to his waist, and drank a tawny elixir from a goblet the Keeper of the Chalice handed to him. It tasted sweet as it covered his palate.

His skin was still agonizing to him. It restrained him. It held him back from exploding into the night and becoming one with the universe, filling the vast void of space with his own consciousness.

The elixir began its work. He became calm, submissive, for a moment. The Chaplain of the Anointing took a beaker filled with oil, the oil of olives, and slowly poured the thick liquid over Tyler's head, letting it move over his shoulders and down his chest and back. "Our sacred text says, '*Bow thy head toward the water, toward the cooling, and become anointed by the oil of comfort, by the oil of strength, by the oil that will always light thy way to the end of thy days, until He, blessèd be, shall arrive and give thee thy blessings in thy tent, in thy abode.*'"

Tyler arose. A tunic, rose and silver, was placed over his head and let to drop. He put his arms through the sleeves, folding his hands almost in prayer at his waist. The hem of the garment floated for an instant before it sank several inches into the current.

The Chaplain of the Anointing helped him step up onto the rocks. A veiled servant of the Crewe of Adelphos placed a golden silk triangle, with the vertex pointing upward, upon Tyler's heart and motioned for him to hold it there. Two of the Potentates of the Inner Circle raised the veil covering the mysterious stranger only slightly, and the shrouded figure prepared to give him the transformational embrace.

At first, a brother formed a triangle made from two index fingers forming the vertex and two thumbs creating the base over the area where Tyler's neck and shoulder come together. The warm breath of life from the veiled stranger passed through the triangle and rested upon his skin. Tyler felt a light bite or pinch on his neck, upon his skin, but he was unable to discern how this was being done. It stung him. He winced for a moment. He felt paralyzed, but he didn't shiver as before when his father had kissed him.

A radiant heat, increasing in intensity, flowed throughout his veins. He began to perspire profusely and he pictured lava slowly snaking its way throughout his body, so searing did it feel. He could clearly see things of the past and shadows and shades of the future. He was now bonded and confirmed to the Crewe forever. He recognized his father's voice from under the veil saying, "Tyler. Accept what you have been given." And then sleep rapidly overtook him. He dropped to the earth near the sea from which life first came, according to the *Kuhduush*.

His next memory was waking up on his bed, sprawled out face down with the whiskey glass in his left hand, still wearing yesterday's clothes.

* * * * * *

Jonathan Adamson, the athlete from Connecticut, was the last person to leave the cove that night of the Perseid showers. The sun was just getting ready to rise up out of the ocean; the stars had vanished after yielding to the breaking dawn. The night had turned cold shortly before sunrise, and fog crept along the coast like white tigers on the prowl. All remnants of the meteor showers had long ceased; the emergence of the new day had triumphed.

Jonathan stood upon the cliffs looking out to sea, watching a massive ship plow through the surging waves in the distance. He thought about how the ship's passing at daybreak was like the Crewe's passing in the darkest hour. People came together, touching each other's lives and moved on to other days and other adventures. People are vessels waiting to be filled, and vessels are filled with people and goods. Both are on a journey that ends at some point, but then people and vessels are ready again to turn and begin once again. New adventures, new destinations, new encounters unite those seeking to understand the passage upon the water and upon life itself.

The sacred rites had spiritually renewed Jonathan on the shore down below the night before. He always perched himself afterwards, however, on a hill somewhere to enjoy the rising warmth of a new day each time he experienced his rejuvenation. Life was his. Life was all there was. And because he was studying medicine, he hoped to be able to heal and comfort those in distress wherever he might encounter them, not only through material medicine but through the touch of life itself.

His neck pinched him for a moment. He turned when he saw his friend approaching from behind. Both smiled, and Jonathan returned to his view of the morning calm. "It will be daybreak in a few minutes. Look out into the infinity of the sea," he said without turning.

"It will be daybreak, but not for you," the voice said. Suddenly, Jonathan felt the muscular arm grab his neck. In a split second, it was over. A crack, actually a snap, caused him to fall limp. His friend, a great betrayer, breathed in deeply and absorbed the life passing from the body. Jonathan's intended purpose in life had been derailed; he had served another's objective. He had fed the famished one.

CHAPTER 11

12 December 2009

The paramedics stripped off Tim's undershirt, stained red, and began to check his vital signs, transmitting the information immediately to the hospital where the emergency staff evaluated and gave advice to the EMS team back at the Academy.

In the classroom, everything seemed to be normal. Materials and books were neatly lined up on carts and bookshelves. The desks were tidy and orderly, but it was a smell that caught Paul's attention first. A candle, not bayberry, left a Christmas scent after having been blown out; the lingering odor permeated the entire classroom. He was certainly aware of the two medical guys working on Tim, but he detached himself from the reality of the situation.

Paul slowly moved around the perimeter of the room, searching the floor with sharply focused eyes. In the back corner, a few scraps of paper, which had avoided the janitor's vacuum cleaner, lay waiting to be picked up another day. One brown tooth from a comb was embedded in the carpet. Everything looked normal.

His own desk had been cleared off because the holidays were coming after exams, and he detested a cluttered desk over break. It didn't bother him most of the year if he couldn't find the right textbook or the correct stack of homework papers, but over Christmas, everything had to be in order.

His mug that read *No More Mr. Nice Guy,* a gift that Chris Markowski, a former student, gave him during his first year of teaching at the Academy was half-filled, he thought, with the water that he constantly kept at his side when he felt dehydration setting in, and he knew that if he didn't empty it out now, he would forget, and there would be enough biology projects growing in it by the end of Christmas break to keep half the school busy at the microscopes. The reddish-brown water within, however, had caught his attention as he raised it to his nose for a sniff. *Almonds,* he thought to himself. *Tea with almond extract. I only drink herbal peppermint.*

Without thinking much about it at the time, he dumped the tea into the plastic-lined wastepaper basket beside his desk, accidentally letting the cup slip from his hand as he flicked his wrist to empty out the liquid. The clunk of the mug falling into the basket caused the paramedics to turn in unison, but they immediately returned to the work at hand.

As Paul fished around for his mug in the trash basket, his hand brushed against some solid waxy objects. He retrieved his mug and two red candles, placing them quietly into his side-drawer before he left the room. Tim opened his eyes and then fell back into his unconscious state.

"Almond tea," he said to the paramedic closest to him. "I think he drank some almond tea or tea with almond extract. He has a nut allergy."

Paul noticed Tim was now wearing a stained undershirt, but earlier he said that he hadn't been wearing one.

* * * * * *

Just after Midnight
13 Dec 2009

At the hospital a few hours after the dance was over, Paul Docket sat in the quiet of Tim's private room. From time to time, he glanced at the various machines that the nurses had attached to monitor pulse and respiration. On the right side of the bed, an I.V. solution dripped down the plastic tube attached to Tim's arm, and the steady drip. . .drip. . .drip was almost hypnotic. All Tim needed, Paul figured, was a quiet night to recuperate.

The prognosis was good, considering that little time had elapsed from the onset of the anaphylactic shock that such allergies can cause, but Paul was somewhat skeptical about the entire incident. It was in his classroom, after all, that Tim had been found lying unconscious on the floor, and it was in his own room that the paramedics had given the first account of what could have been another school tragedy. Had Tim not been found in time, the outcome would have been starkly different.

Paul looked out into the hallway and noticed that the corridor lights had been dimmed. He was now surrounded by yellow and red and blue twinkles emanating from the various machines making an occasional soft, cat-like purring.

Except for a twitching motion every now and then from his left index finger and an occasional flutter of the eyelids that showed he was moving deeper into sleep, Tim remained motionless on the bed. He had purposely been sedated by the resident in charge to let his body gain the rest it needed.

"Hope you can hear me," Mr. Docket began in a voice a little too loud. "Things will turn out fine. They always do."

Paul moved nearer to the bed and stared down at Tim's relaxed face. Tim shifted his leg. Paul noticed the movement and thought it to be a good sign although he wasn't exactly sure why.

Tim had turned his head slightly. All of Paul's whispering and talking and consoling weren't going to make Tim talk. Paul just wanted to be there in case the football team's star linebacker decided to suddenly wake up.

He was lucky to be at Tim's side. Had he not known Dr. Hlivko so well, he wouldn't have been allowed to be in the room at all.

The night nurse made her rounds, checked the charts, took vital signs, read the machines, and nodded to Mr. Docket that all seemed to be well even although she wouldn't be able to tell him if it weren't. At least she was quiet about it all, nothing like the earlier nurse who laughed aloud and snorted like a braying donkey when she accidentally dropped a tray of medicine, scattering the pills to the four corners of the room.

Paul squinted at his watch. A little past 1:30 in the morning. It was time for him to be going home. His coat, scarf, and hat were hanging from the hook on the back of the door, but before he prepared himself for winter's nocturnal assault, he entered the small private bathroom to freshen up a bit. Tim slept. The machines whirred.

Paul was drying off his hands at the basin when he noticed the hospital smell of disinfectants. It wasn't an unpleasant smell by any means, but it reminded him of where he actually was. Because hospitals depressed him terribly, this was the first moment he had to come face to face with the reality that all was not well. He felt his stomach sicken. His whole body was on a swift elevator ride down. The floor gave way, his knees weakened, and he held on to the sink to keep himself from falling completely. He perceived a piercing howl. The creatures of the night were loose. They were close.

Looking up into the mirror, he hardly recognized his own face that was contorted in pain and fear. His eyes were glassed over, staring off into another realm, yet still within the reality of the mirror itself. He studied himself for a moment. The commotion outside broke the silence of a final stare into the glass, but he found himself paralyzed, unable to blink or to move or to react.

Mentally, however, in his mind's eye, he could see Tim thrashing about on the bed like a puppet being jerked about by unseen hands and strings. Tim's eyes opened and snapped shut… opened and snapped shut. His mouth exuded horrible, eerie sounds. The boy's heart was pumping furiously and his breathing was deep and uncontrolled. Tim panted out, "The damn wolf!" The vision ceased.

Tim, however, continued to have spasms. One was so severe his head snapped back against the head of the bed causing him to feel the pain of metal smacking against skin and bone. Then he felt the *wolf* grasp his jaws before a horrific twist to his right caused him to fall into the blackness of a winter's night.

The room went silent for a second. Shortly thereafter, the cardiac monitor set off its piercing alarm. Then it started. The monitors were taking on a life of their own. Soon, nurses and doctors dashed in like a thundering herd, barking orders and checking the beeps and flashes. One nurse stripped off his night shirt with one firm tug as they angled themselves to see what the problem was.

All the action in the room was in fast forward. Hands flew, needles pierced, and dials registered data. The medical team was well-trained; each had the routine under control.

The steady *beeeeeeeeeeeeeeep* of the cardiac monitor that had summoned the medical team in the first place forced Paul to go into immediate denial. The team tried CPR and the "paddles" twice, but it was to no avail. Tim had died alone before they even reached him.

"Call it," Dr. Hlivko said.

"2:05 AM," came the reply.

Paul opened the bathroom door. His spell was broken. The nurse in the green sweater turned to him, thinking that he had been there the whole time, and said, "I'm sorry, but could you wait outside for a few minutes?" She looked around the room in search of something. "Where's your friend?"

"My friend?" Paul asked.

"Yes. He was just here a few minutes ago when I walked by on my way to the nurses' station."

"There was no one in here with me at all."

"Must have been. Saw him. Didn't get a good look at him. He had on a blue shirt," she continued as the staff removed the emergency cart with the defibrillator and electrical coils nestled on the top, quietly poised until they were needed again.

Before Paul left the room to give the doctors more time to complete their jobs, he walked over to Tim. There was a blue triangle drawn on his right hand near the I. V. needle. Its vertex was pointed down toward his fingers. It hadn't been there when he went to the restroom. It shouldn't even be there now.

* * * * * *

Morning, Before Dawn
13 Dec 2009

Coach Jared Hominy, *Grits,* was sitting in his family room watching nothing in particular on the wide-screen TV that took up most of the corner by the brick fireplace. Hoping to find something that would hold his interest, he mechanically surfed the channels, but it was always the same old garbage that he couldn't stand anyway. The news bothered him because it just showed the stupidity of humanity...although he, of course, had all the answers that would change the world. No one, however, knew to ask him about how to solve the planet's maladies.

He liked the sports channels, of course, but many of them showed re-runs of old events that he had previously watched. The other sports on TV weren't really sports to him. Skiing, curling, figure skating (for Gawd's sakes!), and snowboarding were no more sports than knitting and crocheting. He did concede, however, that those sports were much better than golf, a so-called sport akin to watching paint dry on a porch in the hills of West Virginia.

He looked around the room and focused on the tree, a six foot blue spruce that his wife had decorated the night before. Personally, he didn't care if there was a tree or not. The whole season should be outlawed by an act of congress, he felt. He usually went to the mall at the last minute to buy some presents after he had caved in with guilt. Life wouldn't be worth living for him, however, if he didn't produce some trinket for his wife from underneath the tree on Christmas morn.

Because he hadn't had much Christmas joy as a child, Grits didn't have much respect for the Christmas holiday at all. The season was always a time of bickering and fighting between his parents about what the kids *weren't* going to get because there was never enough money. Money was the center of every argument; money, of which there was little, ruled their domestic atmosphere with ballistic force.

He was happy, then, just to have a new football or a bat for baseball, and he never really enjoyed baseball that much. His father had been gruff, even more so during the holidays, and Grits assumed that that was the way he had to be, too, when he grew up. And by the time he had finished college, he had turned into one sour, sober-faced, emotionless individual who sported a twenty-four hour game face even when there was no game in sight, and as far as *joie de vivre* went, he felt that that term was probably an appetizer listed on the left side of a French menu, not that he had ever seen such a thing.

He had been head football coach for about eight seasons at Trinity, but that didn't mean that he had been a successful one. Out of his seventy-two games, he had won only twelve, and it seemed that the school's former reputation was now over and forgotten. The days when coaches from Tyson's Grove, Chesterborough, and upscale schools, such as Liberty Commons and Kessel-Parchment College, came to watch some of the weekend games were over. They no longer tried to hustle new recruits by luring sophomore Trinity boys away from their commitment. No, the only remnants of those moments in school history could be found in journals the graduating students wrote for the school's library as a graduation requirement to be tucked away on the shelves in the archival bookroom.

Grit's wife was dusting off her own bookcase, but her glare was clearly focused on her husband. "You could help, you know," she admonished.

"Just don't start in on me today. I'm tired, and I'm not in the mood for one of your confrontations," he returned.

"What have *you* done to be tired about?" she asked defiantly.

"Leave me alone. I told you, I'm not up for one of your mood swings," he warned, expelling air from his lungs in a long sigh.

"I suppose you're not up to telling me about last night? You went to school, I assume, but you didn't come to bed. Stay out all night, did we?" she pressed. Although she was dusting, she was gearing up to go for the throat.

"Yeah, I went to school. I had some business to attend to. Then I came home a little late. You were asleep, so I slept down here on the couch. Didn't want to wake you." He never took his eyes off the TV and continued to change the channels without paying much attention as to what was being shown.

"How considerate! I do know that you slept on the couch, but I have an observation."

Grits rolled his eyes because he knew that when she had an observation, he was about to be brow beaten.

"And your observation."

"Just how late were you at school?" she asked, setting up the trap.

"I don't know. Didn't look at my watch. "

"And you came home and fell asleep on the couch?"

"I told you that already, woman. Let it go!" he shouted.

"You bet I'll let it go! I came downstairs at 2:30 and you weren't here. Your car wasn't in the garage. So, where were you?"

"Out," he said flatly, almost daring her to probe deeper.

"Just *out*?"

"I had some things to take care of. It ain't none of your business, is it?" he said.

"What would *you* have to take care of at that hour of the morning?"

"You're not my mother!" he shouted even louder than the last time.

"No, but I'm your wife. But I don't know how long I'll even be that," she said as her voice quivered.

Mrs. Harriet Hominy left the family room in a hurry without noticing that Grits had a slightly sarcastic smile on his face. He still controlled the remote, and he still controlled Harriet. Like the remote, she was nothing more than another annoying button he had to push.

Chapter 12

Kennepointe, Maine
12 August 1886

Tyler rolled onto his back, letting the whiskey glass in his hand fall onto the woven rug beside his bed, and he stared without focus at the plaster ceiling in his room until the cold breeze coming in through the open window coaxed him out of bed. The winds in August were often warm and humid, but the temperature on the cliffs had dropped during the night, and the wind was being pushed along by a front coming in from the north, from as far away as Hudson's Bay up in Canada.

His mouth was gamey; his tongue, still coated in the center, felt fuzzy against his palate. He scraped his teeth over the top of his tongue and tried to remove the offending residue, but the taste lingered on.

Everything in his room looked as it did the night before, yet *he* felt different. The sunlight, however, looked atypical for the morning, and his mind couldn't justify the apparent discrepancy.

The memories about the cave and about the ceremony on the shore of the cove were hazy, dreamlike, yet he still remembered being there surrounded by shapes and forms in the darkness, unless the recesses of his mind were lying to him. He looked at his neck in the mirror. The skin was tender to his touch, but it had stopped burning, and for that he was grateful. He remembered a sharp pain and something flowing down into his body, but his skin was now smooth.

His mind and his imagination had combined to teach him a lesson about drinking forbidden whiskey, and he tossed the bottle into the trash for Mrs. Murphy to discard later.

Outside the door he heard her rattling his breakfast plates; she knocked gently once again. He was lucid enough to want to talk to her, yet he wasn't sure what he wanted to convey. "Mrs. Murphy! Could you enter please?" he asked more formerly than he was used to. He gave what she perceived to be a command. He took one last look around the room to make sure that it and he were proper for the early morning visitation, and if things weren't in order, it didn't matter; she entered so fast, she startled him in a way.

"Yes, sir?" she asked before noticing that his attire was still wrinkled, still in that state of disarray from the evening before. It was clear to her that he had fallen asleep after a quick binge with the bottle.

"If Lucas comes by this morning to work on some of his paintings, ask him to visit me. If I am gone on one of my walks, have him meet me at the cove at noon. Not Graydon's Cove, the other one."

"At noon, sir? Not today. It's well after one o'clock already." He looked out the window again and understood why the sunlight didn't look right. "I just came by to collect your breakfast, not to deliver it. You haven't touched it. You were sleeping so soundly when I came in to turn your bed down last night. And this morning, why, I didn't know if you were in or not. I suppose drink has strange effects on some people, wouldn't you say? Not good for a young man to imbibe. This is a Christian house, Mr. Pettigrew."

"I didn't have that much to drink. That I can assure you. I'm not on my way to becoming a sot!" he replied.

She pretended not to hear his last statement. Her first husband, before he drowned at sea during a winter storm in '78, was known to spend far too much time down at the Puss 'n Boots with multiple pints of ale well into the night after a voyage ended before he and his mates had to return home to their marital duties. Her second husband met a similar fate, but she kept the details of the tragedy to herself.

"And as to your friend, Lucas, I'm afraid he left Kennepointe. I met his landlady this morning at the greengrocer's down on Buchanan Street. They have the freshest vegetables in town. Best carrots in the state. Anyway, I think she said he returned to Boston on the mid-morning train." She had a small towel in her hand, and she absent-mindedly dusted the desk and the window sill, often with a snapping motion as though she wanted to scare the dust up and away from the surface instead of containing it within the softness of the cloth. Tyler sneezed. "He was supposed to stay until the end of the month, but he paid in advance and even offered her a gratuity for her services. Fine young man."

After she left, he took out the *Kuhduush* and thumbed through it, but he didn't have any specific place to read that morning. At the beginning of the Book of Khalief, his father had underlined the following passage: *Upon the shores of the waters, where the rocks stand as sentinels to the dawn and as guards to the night, the honoured of old were buried thrice below the billowing depths and raised thrice up and placed upon the shore. The heavens cast down their stars into the abyss, with their own mortality marked as they flashed and became cold. Not so with the Immortali, born to heal, born to comfort, born to assuage the burden of pain. Their twinkling becomes a fire, a conflagration of love, an inferno of affection to those downtrodden by the earth-born. Arise, arise, the morning dawns; the day awaits. Arise, arise! Thy destiny awaits; fulfillment is at hand.*

He sat in his reading chair until about three o'clock, slowly coming to realize that he had been following the ancient script even when he knew nothing about the words contained within beforehand. The rocks, the water, the going down and coming up out of the water was what had happened to him, not to mention the shooting stars that flashed and went cold, yet he had never heard of Kennepointe before, and he didn't comprehend how or why his current experiences matched those in print.

He washed, changed into clean attire, and walked down to Conroy Street. A new photography shop had just opened up for those on holiday to capture their summer moment for posterity's sake. Tyler looked at his reflection in the window, fixed his hair and straightened his cravat before standing for the photographic portrait, as Felix Bashor, the proprietor, called it. He stood perfectly still for a minute, his eyes looking into the lens as though he could see the future, and he promised he'd stop by within the next few days to pick up the picture that he wanted his mother to have.

Further up Conroy Street, he saw Miss Ginger's chaperone, Twyla Langtree, walking at a good clip along the stretch that led from the druggist's shop, her broad hat flopping up and down with each pronounced step. She carried in her right hand a small packet wrapped in brown paper tied with a coarse string, and she gripped her unopened parasol in her left.

"Excuse me, ma'am," he shouted from across the way. Although she turned to see who had addressed her with such brazenness, Twyla kept up her pace. *Such impertinence! One is never to shout at one's elders,* she thought. He caught up to her before she reached the feed store, but she showed no signs of slowing down. She was three times his age, and etiquette did not require her to wait, converse with, or acknowledge one so young. "Excuse me, ma'am. Sorry," he said out of breath. "Is all well with Miss Ginger? I saw you leaving the druggist's."

"Miss Ginger is being doctored. No need for concern," she replied and picked up her pace at a faster gait. It was very clear to him that he was overstepping his bounds, and even though he had been bred with the best of southern manners, he had met his match when it came to trying to break into a society that appeared to be closed to him. She held up the brim of her hat to discern his features; she let the brim drop and thereby concluded her business with Tyler Pettigrew that afternoon.

"Tell her I send my best wishes," he said right before she turned the corner, but he wasn't sure if she had heard him or not.

* * * * * *

That afternoon, some fishermen discovered a body near where the ritual had taken place. As far as ol' Doc Brand, Kennepointe's resident physician during the summer, could tell, Jonathan Adamson's neck had been broken, probably from a fall from the bluffs above, but he couldn't be sure. He had a feeling that the boy was already dead before he landed on the beach. A triangle drawn on the young man's hand, the vertex pointing down, had been etched in India ink. The doctor had seen it before. *Wild college hooligans with fake tattoos,* he often thought to himself. Doc Brand planned to send a telegram to the boy's parents in Connecticut that afternoon.

Tyler heard the news from Mrs. Murphy as the story spread about Kennepointe. Much speculation fueled by gossip and more conjecture kept the village abuzz. Tyler wondered if Jonathan had been to the cove the night before, and he made a mental note to relay the message to Lucas when the two of them met up again.

Around the same time of August each year, a body was discovered on the shore below the bluffs. The locals always attributed those random deaths to the fact that more people came to Kennepointe to find relaxation from their daily lives and were, perhaps, more careless than they should have been around the cliffs; they shouldn't have been so naïve. August often veiled its secrets.

* * * * * *

Kennepointe, Maine
14 August 1886

Two days later, Miss Twyla Langtree sent a messenger to request Tyler's presence at Miss Ginger's summer residence. He splashed some water on his face, a typical ablution on a summer's day, combed his hair, and made his way once again along Conroy Street to where she had taken up residence. He knocked on the door twice, waited, and was received by Miss Langtree, sans floppy hat but still wearing a full skirt, white blouse with ruffles, and a cameo guarding the neck of the blouse, keeping modesty in check that afternoon.

"Miss Ginger is in the sitting room. She has the grippe, fever with chest congestion. The doctor says it may be moving into pneumonia or pleurisy. We let her take the sun. That can dry things up. Follow me, but keep the visit brief."

He followed behind Miss Langtree as a servant would follow the employer, but he knew that this was not the time to ask mundane questions or attempt to initiate a conversation that had no purpose other than to stifle the silence.

In the sitting room off the parlor, Miss Ginger was propped up in a large cushioned chair. Her cheeks were sunken, her brow moist with fever. She managed a smile and motioned for him to approach. He felt the coolness of the shaded room, but he also noticed the smell of illness. It wasn't unpleasant, but it wasn't an odor that normally would be lingering there on a summer afternoon.

"Nice to see you, young Tyler Pettigrew," she said.

"Nice to see you, Miss Ginger," he replied. "How are you?"

"I can't complain. Others are worse off than I am."

Tyler found her answer to be a little too philosophical or altruistic for one her age. When Tyler thought about it, there were others who were certainly worse off than he was, yet he never really thought about the misfortune of others he didn't even know. "Well, I suppose there *are* others worse off than you. What can I do for you?" he asked. He wanted to find out why he had been sent for because he didn't like to be kept in the dark about things. Life was short; mysteries often took too long to solve.

"Lucas told me to send for you. He said you could help," she said.

"You saw him? When?"

"The morning he left. He stuck his head in at the window by the kitchen." Miss Langtree shook her head slightly in disapproval that a young, uninvited man would stick his head in at the kitchen window. . .or *any* window for that matter.

Miss Ginger coughed. She coughed again. "Miss Langtree, could you get me some water from the well? It's so cool and refreshing. I need to apply a fresh cloth to my head. I need something to slake my thirst."

As soon as Twyla left the room to go out into the yard to draw the water, Miss Ginger reached out her hand for Tyler to take. She held his hand in hers for a moment. His neck began to prick him. Slowly, there was a burning sensation again. He reached up and touched the tenderness. He took her hand again, leaned over, and touched her head. "Salan shem ka'lemta," he whispered. She sighed and went somewhat limp, relaxing her head against the back of the chair. Her breathing became slower, but it was regular and stable. His hand became warm, warmer; he felt the fever draining from her and passing through him, dissipating up through his chest. He imagined her healthy, running in Greissing Park and laughing at the butterfly she was trying to catch.

Twyla returned carrying a bowl filled with cold water, a towel draped over her arm. "What are you doing, young man!" she shouted when she observed him touching Miss Ginger's hair. She set the bowl down on a mahogany table, splashing some of the water onto the doily.

"Pardon?" he replied.

"I'm going to ask you to leave. You're no different than all the rest, now are you? Taking advantage of an ill, helpless girl."

"I was just. . ."

"You were just what?" She turned her gaze to her charge. "Miss Ginger, such activity is not..." Twyla Langtree believed

Miss Ginger to be in an apparent state of complete collapse at first. "You did this! What did you do to her?!"

Tyler backed away and let Twyla try to revive the girl, but he knew he had done nothing to her at all. "She just fell asleep and took on a look of complete peace and tranquility, Miss Langtree. Honest. Her complexion is becoming ruddy again, and her brow is no longer moist. Can't you see? "

Miss Langtree noticed the change. She was so astonished that she paraphrased what Tyler had just said. "Look. She appears to be in a deep sleep. Notice how regular her breathing is. See the color coming back to her face."

Tyler backed away as a crab on the beach would do if it encountered something it could not comprehend or control. Miss Ginger opened her eyes and smiled. One long, hard cough cleared her throat, and she felt at ease, one with her environment.

"It's time for another dose of her medicine," Miss Langtree said taking some cool water to the girl. "I must make sure she keeps on it. It appears to be working quite well. It has made her fever break. If you don't mind, perhaps you should let her take her rest." She dismissed him as she had often been dismissed during her career as a domestic.

"I believe you're right," he replied. He nodded to Miss Ginger. He nodded to Miss Langtree and departed the summer home, but he knew the medicine had nothing to do with the recovery, and so did Miss Langtree.

The next time he went to call on Miss Ginger unannounced, he found her and Miss Langtree already gone from their summer hiatus.

CHAPTER 13

Shortly before Dawn
13 Dec 2009

Paul Docket didn't sleep well once again. He didn't have his occasional realistic dreams about plane crashes or realizing that he never attended a particular college class but suddenly had to take the semester exam. He didn't even dream about going on stage and discovering, to his chagrin, that he hadn't learned his lines. Those dreams frustrated him more than anything else. He knew that if the planes didn't crash within nine days, then the accidents wouldn't happen. They would happen or they wouldn't, and there wasn't a thing he could do to stop them. As far as the semester exam and stage debut were concerned, he laughed at the thought of being so unprepared.

No, this time he dreamed of being somewhere in a big house, a mansion with ornate draperies and Victorian furniture, or at least he had the feeling it was such a mansion. In the dream, he knew the people he met; they weren't strangers to him. He liked them. But he also knew that in the world beyond his dreams, they didn't exist in real time. They had appeared in dreams before but remained anonymous.

They could have been members of the Crewe of Adelphos from another place, from another era, because they were dressed in ritual clothing that he had seen before. Like any dream, however, there were parts that didn't seem to be right, but he didn't know just what was not right.

During the dream, one of the strangers, veiled under an ornate cloth, came up to him and seemed to want to whisper something into his ear. Others gathered around and watched. Paul leaned in so he wouldn't miss a word. He was concerned about being polite. Just when he thought the private message was ready to be delivered to him so secretively, the veil was lifted, and he felt a sharp, burning pain driving itself into his neck. He was paralyzed when he tried to wake up. He couldn't escape the throbbing. Molten steel surged through his veins. He was a crucible. After the initial shock of what was happening dissipated, he was awash with peace and contentment. A veil was placed over his head and he fell deeper into slumber.

He turned on his side in his large, comfortable sleigh bed and positioned himself on his side. He had had vampire dreams before, but in previous dreams, they were evil, vile predators who never got a chance to fully bite down to accomplish their task. He was always able to fend them off by a strong verbal rebuke. The people surrounding him this time, though, were trustworthy and not at all malevolent. They did not project a malicious demeanor. He mentally experienced a feeling of calm that he had never experienced before.

He woke for a second, noticed it was only four o'clock, and drifted back into sleep. This time, however, in his second dream of the night, he dreamed about being in his Jeep parked out in the country along a deserted road. A policeman approached the driver's side and asked for his driver's license. They talked for a moment and exchanged pleasantries. Through the open window, he tried to see the man's face, but he couldn't. The voice was familiar to him, but in his dream, he couldn't place it. The stranger asked him if he had ever received the embrace. It was an odd term. Paul didn't know what that meant. He had to answer in the negative.

Without warning, the man grabbed Paul's head, twisted it to the left, leaned in through the window, and sank his teeth into the right side of Paul's neck. This was not like the previous dream earlier that night. Horror filled his mind. He tried to scream out, but he was unable to do. He felt vile. He knew he had been violated and wanted to throw open the door and chase his assailant, but he couldn't. In the quiet of the isolated locale, he looked up into the rearview mirror, and he saw no reflection of himself. It was as though he had ceased to exist.

When he finally woke up, the first thing he did was to touch his neck. Other than some scraggly neck fuzz that would disappear with his morning shave, there was nothing there of a physical nature to validate the dreams at all. The clock read 5:09 AM. He had slept off and on for only a few hours.

Paul Docket stood under the shower trying to wash away the sick feeling that had taken over his body earlier. It was the first time he had noticed the water shooting out like stray bullets hitting his skin, and no matter which way he turned, the shower was anything but relaxing. He twisted the showerhead, but the water still annoyed him. He tried to duck around the hard spray, but it still stung him. He was still thinking about the way Tim had died so suddenly, almost violently, earlier.

He slowly turned the water dial, and with each nudge, he felt the spray beat just a little colder. The water started to invigorate him. Mental questions started to nag him as he shampooed and rinsed, but those questions were flying at him so fast, just like the water jetting from the showerhead. He found it difficult to focus on one thing in particular.

Convinced that he was finally clean and as refreshed as he could be, he tossed open the shower curtain as the *artic air,* as he called it, rushed in from his miserably heated bathroom. Immediately, his arms were covered with goose pimples, and he toweled off quickly before he started to shiver.

The moisture in the air had fogged the mirror, but three good swipes with the towel let him view enough of his face to notice that he had not rested as much as he should have. His eyes were puffy; his pupils were dilated.

Paul snapped a clean red towel off the rack and rubbed his hair dry. By now the mirror had cleared, and he brushed his hair into place, what little hair he had.

In the sitting room down the hall from the master bedroom, he snuggled up in the Queen Anne chair, leaning his head back against one of the wings for comfort. Paul closed his eyes, dreaming for a moment that he was able to fly. He felt himself soar. He let himself float.

At precisely 6:11 AM, his dog, Travis, clamored downstairs, skipping half the steps as he barked a staccato warning at the front door. Paul jerked awake, grabbed his white robe, and made his way down the oaken staircase, holding on to the railing to make sure he didn't fall.

The *bang-thump-thump* on the front door had taken on its own rhythm by the time he arrived, and dragging the dog to the basement took on a circus atmosphere in the foyer off the living room. His shouts of *Be right there!!* didn't stop the percussion section.

Having won the battle with the dog, Paul wiped his hands on the front of his robe, eyed the grandfather clock, and, after walking briskly over the chilled terracotta floor, he absent-mindedly flicked on the porch light that had been burned out since last summer. It was the Coyote.

"Wassup?" the Coyote asked as Mr. Docket just glared at him from behind the storm door.

"What's up! It's not even 6:30 in the morning! What do you mean *What's up?*" Paul shot back.

"Sorry, Mr. D. I know it's really early and all. Can we talk?"

Paul held the door, and the Coyote, keeping his head down to avoid eye contact, walked into the living room, looked around for a second to get his bearings, and removed his neck scarf and coat. A single brown glove hung halfway out of one of his pockets. Paul placed the wraps on a bench in front of the fireplace and pointed to the couch.

"Wow! You've got some neat stuff here! This place is really tight," the Coyote said in a high, excited voice.

"I'm sure you didn't come here to admire the museum! This had better be good."

"I haven't been back to the dorm all night. It's cool. Jax, one of my roommates, is covering for me in case my parents would call or something. My cell conked out a few days ago. My cell always conks out. They don't like it if I stay out all night. Told me once they're not payin' good money to have me traipsin' about."

"Will you get to the crux of the matter?"

"The crux...?" the Coyote asked.

Paul translated, "The nitty-gritty…the skinny…the main *thang!*"

"Oh," he began, "well…"

So far, the two of them had avoided eye contact.

"Mr. D., I'm afraid I might be in big trouble. Really big trouble," Coyote began to explain. "But you gotta promise not to tell anyone."

"You can trust me," Paul said.

"Good," the Coyote replied.

"First, listen, would you like some hot chocolate or something? Don't have much in the way of breakfast."

"Hot chocolate would be cool. Hot…cool. Hah! I made a funny! Sometimes in the winter I get the shakes a little. I need somethin' warm now."

In the kitchen, Paul searched through the cabinets and took out a packet of Swiss Miss, and within three minutes, the microwave had churned out a steaming cup of hot chocolate with little marshmallows floating about on top.

"This ought to do the trick." Paul smiled as he handed the Coyote the mug.

"Thanks, man."

As Coyote sipped the chocolate, Paul flipped on the TV to add some background noise. The living room was too tense at the moment, and both could feel it. If the Coyote wanted to talk, he would when he was ready.

Paul noticed that the Coyote's brown hair was somewhat scruffy. His hands trembled as he warmed them on the mug. His right leg was *nerve-bouncing*.

"Hey, this stuff sure tastes good!"

"Would you like some more?" Paul asked. "You've drained that dry."

"Naw. Should be goin'. Sorry 'bout botherin' you."

Paul was not going to pry this time. Over the years, he had learned that people will talk when they are ready, and no amount of prodding will bring out a confession. It was just as important to be there than to brow-beat someone into spilling his guts.

The Coyote set the mug on the floor by the couch, stood up and stretched like he wanted to delay his departure, but he knew that he was in control, at least in his own mind. He didn't care if Mr. Docket thought he was daft at the moment.

He glanced at the pictures on the mantle as he put on his coat and wrapped his scarf about his neck. From his right pocket, he took out one glove and put it on as he studied a picture of Mr. Docket's grandmother taken in 1914. The left coat pocket was empty, and his eyes focused on the floor to find the missing glove.

"Something wrong?" Paul asked.

"Can't find my other glove. Musta lost it. Always lose things like that in the winter. When I was a kid, my mom used to pin 'em to my sleeves. Maybe I should do it, too."

Paul walked to the guest closet off the living room, rummaged in his own coat, and brought back a glove. The Coyote studied it for a second before he sensed that this was his glove.

"What a joker, Mr. D! I didn't even see you snag it when I came in."

"I found it in the hallway outside Tim's room tonight, or rather this morning, right after he died." The Coyote took the glove, put it into his pocket, and said nothing.

* * * * * *

The early morning storm was just picking up when Paul and the Coyote ventured outside together. They had not gotten to the entire reason for the early morning visit. Paul had coaxed out bits and pieces of why the Coyote had appeared so early, and knew he would have to wait for the rest of the talk to materialize. Christmas lights were twinkling as they drove off to the expressway. Dawn was at least half an hour away.

He pulled over for a second and took out his cell to send a text to Troy, a student and loyal Crewe member. "I was supposed to have some research material for a project he's doing, but I won't be able to assemble it today. Told him I'd be back from the cabin later," Paul explained. He sent the text and drove off again.

"Troy's a good guy. Great athlete. I look up to him," the Coyote admitted. "What's the cabin?" Paul didn't answer.

The snow blowing from open fields off the Interstate forced Paul to drive slowly. It was difficult to judge just how deep some of the mounting drifts were. A snow plow was about a mile behind them closing in as it forced one mound after another to the right of the road. Paul found the exit he wanted and turned east, then south.

"Start at the beginning," Paul began.

"Where are we going? I thought you were taking me back to campus," the Coyote said, twisting his neck from side to side trying to recognize anything familiar.

"Start at the beginning!" Paul repeated.

"I told you. I was out after the dance, and I didn't want to go back to the dorm. I wanted to stay out all night for kicks. A lot of the guys do it, you know. It's legal. I'm over eighteen! It was really late and I was driving around downtown, all three blocks of it! I thought about Tim, so I decided to drop in and see him. The hospital is always open."

"You wanted to visit at such an odd hour? Ever hear of visiting hours?"

"I'm telling you the truth, man," the Coyote continued, looking over at Paul. "I checked downstairs to see what room he was in, and then I took the elevator in the blue section up to his floor. When I got off the elevator, I had second thoughts."

"A nurse told me that she had seen someone in the room," Paul related.

"I wasn't in the room at all, and I didn't see no nurse. I was standin' in a doorway down the hall. I don't know why exactly," the Coyote added.

"I was in the bathroom having one of those crazy spells I told you about once. When I came out, it was all over," Paul explained.

The rolling hills began to be more defined as they drove over the country roads. The snowplows had not been over this section of highway in at least twelve hours, and the drifts were harder to negotiate, even in a Jeep Wrangler.

"Is that why you think you're in trouble…because you were there when Tim began to fail?" Paul asked. Coyote looked out the passenger window and didn't respond. "You're not at fault. He didn't die because you arrived on his floor," Paul continued.

Still no response. Coyote's brown eyes had lost their life. The sparkle of puerile exuberance that he always displayed was absent that morning. He was looking back to the past.

By 7:30, Paul had turned right onto a narrow one-lane road that wound its way back into the deep woods. He shifted the Jeep into first gear to gain better traction. Ten minutes later, they came to a stop in front of a rustic cabin.

"May as well drag in some logs from the porch. We'll need a fire in case the old heater isn't working," Paul instructed. "When I'm inside in the winter, I always like it warm and toasty."

The Coyote stretched again when he stood outside the Jeep, took in a deep breath, and surveyed the area. A small cabin; blackened trees that embraced heavy, wet snow; an axe by a pile of wood on the front porch; no sound except for an occasional blast of wind followed by the deadened hush of the forest.

Paul took a key from his pocket and twisted it a few times in the rusty lock before the door creaked open when he pushed.

"Freezing in here," Paul said slightly above a whisper.

"What *is* this place?" the Coyote asked.

"Just a place where I come to every now and again. Gets me away from the real world."

Paul checked the thermostat, pounded on the wall a couple of times, as if that would do some good, and hoped the built-in electric heater still functioned. He was lucky to have electricity at all, but a new development had been built over the ridge, and he was able to finagle a connection from the electric company, whose CEO was a Crewe member. "We might be in luck. Old cabin needs to be replaced someday. Planning to tear it down and replace it in the spring. A real log cabin would look great here. Put some wood into the fireplace. Don't want to overwork the heater," Paul added as he went to see if the small bath area was in order. "Haven't been here since Thanksgiving." The toilet flushed after he remembered to turn on the water by hand. The insulated pipes had not frozen over. "There won't be any hot water for a while. I usually keep it set on low in case I get the urge to come out here and rough it for a few days. Here, grab a blanket from the chest. Wrap up until it gets warmer."

The Coyote took the blanket and hung it over his shoulders. He blew into his cupped hands and watched his breath escape. He was still shaking, but he didn't know if it was from the cold or from his own nervousness.

"Why don't you tell me what you saw in the hospital," Paul said.

"I already told you."

"Sorta. What you told me wouldn't make you think you were in some sort of trouble." The Coyote stared at Paul for the first time. "What's a *wolf*?" Paul asked.

"A wolf? Just an animal, isn't it?" The Coyote was hedging.

"You played football with Steve and Tim. You never heard them use the term before?"

"I don't think so. Well…maybe. I don't know what it means. They'd sometimes put their hands up to their ears. Looked like a wolf's perked-up ears. Then they'd howl like one and then laugh," the Coyote replied.

It was obvious that the Coyote didn't know what the wolf was, or he was a good liar. "Let me ask you this. Who did you see when you arrived? Better yet, who did you see leaving the floor? He was leaving, wasn't he?" The Coyote remained silent, almost defiant.

Outside the cabin a lone wolf howled. It was dawn.

* * * * * *

At a little past eight o'clock, Paul peered out the cabin window through a slightly opened curtain. The logs crackled in the fireplace. The Coyote was stretched out on the couch covered now by a woolen blanket. He was drifting in and out of sleep peacefully. A log fell in the grate; the Coyote stirred.

Paul shook him on the shoulder. "Listen, son," Paul began, "I'm going to have to leave for a while. I need to buy some food for you. I want you to stay here until I return."

"I still don't know why I'm here. Shouldn't I call the RA or someone? I haven't been in all night long."

"I'll tell Jax. That way if someone wants to find you, he'll let me know. You're safe here."

"Safe?" the Coyote questioned.

"You *know* what I mean. I shouldn't be gone longer than an hour. Hour and a half max," Paul explained.

Paul locked the front door. As he drove to town, he felt as though the Jeep were closing in on him. The whole countryside seemed to be closing in. He was stuck in the center of his own thinking, and there didn't seem to be a way out.

By now, Tim's friends would find out his fate, but as far as they were concerned, it appeared that he had died after suffering a sudden setback. His blood test upon admission to the hospital would confirm that he had ingested nuts or a nut product, and it was obvious that he had died because of his own negligence. Paul hoped that that rumor made the rounds.

Except for the small triangle that had been drawn on his hand, no one would even be aware that a perfect crime had just been committed. It had been planned so.

At the same time that Paul got out of his Jeep in the parking lot at Adam's dormitory, an SUV stopped on the road that led to the cabin. The driver noticed the smoke coming from the brick chimney. He thought for a moment before hiding his vehicle on a road used by the fire patrol in the fall before he headed out on foot to take cover in the woods.

* * * * * *

Adam had pulled into his dorm parking lot at a few minutes after eight that morning. His eyes were tired and pulsing. He had spent most of the night just driving around with some of the guys after hanging out at a pavilion near Heaverly-Allman State Park. They had dumped the girls right after the dance, changed from tuxes into flannel shirts and jeans for the boys' night out where they could "commune with nature."

In the small bathroom of his dorm suite, he shaved off the little bit of stubble on his chin first as he let the water begin to fill up the tub. Then the slow grate of the razor over his face and neck sounded more like a playing card scraping his skin than a razor gliding over his cheeks that he held taut with his free hand. He needed a new blade. Adam rinsed his face with cooler water that was splashing into his cupped hands, and he winced when he slapped on some Hollister cologne. His head ached from lack of sleep. His head ached from other things.

He fished a small plastic-tipped cigar out of his shirt pocket before tossing the wrinkled shirt into the hamper. Easing himself into the filled tub and reclining all the way back, he tried to blow a smoke ring; he coughed and tried again. Adam knew that life was good.

When Mr. Docket rang the bell at student suite 321 in Boggs Hall, Adam was still soaking in the tub. *C'mon, Adam, I know you're there. Your car's parked in the lot,* Paul thought to himself, surveying the area around the dormitory. He rang for a third time.

"Mr. Docket!" Adam exclaimed as he cracked open the entry door. "Just a minute. My roomies are all gone, it appears."

He closed the door and returned after wrapping himself in a grotty towel that hadn't seen the washing machine in weeks.

"Sorry, man. Was in the tub when you rang. Thought it was one of the guys who had forgotten a key. C'mon in. Let me go change."

Paul sat in the living area and noticed that the walls were all bare. Four bedrooms branched off from the living area, and the bath was squeezed in between room one and room two. Adam returned looking scrubbed; his hair was sticking up like porcupine quills…thanks to a handful of gel. Paul related what had happened to Tim at the hospital and brought Adam up to speed.

"So, what are you here for? *I* wasn't anywhere near the hospital," Adam stated defensively, his whole attitude reflecting a mental change.

"No need to think that I'm blaming you. I just feel that we should get together at the cabin and decide what to do. Coyote is in a deep mess at the moment. He could be next," Paul related.

"The Coyote! How could *he* be in trouble?"

"Because he saw who came out of the room while I was in the bathroom. I think he thinks he knows who killed Tim. I'm convinced that Tim didn't have some kind of a relapse. If that person saw the Coyote, it's hard to say what might happen."

"Not sure I can get away to the cabin. I have to start to study for finals. They start in just a couple of days. I've slacked off this term," Adam explained.

"I can't just leave him alone by himself. He needs us."

"Just like Steve and Tim needed us. We didn't do them any good, did we? Where was the Crewe when they needed us?"

"I don't think there's much choice in the matter, is there, Adam? The Crewe is there to help those in distress, but we don't always have a direct line to everyone's life. Have you forgotten your first *Klausur,* as it's known? *To those in danger, help. To those in despair, hope and aspiration. To those in fear, peace and comfort.*"

Adam hastily scrawled a note to his roommates that he had gone out for the rest of the day. His parents were going to call later about making arrangements for a Christmas holiday somewhere warmer than on their estate in Connecticut, but just where was to be a surprise. He didn't know if they'd use his dorm phone or his cell, and it was anybody's guess as to whether the cell would work out in the woods so far from town.

Both went over to the Coyote's room and grabbed some clean clothes out of his dresser. It was obvious that he didn't know what folding meant.

"Let's get him some socks, too," Paul pointed out.

"Uh, never go into a guy's sock drawer!" Adam warned.

"Then you do it! I'm as innocent as the freshly fallen snow," Mr. Docket added dramatically. Adam laughed and fished around for a few pairs of socks.

The main roads that led to the cabin had been plowed that morning, and the driving was certainly easier than it had been before dawn when Paul and the Coyote had ventured out there in such a hurry.

At the entry to the drive that linked the cabin with the rest of the world, Paul slowed down and stopped the Jeep.

"What's wrong?" Adam asked.

"There's been a car along here since I left. You can see that it stopped and backed out and headed up over there. Its tracks haven't been covered over since the storm let up," Paul stated. "It looks like it went back a bit into the woods maybe."

"Probably made a wrong turn," Adam added.

"Who knows?"

The sun had disappeared behind the clouds from the south, and the two passengers suddenly had a chill at the same time.

"Looks different out here than in the summer," Adam noted.

"Sorta isolated, isn't it? I think this is the best place to be at the moment," Paul added. They sat in the Jeep trying to keep the conversation going. "We have to take care of him, you know. He's not a member yet, but we've been preparing him for a long time. We just can't forget him at this point."

"Guess you're right, Mr. Docket. Should we get some of the others out here, too?" Adam asked, appearing to be very mature in his line of thinking.

"It would be easy to rally the troops, but the Coyote wouldn't understand. Besides, most of the brothers are getting geared up for exams and the holidays. We have to stick together on this." Paul and Adam had been keeping each other sane since Steve Gruder decided to have that fatal shower in October. "Do you think you'd be able to spend the night out here? Coyote might have to. I don't want him back on campus where things could happen."

"I don't know if I could stay out here. It's a bit creepy. Since Steve died, everyone is so paranoid about people going off on their own. Let's get inside."

Both slammed the Jeep doors with a loud thud after jumping into the calf-deep snow. Adam quickly took in the environment, inhaling the air as his eyes observed the rustic panorama. He remembered the summer campfires and songs; he longed for the days when things had been safe and secure. The gods of fall were just a memory to him now.

CHAPTER 14

Noon
14 Dec 2009

Inside the cabin, the Coyote was still resting on the couch when he heard Mr. Docket and Adam stomping snow off their boots on the front porch. He sat up with a start, somewhat disoriented as to where he was. Docket and Adam entered the cabin's only room and saw the Coyote rubbing his eyes and giving a big yawn.

"Mr. Docket! Adam!" the Coyote greeted. "Wassup?"

"You look like you've had a good snooze," Paul Docket said.

"Not too bad. It got warm in here after you left. What are you doing here, Adam?"

"Just came to check on you," Adam answered.

"What's there to check on?" the Coyote asked. "Watcha got in the bag, Adam?" It was beginning to sound like twenty questions.

The Coyote was often childlike. He seemed to focus on some things for only a short time and then moved on to other things, and transition between thoughts was unimportant to him.

"Some of your clothes," Paul Docket explained as Adam pulled out a shirt and a pair of jeans. "We snagged them from your dorm room. Now take these and go and get yourself a nice hot shower. There should be more than enough hot water by now, but go easy on it. Hard to tell how long the tank will last!" Paul laughed as he pushed the Coyote in the right direction, watching him until the door shut. He and Adam could soon hear the water splashing against the stall.

"Go back to the Jeep. I bought some food earlier and tossed it into the backseat. We might as well have an early lunch before we begin to explain some ground rules to him," Paul said.

"What are you gonna tell him anyway?" Adam asked.

"Guess I'll have to tell him everything he needs to know. I think he'll be more comfortable with you here."

"But what about the promises we have made? We can't talk about it all to someone who isn't one of us. Even if they're only ceremonial, you know the symbolic penalties," Adam pointed out.

"Not if he becomes one of us first!" Paul announced with a grin. "In the locked drawer over there is a white tunic, the one you wore last summer. Before you go out and get the food, take it out of the drawer. Put it in the bath on the little wooden table. He won't have much of a choice at this point."

"Sure hope you know what you're doin'. You can't be protected from the *wolf* if you don't know he's in the woods!" Adam exclaimed.

Looking out the window, Paul stated, "I have a hunch he's a lot closer than the woods over there at times."

Adam pulled the tunic from the dresser and snapped it to quickly unfold it, and then he quietly entered the bathroom where the Coyote was still showering behind the old plastic curtain covered with pictures of ducks in flight. He draped the tunic over the table by the sink and removed the Coyote's shirt and jeans. Adam smiled to himself as he heard the Coyote singing *You better watch out, you better not cry, you better not pout, I'm tellin' you why...*

When he returned, Paul asked him what the smile was for. "Just the ol' Coyote in there. He's singin' 'Santa Clause is Comin' to Town'!" Both chuckled at the thought of it.

"Let's get busy, Adam. We've got some work to be done ASAP," Paul commanded.

Adam returned from the Jeep with a box full of food that he set down near the couch. He unpacked some of the content to see what Paul had purchased. Because they were items that could be prepared with no cooking, Adam lost his interest in that type of cuisine. *Stuff tastes like cardboard,* he thought to himself.

It wasn't long before Paul was busy setting up the card table in front of the fireplace. Adam searched through another drawer to find the yellow cloth napkin.

Except through an occasional glance, neither communicated verbally. Both knew the routine of induction. Normally, it required a host of brethren, but this was not a normal time for any of them.

"Don't forget to fold the cloth in the form of a triangle," Paul instructed.

The innocent, boyish Coyote would soon discover a world where light and understanding were always being attacked by forces that he couldn't see on his own. He had been chosen to assist his secret brothers long before he had known most of them. Coyote's time had come.

* * * * * *

Paul and Adam became quiet when they heard the Coyote shut off the water and stop his singing. Both stared at each other waiting to see how long it would take before he noticed that his clothes had been replaced. Paul drummed his fingers nervously on the arm of the chair. Adam took a deep breath and stared at an invisible spot on the floor.

"Hey, guys! Where's my stuff?" the Coyote shouted from the bathroom.

Adam replied, "Just put that tunic, that robe thing, on and come out."

"Huh? But where's my clothes?"

No one answered him this time.

When the Coyote opened the door, wisps of steam escaped into the main room and created an almost surreal atmosphere.

"I don't get it," Coyote began. "This looks goofy to me. This isn't some weird religious thing, is it? You're not all waitin' for the Mother Ship to zap us up, are you?"

Paul began to explain the purpose of the entire ritual, and the Coyote, sitting on the couch beside Adam, began to listen. It was as though he knew what was happening. He seemed to be open and trusting.

The ritual began with the often repeated words: *What is the hour? It is the hour to convene.* The letters from the mailmen had to be delivered first. From then on, the rite of passage flowed like a slowly meandering river. Symbolism, mysticism, and allegory intertwined as the ceremony reached its peak with the oath of loyalty.

The red candles were finally extinguished; the solemn handshakes from left to right and back once again sealed the oath and made the Coyote a member of the Crewe of Adelphos. Obedience to truth, one of the lessons taught and sworn to, was the first challenge that the Coyote was to encounter.

"You have promised and sworn unswerving obedience to the truth. You are to meet challenges and overcome them as you progress. Do you understand what you have promised?" Paul asked seriously.

"I don't know," the Coyote replied. He was honest.

Adam was busy putting the yellow cloth away in its place and re-arranging the candles so as not to leave a tell-tale trace of any of the ritualistic settings.

"You are a servant of truth and honor," Paul began. "Being such, I have to ask you who you saw coming out of Tim's room at the hospital."

The Coyote realized he was in a difficult position. He stared around the room as if to see if the perpetrator were actually present. Putting his head back against the couch, he ran his hands through his tussled hair that hadn't quite dried yet.

Adam and Paul leaned over a little closer. "There's nothing to fear here. Steve and Tim were one of us."

The Coyote had put his hands over his face as his emotions reached a catharsis.

"Troy."

"Troy Krueller? The soccer goalie and varsity football kicker?" Adam asked somewhat bewildered.

"Yeah, one and the same." The Coyote continued, "I got off the elevator and didn't know which way to turn. The night lights were on, and the corridor was somewhat dark. I stepped back into a corner area when I heard someone in the hallway. I thought I'd get in trouble. It wasn't visiting hours, but you know that. It was Troy. Funny, he walked right past me in a hurry. Then he got on the elevator. I was getting ready to go on a little further down the hall. A nurse was laughing as she talked on the phone somewhere."

"Did you actually *see* Troy come out of the room?" Adam asked sipping on a soda that he had brought in from the car earlier.

"I don't know what I saw. I'm not sure. Maybe. It was confusing."

"Why did you hide when you knew it was Troy?" Paul asked.

"Because I had this feeling, see. Can't describe it. I just knew that I shouldn't give myself away," the Coyote explained. "Troy is part of Hominy's Pride. I guess they intimidate me."

Adam explained, "Troy is the Crewe's plant *in* the Pride. You can trust him. He'd be the first to tell you that the Pride is a counterfeit crewe. Hominy knew that. He never was in one when he was here as a student, or at least we can't find any proof that he was, and he was always bitter. Nobody in the other crewes wanted him, so when he came here all puffed up because he was the new coach, he selected his Pride, and it was held together by fear, by coercion. We are based on respect and loyalty."

"You never *joined* the Pride," Paul continued. "There was no ritual, no signs, no nothing. Hominy just latched on to you, and you were afraid to disassociate yourself from him. Isn't that the way it was?" Paul asked.

The Coyote responded, "Yeah. I guess so. I never knew crewes, or whatever you call them, existed for certain although I had heard stories. But I did know about the Pride. He ranted and raved about it all the time. Do this! Do that! Be aware when the lion is on the prowl! Never did know what that meant."

"It's somewhat of a code. In the Crewe of Adelphos, when we say that the wolf is loose, it means that something is not right. Our own wolf, or alpha, is always guarding his den. He is never away from his duties," Paul said.

"Is that supposed to comfort me?" the Coyote asked.

"It is," Paul said.

"I took the elevator back down to the lobby. I sat there for a while over in the corner that had the big Christmas tree with the fake gift boxes under it. Those ornaments sure could sparkle! Outside the window, I saw Troy talkin' to Grits. They shook hands, stepped off the sidewalk, and headed out into the darkness together. My gut told me that since I had gone to see Tim in the first place, it was my duty to visit him. Then there's something else you should know. When I got back up to Tim's floor, someone else came out," the Coyote said, staring down at the woven rag rug, "but I don't know who it was. He ran to the right in the other direction rather quickly like he was tryin' to get away. He was dressed in blue, maybe black, the lights were low, and there was a flash on his chest like he was wearing an ID tag or somethin'. That was just when all hell broke loose with the beeps."

* * * * * *

The Coyote finally got dressed in his own clothes, and the three of them were sitting around the fire discussing all that had gone on. One would speculate and the others would discuss and give more theories. Mr. Docket was hoping to find the right moment where he could list the assumptions that he had come up with since last night at the dance. It seemed as though weeks had passed by since then. Things were happening too fast, and he felt that he was out of control for the first time in years.

He needed to ask the Coyote more about the Pride, but something made him want to wait until things had settled down before he approached the topic again.

Adam was making small talk, but his nerves were on edge, too. Any one of them could be in danger at the moment, and it wasn't easy to keep up with the chit-chat that was taking place. At the same moment that Mr. Docket was turning a hissing log in the fireplace, a loud crash caught them off guard. The sound of breaking glass, a flash of fire flying through the air, an exploding bottle, and the quick scent of kerosene had them scrambling in confusion.

"Get outa here!" Paul yelled as he began beating the flames with the blanket the Coyote had been snuggled under earlier. "It's spreading!"

Adam and Coyote began to attack the flames, too, but the more they fought, the faster the flames seemed to spread. The edge of the couch was engulfed. The fire began to mushroom as it spread across the floor near the doorway. The heat became oppressive.

Quickly and instinctively, grabbing their coats piled on the chair by the door, they escaped to the porch. Paul's Jeep was the next goal. There they would be safe from the blaze and the snowstorm that had started up once again. Paul shoved his key into the ignition, but the motor wouldn't turn over. He tried again. Nothing.

The Coyote got out, lifted the hood, and poked and prodded at some wires. "Let's make a run for it to the main road. Maybe this thing's booby trapped!" he shouted to Paul and Adam, who were inside the Jeep.

All three began a synchronized trot in the direction of the highway, turning every now and then to check on the progress of the cabin fire as it flared out around the windows.

Twenty yards into their run, the whiz of a bullet, followed by the loud *kaboom* of a gunshot blast, zipped past Adam. The next shot kicked up the snow in front of the Coyote's feet. The third came too close to Adam, and he fell into the fresh powder and rolled to his left; Paul and the Coyote lay prostrate beside him in the deep snow and looked around trying to see where the shots had come from.

* * * * * *

Jared "Grits" Hominy was relaxing in his rec. room that afternoon when his wife brought a frazzled Troy Krueller downstairs. She tried not to show her festering disgust toward her husband directly, so she compensated by being overly friendly to the boy, asking him about his holiday plans and the health of his mother and family members. She took his coat and neck scarf back upstairs after Grits stared at her for a few seconds with that *get-outa-here* look he was so well-known for.

"How'd it go out there today?" he asked Troy.

Troy looked befuddled. His eyes were the size of a young buck's and just as dark. Maybe he even looked terrified, like a boy who knew that he had done something horrific but didn't want to admit it.

"Not as well as I thought," he said in a soft voice, glancing back toward the stairs to make sure they were alone. "I meant to scare them. That's all," he whispered.

"That's what you were supposed to do, son. That was the plan. Glad you kept your ears open and alerted me as to when they'd be out there. Sad that only three showed up. Only wish the whole lot of 'em would have been there," Grits responded as he poured himself some Scotch. Among all of his vices, Scotch whiskey and bourbon were his biggest.

"I threw the bottle at the cabin. . .just like you said to do. But it went through the window by accident, though, before it exploded. Wooooompf!" Troy recounted, throwing his arms into the air and adding the sound of the muffled explosion. "They ran out like a bunch of scared rabbits. Scared the crap outa 'em! Shoulda seen them stumbling' off the porch! You look rather bushed yourself! What's up with that?"

Grits thought for a second and replied, "Was out shovelin' the snow off the walk. A might frigid out. Cold weather always tires me out." Troy wasn't able to detect the lie. Grits sloshed his Scotch around in the glass. He had that sarcastic grin on his face once again as Troy continued to tell about how he was just going to shoot at them to frighten them off. Grits's brow knitted up with approval.

"It sorta got crazy. I was shootin' around 'em to scare 'em good. Jus' like we planned, but I swear I think I almost hit Adam."

"You what! What the hell you thinkin', boy!" Grits raised his voice and twisted up his face at the same time.

"I thought I was shooting over his head, but suddenly he fell. Musta aimed too close. If I didn't know better, I'd swear someone else was out there, too. Couldn't tell because of all the echoes ricocheting about," Troy explained.

When Grits Hominy became agitated, his neck muscles tensed. His face became distorted. His anger suddenly would go inside, and there it would seethe. He turned away from

Troy and gulped his Scotch as he thought for a second about what had happened.

"Let me pour you one," Grits ordered. "You deserve it. We ain't all perfect." Troy held up a glass as the coach poured the liquid about two fingers full. Slowly, the boy sat down on the Ottoman opposite his coach and stared into the glass, took a gulp, and waited for the coach to continue. "And the cabin?" coach continued. "What about the cabin?"

"It was burning when I left," Troy answered before he took another mouthful.

"And you're sure no one saw you?"

"No one saw me. It was snowing quite a bit out. There was a lot of confusion. I mentioned that before," Troy explained. "I was headin' on back through the woods where I stashed the car."

"Did they try to follow you?"

"Nope. They couldn't get the car started for some reason. The Jeep ain't that old. Don't know why it didn't kick over. Just kept makin' a *chuga-chuga-chuga-shrrrrrrr* sound. From my hideaway I saw them hurrying off in the direction of the main highway off the old Miller Access Road on foot. I had to have a little fun, didn't I?"

"That's good. Damn good, son," Coach Hominy answered, slamming his fist on the arm of the chair.

Coach Hominy was on his second glass of Scotch, and Troy was about ready to join him for another round, but he always made sure the coach was always at least two drinks ahead.

"How could all of this have gone so wrong in the end?" Troy asked after the coach had measured out two fingers again.

"Wrong? Who said it went wrong, boy?" he asked. "Stop your whimpering. You sound like someone's grandmother at a wake, for Gawd's sake. I thought I had made a man out of you over the past couple of years!" Grits began to raise his voice, but he quieted down for fear his wife would hear.

His personal pride, however, swelled at the thought that one of his lions had finally enjoyed his first kill of sorts. His stomach began to churn. He reached for another drink to satisfy his unquenchable thirst.

Troy soon drank his own glass dry, leaving a couple of ice cubes sliding around.

Coach had just tossed on another log and stirred the fire up with a poker. Still seated on the Ottoman, Troy turned head and watched the coach, quietly studying his every move.

Coach Hominy, letting the Scotch speak, said, "They all betrayed me, son. Steve Gruder, that s-o-b.; Tim, the others. Not one of them was grateful for what I did to turn them into men. I suppose you'll turn on me next!"

"No, sir! I won't betray you."

"You better not. Things can happen. I don't like it when those things happen," Grits continued.

"Like the things that happened to Gruder and Tim?"

"You do see the entire picture, boy, don't you? When a member of the pride is weak, the lion sometimes has to kill its own. The stock has to remain healthy and fit. If it's weak, others can come in and destroy it. That's what's happening here."

"So you killed them, coach," Troy stated.

"Me?" His eyes darted around the room for a second; he remained silent. Troy didn't know how to interpret the uncomfortable pause. "Do you really think I could do that?

Maybe. I don't know. Naw. I'm just joshin' ya, boy. But someone saw them as weak, and he came and started thinning out my herd."

"You sound like you're trying to convince yourself of your innocence," Troy observed.

Troy fumbled for a pack of cigarettes in the pocket of his letterman's jacket.

"Smokin' ain't good for you, boy," the coach admonished.

"Scotch ain't either. Besides, I ain't in trainin' now," Troy answered back brashly.

"Guess you're right. Give me one then."

Both sat back and smoked slowly without saying a word. From time to time, Troy would suck an ice cube into his mouth and then crunch down on it, feeling it mold itself to the top of his bottom molar and then melt. After they had finished for the evening, Hominy went to a small safe located in the hallway, returned with $600, pressed it into Troy's hand and said, "You go out there and have a merry little Christmas, son. After the holidays, I'll even let you earn more than that."

Troy took the money and stuffed it into the front pocket of his jeans without counting it. Upstairs he wished Mrs. Hominy a happy holiday. It didn't take her long to return to the rec. room downstairs.

"You didn't learn at the first school you were at, and I doubt if you'll learn now," she said as she emptied the ashtray into the fireplace. "You know what you did to his. . .to his. . . well, you know what you did."

"Don't see how it's any concern of yours as to what I've done," he answered. "I let you live here for free, don't I?"

She returned to the kitchen upstairs, and he sat and reflected about the past after pouring himself another drink. He was disturbed. That gut-wrenching feeling that things were always churning around inside him had given Coach Hominy his outwardly cocky beginning at Trinity. He was the master of the cover-up. To everyone he encountered, he was in control; he was stable. But he wasn't.

He remembered taking the previous year's team and reminisced about the great plans he had for turning the boys into even better, well-disciplined young men. To him, well-disciplined meant being ruled under Spartan law. Ye'SIR! Righ'SIR! Ye'SIR! SIR! SIR! Drop an' gimme twenty, boy! Drop an' gimme forty, son! Ten laps! Twenty laps! Every drill had its cadence. Every athlete had his own drum, but only Coach Hominy got to beat on that drum.

As with any team, there were those who participated only for the glory. Others participated for the sweat, knowing that they gave it 100%. It was the latter group that Grits admired. Perhaps in his own raw way, he adored them. They would be the select, the elect, the Pride. The young cubs would become the lions, the predators, but only those he found worthy. He wanted to mold the select into an unflinching group of rock-hard athletes who knew neither fear nor cowardice. He would teach them how to intimidate, how to rule, and how to step on others before they could be stepped upon.

His selection process began each August after the first sweltering day of practice. Those who didn't throw up or pass out or complain were his targets. He even was known to prowl around the freshmen area, always keeping an eye out for the one who would someday fit into his plan. That's where he first spotted Troy a couple of years back. He remembered it all so well.

"You've got a good arm, Krueller," Coach Hominy had said to break the ice.

"Thanks. I think you're right," Troy answered back without any expression in his voice at all.

It was that cockiness that Grits wanted to capture and form into his own image and likeness. And he had had remarkable success in transforming those he deemed to be worthy. What he didn't know for sure (but always suspected) was that the Crewe of Adelphos was always a recruit ahead of him at every turn.

Having selected about eight or nine young recruits a year, Grits had formed a group that proved to be trustworthy until death, at least as he saw it. With the Coyote and others wandering away from his assertive power, however, he was reliving and reviewing what steps he had to take to make sure no one else defected.

Chapter 15

Christmas Eve: seven o'clock
24 Dec 2009

Greenlawn's wintry nights had been heralding an affluent holiday season for well over a month. Graven images of Santas and elves, reindeer and sleighs, dotted the landscape. Colored lights illumined the homes, trees, and bushes against a Yuletide canvas of frosty, starry nights. Those longing for the memories of a passed youth inhaled, through the evening air, the scents of Christmas etched in pine and in the smoke, sweet smoke from cherry that plumed upward toward the jet sky from a hundred chimneys.

Festive homes bedecked with wreathes and holly silently lined the serpentine streets guarded by magnificent, dormant maples and oaks, their branches casting fragile shadows like boney, arthritic fingers across the snow. Automobiles passed by silently. All was quiet; all was at peace.

Manicured lawns were at rest under their snowy blanket. Hedges were a prickly reminder of last summer's lush growth. A brown rabbit darted across the road near the small lake without looking behind; Scamp, the cat, was spending her winter looking out the side window off the kitchen. Dogs nuzzled their masters who were relaxing in warm dens on plush leather chairs. That's how it was that Christmas Eve in Greenlawn.

Not too far away from the Second Congregational Church, where most of the town worshipped, Buck McDougal kicked the snow off his boots before jumping up into the roomy cab of his maroon Dodge Ram. He shivered when he leaned back against the frigid seat. His chin, peppered with brown stubble, caught itself for a second on the woolen scarf wrapped around his neck when he looked to his left and to his right before starting up the engine.

The truck turned over immediately, and Buck slammed the gear into reverse. He felt the truck vibrate with power when the back wheels, encountering the deep snow, dug in for traction. His boot eased up on the clutch, and the bed of the truck began to swerve to the left. Buck shifted into first to rock it out before hitting reverse once again. His hand and foot, working in tandem with the gearshift and the clutch, forced the rear over a mound of snow at the end of the drive that the city left behind after plowing Packosky Boulevard earlier in the evening.

According to the truck's clock, he was already about fifteen minutes late, and tardiness was one thing that Buck couldn't tolerate. His breath began to steam the windshield with a frosty haze, and as he drove along, he passively observed how the streetlights cast miniscule circular rainbows onto the glass where his breath had filmed over.

Instead of turning on the defroster, he grabbed a stained T-shirt from under the front seat and attempted to wipe the window clean. He finally rolled down the window a bit and inhaled the cold air deep into his lungs. The heater always annoyed him. Made him too warm. Warmth was for homes, not trucks, although his truck was often his home when he went out after dark to socialize with the quiet of the night.

* * * * * *

Parked out between Belman Acres and DeGrand Park, Buck McDougal grabbed a fresh pack of Newports off the dashboard. He had just purchased them at the gas station on Rt. 224 after a mental debate as to whether he wanted to indulge in such a social gaffe. That made his cravings even stronger. Socially unacceptable things were just fine to him; he loved to rattle every cage he could.

Except for the occasional boys' night out, he had quit smoking halfway through his freshman year at the Academy when he was eighteen, but he was under more stress now than when he had three zits on homecoming night during his sophomore year, he remembered with a hardy laugh. And those three zits, by the way, cost him a romantic moment with Tammy Arner when, parked out by the Old Cemetery Road hill with Buck in smooth control, she suddenly came down with a "throbbing" migraine, as she put it, after watching him pop a pustule on his chin while staring into the rearview mirror to zero in on the pubescent problem.

He wanted a release from daily tension, and without much deliberation, he rolled the window down a few inches and lit up the cigarette after he had smacked the hard pack against his palm five times. An older friend, Mike, had introduced him to that vice…actually, several vices when he thought about it…although he discovered booze on his own long ago during a Fourth of July party down by the lake. Of course, perhaps Mike was there for that milestone also.

The wind gusting in the window blew the smoke around the steering wheel. He watched the blue haze spiral and snake its way throughout the cab; the windshield fogged up for a moment. He turned on the defroster this time to clear the smoke away from his view of the natural wilderness. The windows became clear once again. Leaning his head back a bit, he thought about the quiet outside the truck while slowly drawing the smoke in. The menthol felt good at the back of his throat. The tension in his chest began to dissipate; he relaxed and let the accumulated frustrations flow out the cracked window and drift up toward the cloudy sky. According to a spate of text messages from friends and acquaintances, Christmas Eve had officially begun.

This spot out in the woods where the pines formed a crescent around an open meadow was his favorite. It was his place for solitude and introspection when things started crashing down on him. The deed to the property was now in his name. He had bought happiness.

When he first came to Greenlawn, he would drive out to a forest nearby on the other side of the ridge in a pick-up where a friend taught him how to hunt deer. Most of the time, Buck made so much noise that the deer were forewarned as soon as the truck doors slammed shut.

He spent his first night camping out on the other side of the glen in canvas tents with his friends, and, according to their youthful logic, those pup tents could stop wolves, bears, and a wayward moose or two, although the only moose to be seen locally was at the zoo in Ketertown. But it was the skunk attack near the oak tree that really gave him a healthy dose of respect for nature. He never looked at tomato juice the same way again.

The Ram's motor had been idling for a while. Great white curls of exhaust fumes billowed up into the air, and the headlights illumined the dense forest on the opposite side of the field. At the end of his smoke, he shut off the lights and killed the engine. Through a slight break in the clouds, the moon came into view above the tallest spruce over to his left. In just a week's time, that moon would become a blue moon on New Year's Eve, the second full moon of the month. Soft light spilled onto the meadow where darkness had once claimed its territory, and long shadows from the trees veiled the snow. Light. Dark. Always at odds with one another. Always struggling for domination.

A solitary figure made his way along by the split rail fence behind the parked truck. A twig on the ground cracked and broke. Buck cocked his ear, watched him approach in the passenger side mirror, and leaned over, stretching his body over the console, to open up the locked passenger door.

"What is the hour?" Buck asked.

"It is the hour to convene," Paul Docket replied.

Both sat and stared out into the frosted woods through the windshield in silence. Nothing was moving. The wind was calm. Suddenly, an owl sailing across the meadow tried to grasp something in its claws, failed, and flew off to another tree. A fox, perhaps a dog, darted out into the field, turned its head and listened before slowly slinking back into the forest. An awkward silence permeated the cab of the truck.

"They say that the animals can talk at midnight tonight," Paul said, breaking the silence. He didn't really believe that old Norwegian myth, but he had to come up with something to say. The silence was so loud it was annoyingly intimidating.

"And what the hell do you think they'll say, Docks?" Buck retorted. Paul fidgeted on the seat. The only time that

Buck ever called him "Docks" was when a little booze or frustration had come into play.

"How would I know? Just trying to make some conversation here," Paul snapped back. "Smells like you've been out with Jack 'n Jim tonight," Paul said.

"Who's Jack 'n Jim?"

"Daniel's and Beam, Buck. Daniel's and Beam."

"Yeah. The only one missing is Jose! Hey, I'll drink to that! And where's your ride tonight?" Buck asked, lighting up another 'port. He turned his face to the left and blew the smoke out the cracked-open window. The wind blew it back just as fast.

"Ride? Oh, my Jeep. Not repaired yet. First, the battery died out at the cabin. Next, I bought a new battery thinking that the old battery had been the problem, and things were fine until yesterday. Died again. Something's been stopping the battery from re-charging or re-loading. The mechanic still has to tinker around a bit. Can't get the Jeep back until after Christmas."

"That sucks, man. How did you get out here? We're pretty damn far from town."

"I had one of the town guys, Carlos, drive me out. Told him I was going to the Cicione's cabin. They always have a big to-do on Christmas Eve. Fish. Pasta. Soup. There were enough cars parked along the road. Carlos just let me jump out without too many questions. I told him it would be easy to get a ride back. He didn't know that I had other plans. I figured you'd be here. Actually, I didn't figure. . .your message on my cell gave a hint." Ignoring Paul, Buck reached under his seat for a bottle of Christmas cheer. "It wasn't that long of a walk for me from the Cicione's place. What's so urgent you couldn't just stop by the house?" Paul asked. He tended to ramble on far too much. Buck rarely said much, and Paul tried to slow himself down before he wore McDougal out.

"I don't want to be seen with you until...," Buck said without completing his thought.

"Until all this blows over. I understand," Paul replied.

"*Blows* is right. We have to talk. Wanna swig?" Buck held out the bottle and nodded. Paul looked at it for a second, took a healthy gulp to placate Buck, and then grimaced as if he had just swallowed raw lemon juice. Had the passenger side window been open, he would have spit it out. He breathed out a long sigh and stared over at Buck who had a stupid grin on his face. He wasn't going to be labeled an old lady by anyone, especially by one Buck McDougal who measured how virile a man was by how much hooch he could swallow without gagging and retching.

The second mouthful went down better, but it still tasted vile. Paul nodded. Buck nodded. Paul passed the bottle back to Buck, signaling that he had had enough refreshment. Without asking permission, Paul reached over and grabbed a Newport to kill the taste of whatever was in the bottle. Buck thought to himself, *This oughta be good. If you think the booze was strong, wait 'til you suck in the smoke from that baby, yuh wuss,* but Paul showed no adverse reaction. No cough. No contorted face. Nothing. Buck just studied Paul's face and acknowledged to himself that he didn't know Paul at all.

Buck was still a *person of interest* to the police. Because of the fear and the tension still on campus, people avoided paranoia by causing it. No one, it seemed, wanted to be seen with people who were close to the deceased. *Guilt by association.* Statistics show that most murder victims know the person who killed them.

"Whatcha wanna do?" Buck asked, slammin' down another swig from the bottle.

Paul thought for a second and replied, "How about taking out the little Piper Cub, man, and letting me go for a ride!" Buck had his own plane...a real red beauty of a machine that he used for family business or for personal pleasure from time to time, and he had his pilot's license, thanks to one of his older friends encouraging him to hang out at the local airport to learn the ropes from the older guys before he entered high school. Nothing made him happier than a quick flight to anywhere without goal or reason.

"On Christmas Eve? In my present condition? We'd be lucky if the..."

"I think I get the gist," Paul said. "I wouldn't want to crash somewhere in the forest on the other side of Unk Mountain where we wouldn't be found for weeks! I remember stories about the Uruguayan rugby team, or whoever they were, up in the Andes back in the 70s. If you didn't survive and I did, you might cause me some serious indigestion!"

"Take a Nessssium---Nexium!" he exclaimed. He reflected about how he loved to fly his Cub in adverse conditions, often when he was alone at the controls. He could handle a single propeller, and he learned how to dump fuel when required without injuring the environment. He wanted to take hold of a double-prop, but that was only a latent dream. "Nothing like hurling through space in a rainstorm and wondering if there's a mountain out there with your name on it!" he said once to a group of fresh recruits at flight school who were still trying to learn the flight manual on their own. Buck continued, "Seriously, man, let's book outa here. We'll save the Cubster for another day. I promise."

"We can't go to the Crewe cabin anymore. That's out of the question," Paul said.

"Hell, no, mo-jo. Ain't nothing' out of the question. I got me a place off Route 18. It beats the old one we used for the Crewe anyway, but since we ain't got nowhere else to go, we might have to use this one. I hope no one will toss in a Molotov cocktail," he said, laughing after he said *cocktail,* and then he put the bottle to his lips once again.

"It's gotta be bigger than the old place. Let's get out of here and head over there then, and it better have heat," Paul warned.

"And if it don't?"

"If it *don't,* you won't get the talk you seem so eager to have."

"It's got heat. Don't get your knickers in a knot. It's all good."

"I don't wear knickers," Paul explained.

"You don't! Really? More than I want to know."

"Do you?" Paul asked.

"Dunno. I'm not sure what they are! But if I do, I'm sure they're not knotted!" Buck laughed loud and hard, smacked the dashboard, and turned on the engine.

It may have been all good, but Paul changed places with Buck, nonetheless, against Buck's belligerent pleading that he drove best after downing a few, and the two wended their way through rough terrain and thicket with Paul driving the Ram with the four-wheel drive engaged. The log cabin with the heat appeared between the blue spruces, their branches drooping over from snow that had fallen in the past week.

Chapter 16

Christmas Eve: eight o'clock
24 December 2009

Grits's wife had gone out to the eight o'clock candlelight services at the Presbyterian church over on 6th Avenue where Rev. Calvin Knox orchestrated the raising of the candles at various times during the community's singing of "Silent Night." Some in the congregation were obedient and raised their candles high into the air during the last two lines of each verse. Others were sure that this really wasn't Presbyterian doctrine and pretended not to notice the candle-rise and candle-set action of those around them.

On the other side of town, Grits was watching his favorite rerun of a Super Bowl game featuring the Steelers that Christmas Eve at home. "DEE-fense! DEE-fense!" he yelled from time to time as though the players on the big screen could actually hear him and heed his words. It wasn't the first time he had ever seen that play; he had all the plays memorized anyway just by watching and re-watching the same old defensive moves. It just felt good to take out his repressed aggression knowing that when he yelled *DEE-fense,* the players did just that. . .employed defensive strategies that would turn the play around and head the Steelers to victory again...and again...and again...as often as he played the same game on the TV.

Troy Krueller, sloshing his bourbon over and around the ice cubes in his glass before draining his drink down his open throat, sat on the recliner engrossed in the same game as much as Grits. The coach had called him an hour before and said he had some philosophical things to discuss with the boy. Troy was curious as to what Grits would consider philosophical.

Grits mumbled to himself, "They think they're immortal."

"The Steelers? They are immortal, man!" Troy shouted out.

He stared at Troy, shook his head, and replied, "No, yuh dip, the Crewe of Adelphos, or whatever they are."

"Immortal? Like forever?" Troy asked. "Field goal! Did ya see that, coach! What a sweet kick!"

"It's not live. You don't hav'ta yell at the top of your lungs," Grits admonished.

"You yell '*DEE*-fense' every two minutes." Troy was able to mock out the coach and get away with it especially when the coach was trying to make a point. Grits had a one track mind and couldn't process too many bytes of information at once.

"But it's *my* film. I can do what I freakin' want to do! Yeah, like forever. That's what immortal is, yuh dumb wad. Steve Gruder was ramblin' on about that once. Seems to me he was. I think he was one of them. One of them Adelphoids. He wanted to confide in me after he got liquored up after a game one night. I think he got liquored up. Maybe he didn't. They all confide in me, boy. Anyway, he'd heard some of 'em talking in the locker room...maybe it was in the dorm; I don't remember exactly. I think it was him. Maybe wasn't. If it wasn't him, it was someone. I'm sure he was one of them. Just said that a second ago, didn't I? You're confusin' me, boy. Stop confusin' me. Betrayed me, he did. I've heard strange things over the years, but nothin' like bein' immortal. No, sir. That's downright scary."

"How could Gruder be immortal? He died in the shower! Don't sound like *immortal* to me," Troy said, making those annoying quotation marks in the air. He scratched his stomach absent-mindedly, stuck his hand under his waistband, and stretched out his legs, and sighed, perhaps out of boredom.

"And Tim, too. He was one of them. They can't put much over on me. For all I know, you could be one of them, boy," Grits said. He poured himself more bourbon and motioned for Troy, who was only too happy to accept the coach's invitation, to do the same.

"He died, too, didn't he? If you ask me, not much *immortality* for Tim," Troy said, repeating his quotation marks in the air.

"Don't you get it, son. They hide it. They hide it from us. They're sneaky about it. They're all sneaky. I want to have what they've got!!" Coach Hominy slammed his fist on the arm of the couch. "I want what those s-o-bs have!"

Trying to maintain some sense of calm, Troy said, "Steve's gone, and so is Tim. They don't have nothin' to give as I see it. Even if there was somethin', how did they get it? How did they *get* immortality? Someone's makin' up a tall tale." Troy watched Grits out of the corner of his eye. The coach had turned off the game and sauntered off to the bathroom. The toilet flushed, and the coach returned, shuffling his feet on the carpet.

Grits made a V sign, motioning for a cigarette. "Hurry up, boy, before the old bag gets back from her mystical moment with the reverend! Ought to be here by nine if the pastor ain't too long-winded. She'll be hummin' hymns for the next three days. When she gets religion, I get nothing'... if you follow my drift." Troy tossed him one from the pack in his jacket pocket and watched Grits light it from a candle his wife had placed on the table earlier in the evening. "How did you ever get hooked on Marlboro reds anyway? Awfully strong stuff, boy." Troy ignored the coach's question.

"So don't smoke it," he answered sarcastically. "Anyway, the whole concept of the immortality thing is from science fiction. You've read one too many of them spooky books, haven't you?"

"Haven't read a thing in years," Grits announced proudly. The last time he attempted to read a book, any book, was *The Catcher in the Rye* when he was a freshman in college. He never made it past page two, and had it not been for Candy Lambert's late evening tutorials at Kuyper's Bar, he would never have earned a D- on the final exam.

"For argument's sake," Troy began after sipping some more bourbon, "how would you know if someone was immortal or not?"

"Guess you'd have to wait to see if they die," Coach replied.

"Or try to kill them to see what happens. Right, Coach?"

"You *do* think that I..."

"Hey, they ain't comin' back, now are they? So what difference does it make who did 'em in? Perhaps you proved to yourself that they ain't immortal. You know where my loyalty lies, don't you? Don'tcha, coach?"

"Yeah, loyalty schmoyalty." Grits sipped some more booze. "Not unless they're zombies or vampires. Nothin' like that's happened since that book by Brad Stober," Coach said.

"Bram Stoker. *Dracula* was written by Bram Stoker," Troy said, correcting him politely.

"Brad, Bram, potato, potahto. Educated, ain't you, son. Who cares?" He flicked an ash onto the carpet just for the fun of it. "Yuh know, you're like the son I never had. Want you to know that, boy."

"Yeah. And you're the dad I never had." Troy stood up to get some more ice and softly repeated to himself, "The dad I never had."

Troy and the coach both heard the keys jingling at the lock and knew that Mrs. Hominy had just returned from her spiritual experience under Rev. Calvin Knox's tutelage. The coach quickly tossed his smoke into the fireplace to destroy the evidence; Troy took the visual blame. A guy can't do much when he's caught in mid-inhale. She acknowledged Troy's presence by a nod and a shake of her head disapproving of his habit, stared at her husband's drink when he began to down it after she entered the room, and went upstairs to the kitchen to make a pot of tea before bedtime humming "O Little Town of Bethlehem."

"Oh, Lawd, she's hummin' hymns again. Didn't I tell you?" Grits pointed out smugly.

"I think that's my cue to go, Coach. I have to get out and about before I head home for the holidays tomorrow. Mom and her parents on a cruise until the day after, and I thought I'd just stay here at school. We're all meeting up in New York for a few days before going home to the city. I'll keep my ears open. Maybe I can uncover some things for you.

Remember, life's a slippery slope sometimes. You might not want to uncover the truth."

"They're not immortal. Can't be. Naw, I don't care what they say. They're just like us. Gotta be," Grits said. He watched the moon appear through the bay window. "They are like us, aren't they?"

"Yeah. Just like us," Troy said buttoning up his coat and tying his plaid scarf around his neck.

Chapter 17

Christmas Eve: ten o'clock
24 December 2009

Buck McDougal was tossing some logs into the fireplace, and Paul was in the kitchen area making some cocoa to replace Buck's attack on the spirits of Christmas present. The log cabin was nothing that Lincoln would recognize; it was too modern on the inside, its wood polished and protected by a coating of glossy preservative, and no convenience had been overlooked. The outside, however, was more rustic. Darkened split logs, window boxes awaiting the spring, and French windows encouraged the weary traveler to draw near and enjoy the comfort within.

The first floor was an open grand room, and the two bedroom lofts kept watch over spindled railings. And the best part was the heat. No asthmatic water heater and primitive electric furnace. No leaky windows that blew the curtains when the wind kicked up!

Paul busied himself in the kitchen and from time to time he wondered about Buck and what made him Buck. Docket and McDougal, it is true, had nothing in common, other than the Crewe, and they had never had a discussion about anything of importance. Neither knew much about the other, except for a few snippets, and that type of relationship seemed to be acceptable to them, but with all the tragedy they had been plunged into, it was time to have a long talk about what was going on. It was time to dump the superfluous and focus on the internal.

"The more I look around here, the more I'm amazed as to how you designed strength and endurance into the plans."

Buck just nodded but failed to reply. He drank the cocoa making loud slurping sounds. "This stuff isn't too bad. Put anything in it?"

"Nope. Just milk. Why have you kept this place so secret?" Paul asked.

"Dunno. I've had some of the Crewe over from time to time. You know how I like those rituals! Never came out here with others very often, so this cabin is not part of my history with others except for the Crewe. Even Lisa, when we were still going together, never ventured out here. A couple of the guys and I were out at Thanksgiving trying to put things into perspective. I came out here yesterday and brought provisions in case I wanted to stay over for the holidays."

"Wish you had brought me along in November. I could have used a retreat," Paul said.

"We'll have to have everyone over after the holidays. I can see us all sittin' around right here in front of the fireplace!"

Buck reflected back that it was during his junior year at the Academy he was tapped in the middle of the night while asleep and was hustled out of bed to some sequestered area south of the football field. Blindfolded, he met the mailman. He played football then, starting defense, and he was what the Crewe wanted, and he became a member of the Crewe of

Adelphos. Now he has returned to teach at the Academy that has meant so much to him.

His first Crewe responsibility was to assist the historian, and that meant learning the oral history. Any written history, and that included the *Kuhduush,* had been lost decades ago, or so the Crewe thought. Any office within the organization had to be learned quickly because members were only on campus for a couple of years before moving out and beginning new lives, so they had to learn their new function and then pass on what they knew to others. He memorized the history and made it come alive to the others.

Paul found the Crewe during his second year teaching. Nobody knows the entire story, but some of his students found him *worthy,* as they put it, and soon the mail was delivered even on a Sunday when he was taking a walk through the woods off campus.

"They were always around," Paul said. "I didn't have to do anything because they just found me. I remember having to memorize the letters not knowing how many there were or what the purpose of it all was. I always felt watched, yet protected. You?"

"At first," Buck said, "I just thought it was a fraternity. It is, I guess, sorta. It's like an onion. You can just keep peeling and peeling hoping you'll get to the center of it all."

Paul hedged, not knowing if he wanted to get into the deeper aspects of the Crewe. "Well, you're right. Sometimes I just feel that. . .well, I just feel that I'm not sure of what it's all about. I often get the impression that there's more, but I don't have a clue as to what the *more* is. By the by, I've got something you need to take a look at." Paul took out a small packet and tossed it onto the glass table. "Go ahead, Buck, and open it. I've thumbed through some of it."

"It ain't some sappy special from Borders, is it? You know I ain't a great reader," Buck replied.

"Boy, look upon the *Kuhduush*. It's real and not just some memorized mumbo jumbo that we had to learn bits and pieces of by oral tradition," Paul explained.

Buck sat and looked at the wrapped packet; he didn't want to actually touch it. He laughed nervously and then cleared his throat. Paul said, "Buck, you open it. You're the youngest. The *Kuhduush* says that '*He who is the youngest shall bring wisdom to the elders. He who is the youngest will teach the Sons of Adelphos the ways of honesty, openness, obedience, and determination, four words upon which our wisdom hangs.*' Don't remember where in the *Kuhduush* that comes from exactly. I had to learn it once for one of the degrees."

McDougal slowly removed the paper, and after he finished touching its leather, feeling its smoothness, and quickly glancing through it, he passed it back to Paul with reverence, who then flipped through the sacred text, explaining how it had been returned through young Joel Garret, the great-great-great grandson of Tyler Pettigrew, son of Beauregard Pettigrew, son of Harland Pettigrew.

Paul said, "Joel's a student of mine. Took out some materials from the archives, and I spied it. I snagged it from his room about three and a half weeks ago. I've spent some time going through this. You'd be surprised how accurate our memorized quotes are to the original text."

Buck pictured the onion analogy and wanted to approach Paul at that very moment. He wanted to strip away some of those layers and lay some things bare, but the time had to be perfect, almost to the second. This could be that moment because Buck was ready to pass on inner secrets that he had sworn to protect, but the sound of someone stomping up the porch steps trying to knock the snow off his boots halted the conversation that both had been planning to have for months.

Paul pulled back the curtains on the door, peered out, fidgeted around with the lock, and let Troy in.

"Wow! I don't remember it being so nice out here. I'm so used to the Crewe cabin, but that's all over," Troy said.

"Yeah, it is," Buck said. "Thanks for the Molotov cocktail, guy. I'm sure the entire Crewe thanks you! I remember when the only thing you could ever toss right were your cookies!" Paul and Troy laughed.

"Sorry, but I only meant to set the side of the porch on fire. That's what Coach wanted. Just enough to scare you. Glad I got your text message and knew where you were. It all worked out fine. He had been after me to somehow get you all out to the cabin and then let the fireworks begin! He didn't know you were going to tear down the old hovel in the spring anyway. I don't feel bad about torching the place because you were going to destroy it yourself to re-build it. But I goofed it up bad. It seems I always goof things up. I could have killed all of you. And I never touched your Jeep. Really. And I shot *near* Adam not *at* him. Don't understand how I came so close to almost injuring him," Troy stated and then tried to shut himself up. He was rambling and he knew it.

"What brings you out here tonight? Thought you had some Pride bonding to do with the Gritster," Paul said.

Buck made his hands paw the air like a giant cat. "How is the Lion's Pride these days, Troy? Am I supposed to growl or maul you or something at this point?" All three gave each other a high five and guffawed at how ridiculous Buck looked.

"Well," Troy said, "Grits got toasted tonight. Wife was out at church, and I was there to offer him some type of moral support as usual. He was rambling on about the Crewe's members being immortal." Buck tossed another log into the fireplace, and Paul, listening intently to what Troy was saying, shifted in his chair. "I said that all the immortal stuff was hogwash because Gruder and Tim were dead, and then I asked him how you could be immortal if you're no longer around."

"Maybe he just believes that when you die your spirit just goes somewhere. Isn't that being immortal?" Paul asked.

"Not sure what he believes. He's not spiritual. At least as far as I can tell. Too bitter to be spiritual. But I think he means that being immortal is when you don't pass through death at all. I've never heard anything so dumb in my life," Troy explained. Buck looked at the fireplace.

Paul shrugged his shoulders and said, "This life isn't a dress rehearsal. When it's over, well, it's over. Where do people get such lame ideas?"

"Do you suppose he killed Steve and Tim just to test out his theory? They died, so he must know they weren't immortal," Buck said. He tossed on a fresh log.

"He stopped just short of saying that," Troy said. "I think he's coming apart at the seams. His marriage is in a mess. His Pride is falling apart. I'm the only guy who ever goes over there except for Roger, his new buddy. Grits doesn't know who to trust any longer. He's grasping for something, but he doesn't know what he wants to grab."

"It's him or us, Troy. He's about to cause us major problems if he keeps talking that nonsense. You know what you have to do," Buck said. "Let him go over the edge."

"Shouldn't be too hard to do. Hey, what's that?" Troy asked before he reached over the table and picked up the small book.

"That? Nothin'. Paul found it somewhere and gave it to me. It will look good on the mantle beside those other books," Buck explained. "Nothin' like a good leather-bound book and a roaring fire!"

Troy opened it up, glanced at the page headings, and put it back onto the table. Buck quickly moved on to other things, and Paul supported him in the transition. They sat and talked about the possibility of acquiring new recruits for after the holidays. All three watched the fire devour the logs, and well after midnight, Paul hitched a ride back to his own home with Troy at the wheel, who then continued on to his dorm room where he collapsed wondering how he had gotten involved with it all. And Paul, before he drifted off to sleep, wondered what new layer of the onion he had almost opened.

Buck snoozed and snored up in the log cabin's loft. He turned in his sleep, touched his neck where it burned a bit and remembered. It had turned into a silent night after all.

Chapter 18

New Year's Eve
31 Dec 2009

Roger Honeycutt, drying his sopping black hair with a dark-blue fluffy towel containing specks of lint, stood in front of his antique Tuscan dresser and mirror, an heirloom, he once told his friends. He wrapped the wet terry cloth tightly around his waist, laid out his underwear on the dark green marble insert, massaged a foamy dollop of mousse into his hair, and went back into the bathroom to shave. His Gillette razor made well-controlled strokes over his face and neck before making a few random swipes down his chest and stomach as he touched up his previous attempts at being well-groomed. Stepping back and scrutinizing his work, he passed inspection once again. But he always passed inspection.

Roger studied his face in the mirror, noticed the tender spot on his neck that had started to bother him recently, massaged it for a moment, and tossed his wet towel over the shower rod, where it would hang and dry whether his roommates liked it or not. He mechanically pulled the rest of his evening supplies out of the medicine cabinet, lining them up like soldiers in formation on the sink.

He slicked some deodorant generously around his underarms, sniffed his right armpit to make sure it smelled good (he never checked out his left), slapped a handful of talcum hither and yon (more hither than yon), applied the Axe body spray his friend Phil had given him in a grand arc that he stepped into, coughing mildly after inhaling the various concoctions floating in the air around him, and winked at himself in the mirror. Shave, slick, sniff, slap and spray. It couldn't get simpler than that. He was ready. He was fresh. He was cocksure as to who he was and what he was about.

He started college when he was twenty because he first wanted to go out and find himself, whatever that meant. He was always finding himself and re-inventing himself. He was so good at re-inventing himself that he wanted to change his name to Edison Honeycutt once. He wasn't sure what he had found in all that searching, but he was ready to major in life's fast lane, hoping more for a master's than a bachelor's.

He often tried to make himself look a year or two younger to fit in more with the guys. Taking one final look in the mirror by the door, he realized that he frequently tried to make himself look a year or two older, so the college women would notice him more, but they always did, no matter what his real age was. That New Year's Eve, he just wanted to look himself, and as far as he was concerned, he hadn't looked himself in years.

The last night of December was usually a prolonged night for him, as most of the winter evenings were, and he had already made plans to be with Leslie Morehouse, a rather aggressive young lady. Although she didn't know it, it would be her last hook up with him. They had been out twice before, and his third-time-is-a-charm rule would take effect shortly after the soirée ended with the final toss of the confetti and the last duck-like hoot of the striped cardboard horns. Were he honest with himself, he would have to admit that he liked her, but he continually attracted the ones who were possessive or those who wanted to change him in some way. As far as he was concerned, he wasn't about to become anybody's trophy. Leslie's trophy shelf that kept her ego satiated had filled up long ago.

He had spent Christmas on campus. Although no one was sure about the real reason, some said he had had a falling out with his father shortly before the holidays. But on the twenty-seventh, he returned to the pizza parlor to offer some help because he needed the extra cash for New Year's Eve, and when the owner had to rush to Iowa to be with his ailing mother, Rocco's Pizza and Sub Shoppe had to close early for the rest of the holiday season. In a way, that was a boon for Honeycutt because he had a chance to relax, prepare for the new semester, and go out and sow a bushel or two of wild oats before the discipline of work and study took over his life once again. Actually, he wanted to focus on the wild oats at the moment, and he knew it wasn't going to be with Leslie Morehouse.

His little Mazda hummed along with each shift of the gears, its muffler roaring to a crescendo when he changed from first to second and from second to third, an exaggerated sound he created on purpose to impress any sport car aficionado within earshot. The town's 35 mph speed limit didn't mean much to him. Actually, it didn't mean much to anyone. There was only one police car in the vicinity, and Tommy the cop was always parked at the Denny's south of the 434 junction in case one of the locals needed to get a hold of the law.

At Umaña's liquor store, Honeycutt purchased a fifth of whiskey to mix with cola or ginger ale at the party where he was to meet Leslie. Being twenty-one wasn't so exciting anymore, he came to realize. It had been more fun trying to snag some illegal booze when he was nineteen, but now the proprietors just carded him, an annoying little procedure, and he was free to buy as much as he wanted without any questions. The ID routine would be passé when he was no longer required to produce his driver's license because he looked his age for once.

From time to time, a high school kid hung around the parking lot trying to cajole someone into purchasing a bottle of the hard stuff, but Roger didn't oblige at all. In fact, he appeared to have become somewhat of a born-again Victorian when it came to keeping the younger ones on the road to sobriety. He didn't feel like imbibing that night himself. In fact, he rarely drank at all.

The party over at the Buttery's home was going full tilt when he arrived at nine o'clock, the time he had promised Leslie that he would. She had had her eyes set on bagging Roger since he first stepped out onto the football field last fall. When he looked up into the stands and nodded, giving his signature wink at the same time, she was sure it was meant for her. His charismatic projections, however, were meant for Abigail van Blad, the girl who usually sat in the bleacher row behind Leslie.

To wrangle her first date with him shortly before the Christmas dance required a great deal of maneuvering, and now that it was New Year's Eve, she had plans for the midnight hour. He, of course, had a few plans of his own, one of which was losing her before heading to some more fun with the Crewe out at the state park where they'd build a fire, celebrate, and crawl into down-filled sleeping bags strewn over the picnic tables in the Gresslauer Pavilion after balancing the rites of manhood with the bitter cold that Greenlawn could deliver on such a night.

Arriving late, 10:04 to be exact, Miss Leslie Morehouse tried to make a well-executed entrance. Her mother had always taught her, as mothers tend to do, that the entrance was the most important part of the evening.

And at that precise moment, as Leslie walked into the dining room with a big smile on her face, her right hand upraised and waving at nobody in particular, Sharon Dellasandra, who had had too much cheer and beer over at Ricky Mayhew's house earlier, rudely vomited all over the table laden with snacks. Party guests, oblivious to Leslie's arrival, ran to and fro in the confusion trying to salvage whatever they could from the buffet table. Poor Sharon's date dragged her to a sofa as if that would sober her up. Roger swiftly carried the punch bowl, its contents sloshing up and over the rim, to a table in the kitchen, convinced that the sangria had remained unscathed during the final blast that the Dellasandra girl spewed forth from her mouth before the dry heaves set in. He didn't even notice his date in the dining room.

"We're gonna need some more punch. I don't trust that stuff, Roger," Angela Buttery, the official hostess of the evening, said. "Here, take some money and go to the store over on Danforth. Buy some cheese and crackers, too. They'll be open all night. Never could stand a girl who couldn't hold her liquor. Geesh."

"My date's arriving soon and…," he said.

"She'll be fine. She can mix and mingle with the rest until you get back. Now skidoo!"

There wasn't much traffic that night. Most of the town's citizens were either staying home for the evening, or they had already arrived at their destinations. The most popular place that year was the Samples Motel at the northern end of town. According to the paper, they offered an early dinner, midnight buffet, dancing, noisemakers, party hats, complementary champagne at midnight only, and a room with Jacuzzi for two for under $150 per couple. Katzenmeyer's Restaurant, on the other hand, offered the same package without the room and Jacuzzi for $65.00 a couple, and once again, the locals were forced to take out their calculators to see which bargain was really the best.

Two blocks east of Danny Shisler's Convenience Store and Cheese Barn, Roger slowed down when he saw a man stumbling and struggling to make his way through some of the snowdrifts along the side of the road that the plows had left a few days earlier. The headlights illumined the guy who lost his balance on a clump of ice, fell, and sprawled out alongside the winding road, the left side of his face buried in the slush.

Roger pulled over as far to the right as he could because he didn't want some reveler to rear-end him. The man, wallowing in the elements, turned on his side when Roger approached and looked up, his face illumined by a streetlight.

"Coach? Coach Hominy? What the hell are…," Roger said.

"Glad you stopped, boy. It's cold." The coach began to shake from the frigid temperatures; he was wearing a shirt and pants, some old slippers, but no coat. His face had at least two days' worth of stubble, and his knuckles showed signs of being cut and scraped from when he fell onto the road.

"What are you doing out here? I bet you're freezing."

"I, my, uh, my car broke down. I think it broke down. I got out to fix it. No, not fix it. To see what was wrong. Was their something wrong? There's always something wrong. Something's so wrong. Don't you see it, boy? Don't you feel it, son?"

Roger stared at Grits. Mud caked the coach's shirt, and his pants were wet and torn where he had fallen. Grits reached up, stretching out his hands and arms for Roger to assist him.

"You're not making sense. Where's your car?" Roger asked, helping the coach to his feet.

"My car. Dunno. Maybe they took it. Maybe they made it immortal. Just like they are," he mumbled.

Roger opened up the passenger side door and helped the coach get situated on the seat. The smell of alcohol on Grits's breath was obvious. "I'm going to take you home, man. You can find your car tomorrow, but for now, you need to get home and keep warm. You'll catch your death out here." Grits just sat and stared out the window as the trees and the streetlights passed by in a blur. His whole body hurt; his fingers were numb. The heater began to work its magic, but in doing so, his hands and feet began to sting as they thawed. "How long have you been wandering about anyway? It's well after 10 o'clock."

"Hippy New Year!" Grits announced with a burst of glee. He clapped his hands together and began to sing "Auld Lang Syne."

"Hey, big guy, I didn't say it was midnight, yet," Roger said. He forced a nervous laugh.

Roger drove right past the convenience store on Danforth, forgetting the dictum of picking up more punch for the party. What's worse, he forgot about Leslie Morehouse waiting back at the Buttery's. As far as she was concerned, the midnight kiss was going to seal Roger's fate, linking the two of them together for at least a few more hours, and if it didn't happen the way she had envisioned, after all the conniving schemes she had laid, then she'd have to find another loving cup.

"I'm takin' you home," Roger repeated, this time a little slower and louder. That's what one does with foreigners and people who appear to be hurt or sick or partially deaf. If you speak slower and louder, they are bound to understand. The coach wasn't a foreigner, and he certainly wasn't hearing impaired, although he was injured. "Is that all right with you?"

"Don't take me home, son. I don't want to go home. Take me out to the quarry. The old stone quarry."

"Why would you want to go out there?" Roger asked.

"Just take me. I have business there," he instructed the boy. "You gotta trust me on this, man. You have to trust me. I ain't never steered you wrong before. Not goin' to start now."

"We have to get you cleaned up first."

"No time for all that. No time," Grits said.

Roger turned left at Bryson's Lane, against his better judgment, and headed out into the country where the old stone quarry sat surrounded by naked trees and huge boulders. The only time anyone ever went out to the quarry was in the summer for a good, healty skinny dip, but even then it was dangerous because of the submerged rocks. Someone always ended up being paralyzed or worse by making a miscalculated dive into the murky waters from suicide ridge, a ledge about twenty feet up. The community had put a fence around the perimeter several times over the years, but a good pair of wire clippers from Jost's Hardware foiled the attempts of the city fathers to keep all out of harm's way. In some places, the city fathers can't legislate morality. In Greenlawn, they can't legislate common sense.

"There! There! Pull the car over to the side of the road," he yelled. "We'll take the path down through those rocks. Used to go that way when I was a boy your age. The bluff's right above the quarry." Grits gasped for breath. His eyes were wild, his speech incoherent at times. Roger assisted him along the narrow way that led through the underbrush until they were standing twenty feet away from the precipice. A gaping hole in the fence opened up its jaws to let them trespass to the edge. "Troy Krueller says this is where it happens. This is where they become immortal! Krueller's one of mine. He knows!" Roger had to steady the coach. The ground was slippery, and old branches and twigs from fall protruded up through the snow. Grits didn't seem to care about the terrain and forged onward, a man driven.

"Where *who* becomes immortal?" Roger asked. His neck began to pulse ever so slightly.

"The Crewe of Adonis or Adelphos or whatever the hell they call themselves. It's here they become the gods of fall! Right here at the quarry. It is so obvious!"

"The Crewe of Adelphos? What are you talking about?"

"Don't you ever understand nothin' except how to throw a ball?! Krueller told me all about it tonight on the phone. Hah! I made him confide. They all confide in me. I know the secret! You have to yell *Halleeeee halluuuuu*! That's the secret yell. I have to find out for myself," Grits shouted out, his voice echoing off the rocks in the darkness.

"Krueller doesn't know anything. He's just an affiliate member, man. He's nowhere near the Inner Circle. I've told you too much anyway. Someone's playin' you," Roger said. He held on to Hominy's arm, but the coach pulled his arm away with a sudden jerk.

"A filiate? I don't know nothing' 'bout no filiate."

"Not *filiate. Uh-filiate,*" Roger enunciated.

"Just like Gruder and Tim, I suppose. They all hide who they are behind the innocent ones. The others become their sacrificial lambs. Lambs! Lambs! Mary had a little lamb; its fleas were white as snow!" Grits shouted.

"Fleas! Sacrificial lambs? You don't make any sense."

"I killed Gruder and Tim. Didn't you figure it out? Are yuh that damn dumb, boy? Don't remember it all, though, myself so much. Krueller said I did it. I must have. They died. How would he know 'less I told him. They showed me they were false. Not immortal. But that still doesn't mean that the rest ain't." He held on to Roger's hand for a moment. "Those two never trusted me. The herd had to be thinned out. My Pride had to be protected. Shot at that boy Adam out at their old cabin. Yuh shoulda seen 'em all hit the deck in the snow! Had to make sure Krueller did what I told him to do, you know. I was there hiding in the woods to make sure he didn't botch it. I had to know. I had to know! They got the Coyote in their grasp. He turned his back on me long ago!" Grits began to shake as though he were experiencing some type of withdrawal, yet he kept his eyes focused on Roger. "You're one of them, boy. Aren't you, son?" he asked. "Yeah, you are. I can see it in your eyes. They all have compassion in their eyes! Stinkin' compassion!"

"Yeah, I'm one of 'em. I've always been one of 'em. I don't understand about this quarry. I wish I could help you or tell you more, but I can't. Not now. But let me get you home where you can think things through. Where we can think things through. C'mon, coach. Swallow your pride and let me help."

"Krueller was right. You all have the secret. I must have it! It's unfair! Think of everything I've done for all of you. Where would you be without me, son?" Coach Hominy was looking around in the dark as though he could see invisible hosts arriving and departing.

The chilling wind began to pick up. Roger touched his own neck. The burning started. It was a warning, but he knew not of what. He wrapped his scarf tighter to hide the pulsating beats that he was sure the whole world could see even out near the abyss. The full moon, the blue moon that New Year's Eve, now splashed its soft light round about the quarry to stave off the darkness, and Roger clearly saw the terror and confusion in Hominy's eyes. "They can't cheat me again by their lies," Grits confided. "I know the secret even if they won't tell! *Halleeeee hallooooo!*" the coach shouted into the night. And with that last cry of frenzied agitation, Coach Hominy plunged himself silently into the depth of the quarry's chasm before Roger Honeycutt could reach out and grab him.

CHAPTER 19

Boston
September 1886

Maine was more than a distant memory; it was still very much a reality when Tyler returned to Boston directly from Kennepointe that first week in September. A trip to New Orleans first was out of the question. It would demand too much of his time, and he would only be there for a week or so before having to return to Boston, and the arduous journey wasn't to his suiting. His mother was most gracious when she penned him a few lines saying that he should return over Christmas if he wanted to do so, but since the death of his father, she had come down with *Wanderlust* and began to crisscross the area seeking out relatives and friends she had lost contact with during the War Between the States, as she referred to it.

Tyler surmised that she was trying to fulfill the void in her life left by the untimely death of his father, and he kept in touch with her at least once a week, hoping that his letters would catch up with her before her next jaunt. He also came to realize that she was trying to cut the apron strings and let him find his own level and his own path in life. But his path was about to take a new turn.

As always, he attended the opening convocation, but as he was leaving the church after Rev. Entwhistle's inspiring sermon, the same one he gave each year, he came to find out, he saw Sarah Garret sitting on a bench in the sun.

"Hello, Tyler," she said.

"Well, hello, Sarah. What have we got here? A little niece or nephew?" he asked.

"No. That would make it all too convenient. This baby, Barley by name, innocent and unaware of the circumstances life has conferred upon him, was conceived on that November eve when you came to me for comfort. He came into this dreary world just a few weeks ago."

"I'm afraid you must err, Miss Sarah," he began to explain. "I'm afraid I'm too young to be a father."

"And am I too young to be a mother? You weren't too young to seek consolation from me. I kept myself hidden away until the time of my delivery. Deception has compounded deception. I've told people that my cousin passed away and there were no other relatives who would take the waif in but for me."

"Sarah, I...," Tyler began.

"Not now. It's not the time and place. I'll send for you. I'll receive you on my own terms." And she walked across the lawn, the same lawn that Tyler and Prof. Collins had walked across a year earlier when Boston and learning were still green and fresh to him. This time, the grass didn't seem as lush, and the air had taken on a sudden chill.

Professor Collins observed Tyler Pettigrew watching Sarah walk away. "Glad to have you back," he told Tyler, who didn't respond the first time. "Your third year already!" Both walked slowly down towards the river, but Tyler wanted a place to sit down, a place where he could talk without being distracted by others milling about. Collins' office provided just the perfect spot. The leather chairs and the paneling provided the security he wanted. He wasn't so concerned about Sarah, but he was concerned as to if and when he should reveal the facts to his mother, who would certainly disapprove of such carnal impropriety.

Both Prof. Collins and he discussed Sarah's revelation in depth, and Tyler came to see that he would be responsible for supporting mother and child, but he was not in a rush to run out and "make things right by him." He was caught between the typical male reaction of denial and wanting to uphold society's norms. No solution could be worked out if he didn't have the chance to talk to Sarah herself, and that wasn't going to happen until he was summoned. He did calculate the time between their encounter in November and the birth in August several times on paper in the professor's office. The figures did add up for him, but in the back of his mind, he was still hoping there was another explanation.

"And there's another thing that is bothering me. No, disturbing me," Tyler said. "What's this ritual with the rose and silver robe, the elixir in the goblet, the meteor showers and the neck?"

Professor Collins stared at Tyler who related the events of the night of the Perseids in detail. "And then you woke up in bed just as you had gone to bed the night before?"

"Yes, sir. I'm certain of that much. Still had the glass from my little session with the bottle in my hand."

"Where I come from, we call that having a dream! You must have had some mighty powerful drink in your room to set off a series of phantasms that odd. We've all had dreams that were very realistic, but we know that they couldn't be. That's the nature of dreams."

Tyler couldn't tell if Prof. Collins was avoiding something or sizing him up as being some young man who imbibed on too much alcohol. "It was so real, Prof. Collins. Really." Tyler shifted in the leather chair. He wanted to tell about his father and the kiss, about the throbbing on the neck at certain times, but the felt this wasn't the time or place. The *Kuhduush* was out of the question. The person he had to find was Lucas Granville, but he wasn't living in the *Cloisters* any longer.

"And then there was the healing of Miss Ginger," he said. A long treatise followed about how they had met, how he had sought after her in a way but not the way he had sought after Sarah Garret. "When I touched her, I felt what she felt. It was as though I absorbed her illness and then expelled it. Am I losing the foundations of sanity?"

"I think you have a great imagination. A marvelous imagination! Maybe I've been making you work too hard on new ideas for writing creative fancies! I wish I could turn back summer's clock and let you begin all over again. Perhaps you would have a new perspective." Prof. Collins smiled, arose from behind his desk, and led Tyler to the door. When he was sure that Tyler had moved on down the hall, he opened his closet, took out his rose and silver robe, folded it neatly, and placed it in a valise before attaching a small lock to keep the contents secure.

CHAPTER 20

04 January 2010

With his tail between his legs, Troy Krueller scampered over to Buck's cabin as soon as he had returned from Christmas break in New York after hearing what had happened to Grits.

"And this is my business because...," Buck began.

"Because you told me to push him over the edge."

"Actually, I told you to *let* him go over the edge...not *push* him. Apparently, he literally went over the ledge without you being there. What caused him to freak?" Buck asked

"I called him from New York a couple of times. You know, just to keep him where I wanted him. He was drunk, really sauced. Boy, could he pound 'em down! When he gets into that state, he goes on about this immortality nonsense and how he musta killed Gruder and Tim because... because...because. He kept comin' up with weird scenarios as to how it happened and why. He couldn't trust nobody, see. Just me. Awkward."

"Yeah, yeah. Same old," Buck said impatiently.

"How am I supposed to know what he was thinking? So I just kept adding fuel to the fire. I told him that he wanted to see if they were immortal, and he found out they weren't. I had told him that before over and over again. I think he really believed he had done them both in. I assured him that even if he was guilty, I wasn't goin' to snitch on him."

Buck fetched some of the cheer of Christmas past and poured both a healthy measure.

"Thanks, man, but I only drink around Grits to get him to let his guard down, and that won't happen again," Troy said. "I told him that they all become immortal out at the old quarry. It was the most forsaken place I could think of. Once I saw where his mind was at, I just kept on creating one supernatural scene after the other. Then I made up some hair-raising yell that you have to do when you jump off the cliff before you morph into some divine creature that ends up floating down gently. *Halleeeee halluuuuu!*"

"And he bought it?"

"Apparently," Troy laughed. "I bet he yelled out the magic words before he crashed down upon the rocks below! What a yutz. Then I wished him *Happy New Year!* and hung up the phone. You know the rest."

"Yeah, I know the rest," Buck said, "but I don't understand why you had such a vendetta out against him. What did he ever do to you?"

"That's a story for another time. *Vendetta*. . .that's a mighty big word for the Buckster!"

"The *Buckster*?! I'm a member of the faculty, you twit, so watch your step, or I'll *halleeeee halluuuuu* you right out of here. Get my drift, boy?"

"Yes, sir," Troy replied.

* * * * * *

10 January 2010

Greenlawn and its citizens had already begun to move on after the tragic death of one Jared "Grits" Hominy that New Year's Eve in the cold quarry off Bryson's Lane, his burial following shortly thereafter. Rumors multiplied; speculations grew. Only Roger Honeycutt knew the truth of the final moments, and he was tired of having to recount the details of the story. As stated in his deposition, he called Tommy Masheck, the town's only sworn-in officer-of-the-law, by cell phone immediately after the incident occurred. Tommy then alerted those higher up the law chain in Culver City as quickly as possible, and Inspector Milo Vasilovich knew the way to Greenlawn by heart.

At first, Roger was afraid that Tommy would think that he had had something to do with Grits's death, but Masheck was most understanding when he explained the bizarre behavior that led up to the unfortunate moment. Besides, Tommy was a loyal Crewe member, and he trusted Roger implicitly, as any brother would do in similar circumstances.

Tommy had taken the initial report that night before turning it over to Vasilovich, who read the document and decided to interview Roger the following day. Roger was very forthcoming about finding Grits crawling on the road in the snow and slush, about the alcohol on his breath, and about his mental state just before he flung himself off the cliff into oblivion. What he didn't include was the part about the Immortali and Grits's desire to possess what they had. Roger deliberated about revealing that part of the incident, but he felt that emphasizing Coach's mental state was more important than anything else.

A week after Hominy's funeral, the tenth, Roger was walking across campus after his class in Italian and Greek literature. Tommy Masheck approached him, and they began to regurgitate the night Grits died. "Yes, Tommy, he did confess to killing Gruder and Tim. In a confused way, he confessed. How many times do I have to go over this with you again?" This was the first time Tommy and Roger had been alone together since the initial interview New Year's Eve. They had met a few times later, but others were always present trying to piece together what their instincts told them was still a puzzle and a very private matter for the Crewe.

"In a confused way? How so?" Masheck asked, tapping his notebook with the eraser end of the pencil after they sat down in the student union. He always tapped his notebook.

Roger said, "You can't beat truth from a piece of paper, but it helps when no ideas form, doesn't it? Grits said that Troy Krueller had convinced him that he, Grits, had committed the crime."

"Our Krueller? Of course. How many are there? How do you convince someone they committed a crime? Seems to me you'd know if you did two people in or not."

Roger thought for a second. "Dunno."

"See. We keep going around the same circle, but there is something I haven't told anyone. Not wearing a wire, are you? Ha-ha...a little police humor. I do know that Grits didn't kill nobody," Masheck pointed out.

"And you know that how?" Roger wondered.

"The day Gruder died, Grits was having breakfast with me at Denny's. He arrived at school just when the body was discovered. The night Tim died, he stopped at school to pick up some footballs and basketballs. At about the time Tim took ill, Hominy was at my place wrapping those gifts for some of the poor kids over at the orphanage in Culver City."

"You're telling me that Grits had a heart?!"

"Not a big one, but he had one," Tommy replied.

"And why haven't you told anyone?"

"Never felt a need to. Didn't want to be melodramatic about what a 'swell' guy Grits was," Masheck said.

"Melodramatic? Great vocabulary for a local cop! Look. Gotta book for now. Don't wanna stay out in plain sight too long. Hear that Leslie is still trying to track me down! She's onto my scent, man. Maybe I'll introduce you two!" Both laughed and went their separate ways.

Harriet, Grits's wife and widow, had also been most cooperative during the brief investigation which began shortly after her husband's body was dragged up the sides of the quarry in a wire basket. She explained to the officials how her husband had begun drinking in the early hours of the evening, actually beginning in the evening before, and she related how, after a phone call from Troy Krueller, Grits began to pace back and forth like a caged panther.

Without as much as saying a word, he went to his car and drove off, not even bothering to don his winter clothes. She watched his taillights going around the corner on Hammer Street before heading across the bridge over Diggum's Creek into the night. "I really don't know what happened to him," she said. "He just snapped, but he had been snapping for months. His verbal domestic abuse had increased to the point where I was prepared to leave him. Now the abuse has stopped forever. I think we're both at peace now."

* * * * * *

13 January 2010

It wasn't long, maybe a week or so after the new semester started at the Academy, that Troy, Joel, and Roger were sitting around a table at the student union sipping on some herbal drink. Although Roger preferred his warm cider, the Green Society had slapped together some concoction to lure "cause-oriented" college kids into their web to raise the consciousness about the fate of some obscure owl in Oregon.

"Hey, Roger," Joel said, "I was going through some things at the library archives before Christmas and made a few copies of documents from Tyler Pettigrew's collection. Take a look at this!" He removed a copy of Tyler's photograph that had been taken in the 1880s in Maine and passed it over to Roger via Troy. "The resemblance between you and him is uncanny, eh?"

"Wow, you're right," Troy interrupted. "Except for the old fashioned hairstyle, Roger, the two of you could be brothers!"

"And get a load of this," Joel said, producing another picture. "This one marked *Lucas Granville* on the back, taken about the same time, I'd guess, sure looks like Tommy Masheck, doesn't it?"

Roger studied the pictures in silence. "What are you doing with these in the first place?" he asked before turning both pictures face down.

"I'm doing family history research. Docket said he mentioned it to you for some reason. Maybe it was about my link to Tyler Pettigrew," Joel explained. "It seems that this Pettigrew guy is my 3G grandfather. Ain't that a hoot! You should see all the documents he left behind in the archives. Had to suck up to ol' Mrs. Woodburn to gain access. "

"How do you know you're his, well, whatever the relationship is exactly?" Roger wanted to know.

"He had a son named Barley, who had a son, who had a son, and so forth." Joel explained. "I documented it back step by step. Have Barley's birth record from Boston that links him not only to Tyler Pettigrew but to Tyler's father and grandfather. One neat little package. I'm still trying to prove that Pettigrew sent money to support the child because he knew it was his."

"A regular little private dick," Roger said.

"Huh?"

"*Detective,*" Roger explained.

"Oh. Mr. Docket has been helping me a lot. He knows his stuff, dude," Joel said with emphasis.

"So you come down from this Barley Pettigrew?" Roger asked.

"Barley, yes. Pettigrew, no. Barley was the illegitimate son of Tyler Pettigrew and Sarah Garret. They never married, so Barley kept her name."

"And Barley's son was?"

Joel had to think for a moment. "Ok, Barley begat Harold. Sounds so biblical, huh? Harold begat Daniel, my grandfather. I think that's right. Daniel begat my father, William. William begat me."

Roger and Joel stared at each other for a moment before both felt a slight neck spasm. Roger noticed Joel's concern or surprise, he couldn't tell which. "Don't worry. It'll pass," Roger said before he got up from the table and walked away thinking about what had to be done.

CHAPTER 21

The Unveiling
16 January 2010

Roger slid in behind the wheel of his Mazda and drove out to Gresslauer Park, the pavilion on the lake where he always went to think about his life and what his plans for the future were. It was here that he was supposed to be with the Crewe on New Year's Eve, but Grits's death had put that tradition on hold. He often wondered if he could have done something to stop Grits from the fatal plunge, but he didn't have a clear vision as to what was about to transpire.

His neck had sent off a warning to be alert, but he didn't know what he had to be alert about. He thought that perhaps another of the Immortali was in the area by chance, but why would anyone be out at the old quarry on the last night of the year? The place was so desolate that no one would have a reason to be there at that time of year. Yet…he was there; Grits was there. In the Theatre of the Absurd, his favorite playhouse of late, all things were possible.

He had kept quiet to others about his last conversation with the coach, not because he was secretive, but because he saw a problem that had to be handled quickly and quietly. How could Coach Hominy, a grown man be taken in by

Krueller's story to the point where suicide was the only option? Of course, if Grits really believed that the plunge would make him immortal, then perhaps it wasn't suicide after all. It could be called *lunicide* because the whole thing was insane and took place under the influence of the blue moon (luna). Grits was known for his tenacity, his strength. He never kowtowed to anyone in his life, yet there he was, groveling to some young upstart who seemed to have him wrapped up like a spitball in his fist.

Too many things had gone wrong; too many things were out of control, and Roger had to be in charge of his life. That was the first commandment: *Be in control!* On the football field, he called the plays; he fired off the passes. In his own life, he made the decisions, but when others were intruding on his past, and stories about the other side of the Crewe began to surface, it could all collapse before he knew it had done so.

He had to approach Joel Garret at some point. Joel had a right to know the story. He was part of the story already. But how do you approach someone with a story that is so bizarre in the first place? The right moment is the key, but how do you maneuver someone into that right moment? Is there a right moment?

Roger, of course, didn't ask to be one of the Immortali. Had he known what was involved, he would have thought long and hard about accepting his sealed fate. In a way, he felt it was unfair that he didn't know or understand what had befallen him.

He thought of others that he had given the first embrace to over the years and then witnessed them on the shore accepting their anointing the night the meteors streaked across the heavens in their dazzling splendor. Were those brothers grateful, or did they secretly curse the Crewe for what they had become? He wondered how many were not even aware of who they were until that one moment when they passed on. Were they appreciative then?

Roger didn't seek to continue on living generation after generation with new names and new places either. None of the Immortali had sought that. None had ever been given the choice to accept or reject what lay in store. Those in charge of the Inner Circle had just assumed that the brothers who were given the embrace worthily would be ready at some future time for the anointing.

He certainly remembered being Tyler Pettigrew. That name had always been his true identity. He remembered every detail of his life in New Orleans and Boston. Without giving him a blueprint, other than the *Kuhduush,* his father passed on the first stage to him that November night in New Orleans in 1885, and even that didn't make much sense until after something transpired later, drawing him to seek counsel within the text's framework. Perhaps, he was afraid his son would not accept the blessings of what being an Immortali was. Even when Tyler stood and looked at his own grave on campus recently, he knew that just the old body was there. His new body looked the same. And with each transformation, he was the same, right down to his smile, that captivating smile.

After a while, his body became ill, just like those who were mortal; he fell into what some might term *death,* but suddenly he would appear in a new place away from others. The spiritual body would "solidify", as he called it, and he was ready to begin all over again at the age he was when he was first initiated at the cove. Always starting life anew was complex, just as it was mysterious to him. He was happy he didn't have to repeat infancy, junior high school, or the time of pubescent perturbation.

That first stage, the kiss or embrace, however, had only marked him as a potential candidate. That embrace signaled what he was to become if he remained true to himself and to the Crewe. He, however, wasn't complete in either his training or in his initiation. He had no other abilities at first except to be able to be aware of the others around him who were so destined. In the beginning, he still had no idea as to what that destination was.

The slight burning or twitching of the neck near the jugular vein was annoying. He hadn't learned how to interpret it then; even now, after all this time, he still had difficulties. It usually was a sign that another of the embraced Immortali was near or that someone would make an excellent candidate for the Crewe. Often, the burning could be a warning of danger. He never conceptualized that a member of the Krewe of Orestus, those traitors from so many years ago, could be nearby, ready to pounce and take what blessings they all had enjoyed. To him, the Krewe of Orestus was only a veiled warning his father had given him.

The second stage, complete entrance into the brotherhood, was given to him the night the stars fell from the heavens and the oil of olives washed his skin pure. He was now able to watch more of life unfold. He could step back and see more of the picture of humanity with its joy and grief. Although he would change every twenty or thirty years or so, nothing prepared him for watching his own generation turn old and pass from the scene. In the next generation, he repeated the cycle, yet he was still a spectator, always a spectator running along the shores of time trying to find himself and where he fit in.

After his anointing at the cove by his father in 1886, or, for a lack of a better term, his father *transformed,* he thought about the dream state it had induced. Prof. Collins had assured him that it all was, indeed, a phantasm and nothing more because common sense dictated that such things don't transpire except in novels and in the creative fantasies of tortured psyches trying to put a puzzle together where there never was a puzzle in the first place. Prof. Collins should have been more forthcoming with him, but the unwritten law of the Crewe stated that one had to discover for oneself what was and is and shall be. And until the first change, no other can take the journey for the member; he must do it himself.

Tyler had come to realize that within the Crewe, there were those who were general members, affiliates, who enjoyed fraternal ideals. Then there were those who had been initiated into things that even they couldn't explain to themselves and which had to be kept from others. This dichotomy was difficult to reconcile. He felt he was betraying the ones who were only social members. They had the right to know, he believed, what the organization was about, but most would be skeptical at best. The real world, in time, became a world of shapes and forms, shadows and blurred images to him.

For example, Professor Docket was just an affiliate member…a man of virtue to be sure…, but he had gone no further than most of the members who had been tapped at some juncture in life and met up with mailmen who seemed to know all about the new recruits. McDougal was a conduit to teach and lead others to higher levels of being, but even as an anointed Immortali, he had become sluggish and irresponsible in his own personal life from time to time. The Immortali were indeed just that, immortal, but they were mortals still, in a manner of speaking, who still had to fight temptation and live with disappointment over and over again.

But they all had a higher calling after the anointing. They were to bind up suffering humanity and lead others to their true potential. If they failed in assisting others to overcome fear and doubts and illness, then the whole brotherhood failed. They not only had to be there for themselves, they had the responsibility to assist all who needed their aid.

At Gresslauer Park that chilly winter day, he thought about what had made him become so retrospective back in Maine: the sudden healing of Miss Ginger. He could still feel her illness pass up through him and dissipate. It wasn't an unpleasant feeling at all, he recollected, but it seemed to relieve him of mental anguish. He wondered where the anguish had come from.

Once, a friend was in the hospital with a broken leg back in 1897 south of Athens, Greece, a year after Tyler's first transformation. Then known as Haralambos, he had just completed visiting his hiking companion who had fallen going down a small path above the sea. For some inexplicable reason, he received no spiritual inclination to heal him as he had in the case of Miss Ginger, but in a room down the hall from his injured friend, a family had gathered around the grandmother, the matriarch, who, in her nineties, was about to pass on her regal title to another generation. He felt the anguish of their loss and the pain of being utterly helpless. Tears of mourning had already begun, and perhaps it was a blessing that the dear woman was comatose. She wouldn't, therefore, have to listen to the death knell her well-meaning family was giving her.

Tyler-Haralambos walked in, and stood in silence for a few moments. The family, thinking he was perhaps a doctor, moved aside. He ran his hand up and down her arm, and said, "Kuhduush sem d'chaimu. Eloth ram hannel. Men h'alachu; men hallel." Her breathing became a little erratic, but soon she was drawing deep, cleansing breaths. She opened her eyes and stared at the people looking down upon her, their faces still wet from tears and drawn from personal misery.

"Get out of here! I want to wash up. I need my privacy," she ordered with the wave of a hand. The family was astounded; Tyler-Haralambos was pleased. The matriarch could rule the roost for another day. Perhaps for another year.

He had felt the same internal anguish for someone in danger while swimming off the coast of Venice once in 1936. He called himself Gianvincenzo, a student of Italian language and culture, who had come from America during the turbulent time of the Depression. All of Europe seemed to have gone mad with inherent political ecstasy. A flurry of activity over near the Lido, the public strand, caught his attention. A young man had been dragged onto the beach after a lady saw him floating upon the water. "At first, I thought it was some flotsam. Then I thought it was a large fish," she explained to anyone within hearing range. Gianvincenzo turned the boy onto his back. The crowd told him to turn him onto his stomach. But Gianvincenzo remained calm and followed what his mind was processing. He placed his hands upon the boy's chest. Suddenly, he himself felt asphyxiated; pain rushed from his stomach up into his chest before gushing out into the air in front of him. The lifeless lad, unconsciously imitating his rescuer, sucked in a gulp of air, choked, spit up water, and choked again. Soon, he was sitting on the beach, a little pale, but healthy.

"Grazie," the boy said as if he knew what had happened.

"Prego," Tyler-Gianvincenzo replied. "Prego."

Through these events, was he absorbing what others felt, or was he just imagining something that he couldn't explain? All those he met in the world of the Immortali had experienced the same thing: taking on the pain and suffering of others and helping them to heal either mentally or physically. The moving on and not turning back was difficult. Always moving. Never turning back. Yet he did return to the Academy. Did he transgress a law that the *Kuhduush* didn't elaborate on in order for him to re-learn an old lesson? He was there; perhaps at the Academy, he would break the cycle. Maybe they all could break the cycle now. Perhaps they all had to return to a particular place and make final decisions. They had been called to Greenlawn for a purpose.

The park was quiet. The air was cold. Not even the squirrels were to be seen. Roger mentally delved more into his past, and he found particular distress in his memories about Sarah Garret and her son, Barley---Tyler's son---his son. She never did call for him as she had promised that September day seated on the bench outside the church in Boston. He waited, often impatiently. When he sought her out, he discovered she had left Boston for good without telling anyone as to her whereabouts. Tyler was unaware that she and Barley had gone to New Orleans, at first, where she hoped to start a new life. Perhaps she had some romantic notion about life along the Mississippi. Tyler had often told her tales about his life there. Perhaps she wanted to stay close to where he had his roots. It was hard to say.

In time, however, she did contact him by mail, but she never invited him to meet her or her son. He sent her money for supplies, always careful about how he worded his documents. She was always most gracious to receive the money, of course, and he knew he had done the right thing.

He often wondered what his son knew about him. Did they look alike? Did they have the same interests? What did he aspire to be? One year in mid-August, he wrote his son a long letter about his heritage, but he never mailed it. It wouldn't be polite to intrude, and it was quite possible that Sarah had told Barley an entirely different story about his mortal origins.

In one world, he had been Tyler Pettigrew, the young man he knew he was; now he had presently given birth to Roger Honeycutt, athlete at the Academy he started over a century before. Life was an unending cycle to him, and sometimes he had difficulty remembering what he knew, what he was supposed to forget, and what he had to look forward to. He considered it to be rather ironic that he now had returned to the place where his heart had always been. His travels had taken him everywhere he wanted to go, but there was the loneliness that set in when he came to realize that he would be living a life that he had never chosen, and he would have to live that life alone, for who would understand and accept him?

He didn't view himself as being a time traveler because he didn't travel between ages and centuries and then go back and forth again. He was on a straight line of time. In philosophical terms, he lived in the ever-present *Now.* Not able to go back and rectify past mistakes, he had to learn from those mistakes and try not to perpetuate them.

He did seek out other Immortali who had positions of authority and who provided him with documents and appropriate records. Obtaining those vital records was once an easy job, but in the age of technology, it became more and more difficult. Connections were still spread out wherever they went to provide assistance to each other, but everything to him was just formal business. Get a birth record, acquire a college transcript, and find job references. Joy wasn't present like it used to be.

Seated on one of the tables at the pavilion, he no longer noticed the coldness that January always wrapped itself in. Heat, cold, joy, sadness, light, darkness. This is what his post-Garden-of-Eden-world had become. His early years were somewhat paradisiacal. He was protected and comforted by his family and friends. New Orleans kept some of the realities of existence at bay. But now, the world of opposites swirled around him. He often thought he lived in one of those snow-globes he often saw in the stores at Christmas time. And if he just waited, biding his time, things always calmed down, but he wasn't sure now.

Over in the parking area, Tommy Masheck got out of his police car. He was carrying a bag of doughnuts from the café near Cedar Bay Road.

"Roger," Tommy greeted.

Nodding his head, Roger returned, "Tommy."

Both talked. Tommy ate. Occasionally, they would laugh.

"We might have some trouble. Joel Garret has a picture of me taken in Maine in 1886. He's been showing it around. Remember that summer, Tommy? Actually, you were Lucas then, weren't you? I lose track. I've been avoiding pictures for most of my life. Can't risk someone making a link."

Tommy became somewhat paranoid processing the information that Roger just laid out before him. He placed the doughnut down on the table and wiped his mouth with a paper napkin. "Why did you keep your picture? How did you get mine? I don't remember ever having to sit for one?"

"You did sit for one, but you left Kennepointe so abruptly after the night at the cove. The photographer gave me yours when I went in to pick up mine. I told him I'd get it to you. I wrapped them both up in paper, and when I got on with my life, I completely forgot about them. I never knew they would archive all my private papers. I didn't know anything about the change, the transformation. We should have stayed in more contact over the years."

"I'm not always easy to find. I always keep on guard. A mysterious artist in Kennepointe, a writing major in college in Chicago, a minister---you remember that, a doctor, a novelist, and a cop here. Go figure!"

"Yeah, Tommy, just a regular little Houdini! I should call you Harry!"

"I think I was Harry once back in the 30s! Like a magician, I come and go more often than some of your girlfriends' headaches!" Tommy jabbed.

"At least I have some!"

"Headaches or girlfriends?" Tommy asked.

"Ouch! You got me, man."

Roger took off his woolen gloves and grabbed one of the doughnuts out of the bag and began to nibble around the edge. His father always started out eating pastries that way on the veranda overlooking the estate. Many things he did over the years reminded him of his father, even things that he had perfected since the 1880s. And all those memories always caused him to remember his father lying on the bed talking about a change or transformation.

He thought he was referring to death in a poetic manner, as well-bred southerners were wont to do, and he admired his father for being such a stoic. In perusing the *Kuhduush,* he began to understand. *The Angel of Termination shall not touch one so marked. In a moment one shall pass from material existence into material existence.* The *Kuhduush* went on to explain that when illness or accident strikes, one submits, but because of the lineage created by the Immortali, life does not come to an end on this side of the veil for those so selected. *"For some, their posterity, from generation unto generation, remains unscathed. The wretchedness of death and decay abates. The grave cannot hold the spirit after being fed the mortal carrion. The mortal carrion yields its spiritual fruit to new life, renewed in the covenant of the Ancients are they.*

"I often wonder about our purpose," Roger said.

"Purpose? The Crewe gets to stay and help those who need help," Tommy said.

Roger commented, "How altruistic! Didn't do Grits much good, did it?"

"It would have been impossible for you to find him in the dark after he took his infamous leap of faith. You can't save the world! But you can help alleviate some of the pain. You're here so that others might live," Tommy said. "You didn't ask for this. It was passed on to you."

"And to you, too," Roger said.

"I suppose."

"You suppose? Don't you know?" Roger asked.

Tommy looked down at the picnic table and wondered how many times he and Roger had come here to talk regardless of the season, but he had to push Roger away when he zeroed in on some things he couldn't discuss with him. He was always afraid of giving too much of himself away.

"I suppose," Tommy repeated again. He became silent, almost reclusive. Tommy studied the doughnut he was about to devour and realized that the cream was oozing out of its center. He licked his thumb and index finger before speaking. "I often have wondered where all of this Crewe stuff comes from. Is the *Kuhduush* true about members descending from mystical origins back at the beginning of time? Actually, who cares where all this comes from!" He squeezed around the edges of the doughnut and licked more of the cream out of the center. "We're here. I guess the cycle just goes on until we decide to break it," Tommy explained. His onslaught on the leaky doughnut made him concentrate on several things at once, and continuity didn't follow suit.

"Will you ever break the cycle?" Roger asked.

"I don't know. I don't know how."

"My father told me in one of those dream things once that I could break the cycle. I don't know what he meant, but I think he meant that we can select to move on to other places, other realms, if we so desire. We don't have to come back on this earth somewhere, but I don't know how to do that either."

"I hate having to make up other existences," Tommy said, not making a good segue. "I'm afraid that someone will go check to see if I'm telling the truth. I'm tired of it all, to be frank. You asked if I ever thought about ending the cycle. I wasn't forthcoming with the answer. I've already worked on some theories about how to stop it."

Roger laughed. "Maybe it's time. You know what I hate? I don't like having to make up lies all the time either. I'm always telling people that my father and I are on the outs, and that's why we don't have much contact. Imagine the look on their faces if they knew he was born back in 1842!"

"Do you ever see him?"

"Only that night at the cove up in Maine. I told you before that sometimes in dreams, I feel I can fly, and I soar, really soar. Eventually, I land and we find each other for a moment. I sometimes think I see Miss Ginger, not in dreams but in reality, but I don't. She's long gone. I did find her once around 1915 or so, but she just gave me a long look as though she were trying to place me in time. She wanted to say something, but then she moved on by without saying anything. She must have been around fifty then. I could still recognize her around the eyes. The eyes rarely change, I've come to learn. She couldn't place me because I was far too young looking to have been her mysterious Tyler."

"There was a girl down at the marina one year, Helen, I believe, back in the 1940s," Tommy began, "who spent some time with me. We would go dancing and walking along the boardwalk, but I knew I couldn't lead her on any longer. Had I told her, she wouldn't have believed it, and if she did find her way to see that I had told the truth, then she would want it. But I wouldn't know how to pass it on to her anyway. It all centers on the Crewe and the rituals that lead up to the point of acceptance. There are lots of people who would want what your father gave you, I guess."

Roger took a sip of root beer that he had taken along and said, "That *grass is always greener* saying is true. That's for sure. Maybe there's a group of Crewettes out there somewhere, and we're just too dumb to discover them!"

Tommy added, "When you were talking about your father a bit ago, I thought about mine. I see him from time to time when the Perseid meteor showers descend in August, but only at a distance. He's always far off from the activity. When I go to join him, he's gone. He has given me his gift, but we don't seem to be able to be with the former generations at all. That bothers me."

"The Book of Kenduúr says: *Thou art bound to those who gifted thee throughout worlds upon worlds, but thou art separate in being and affection until the final day of rest and ascent.* Whatever that means," Roger said.

"You seem to know your stuff, man," Tommy pointed out.

"Yeah. Enough to know it's time to break this up and get back to more work."

Their snack finished, they separated and returned to various activities. Roger wanted to remove the pictures from circulation as quickly as he could, and a trip to visit Joel Garret or Racine Woodburn was in order, but he wasn't sure how to approach the whole thing with Joel. And once Paul Docket began snooping around family trees and forgotten histories, it wouldn't be long until certain things would be brought to light.

* * * * * *

Troy Krueller turned a couple of times, entrapping himself in the warmth of his blanket. He began to snore, expelling the air out his mouth; his lips vibrated like an Evinrude motor. The long night had turned into an even longer morning. The radiator pipes began their cacophony of bangs and clanks, and he opened his eyes and cursed the mid-morning light.

In the bathroom, he stood at the sink wearing his blue terry cloth robe trying to decide if he wanted to shave or not. Maybe a quick once-over with an electric trimmer wouldn't hurt, but he wanted to keep himself looking scruffy until he had a reason to be well-groomed. He squinted into the mirror to see better, but that didn't help much. He eventually leaned closer to the glass to make sure that he didn't botch the job. The art of looking unkempt was often complex.

It's funny what will go through a man's head while he's staring into the mirror, though. His soul (and the partial darkness thereof) reflected back at him with horrific intensity. In the reflection, he watched the final night with Grits on Christmas Eve play itself out when he convinced his coach that he was the father he never had. Odd. Cathartic. Lethally deceptive.

Even though the true story about his own father had been relayed to Troy by his mother only a few years ago when he was in high school, the vision that trapped his thoughts that morning in the mirror had begun several months before Troy was even born.

His father, Derrick Thomas Krueller, took his own life shortly before Troy's mother went into labor. His father was only nineteen, a freshman at a junior college in Easterling Glen, with a good future if he landed the athletic scholarship to a state college he so desperately needed. Everyone liked him. They recognized his talent, not only for football but for baseball, too. Some believed he could make it into the major baseball leagues or the NFL if he set higher goals for himself than just a scholarship.

His coach at the time, a very young, very inexperienced, and very paranoid Jared Hominy, however, had other ideas. Derrick Krueller was independent, well-mannered, and had no time for Hominy's mental games, which were just as important to young Grits as the games played on the field. In fact, more scouts fawned over Derrick Krueller than had ever fawned over Hominy at the height of his own college playing career, and such groveling bred jealousy, an insidious beast that, once fed, can never be satiated.

At the game that was to showcase Krueller's talent as a wide receiver and cornerback, securing his future as a pro-baller, Hominy never sent the boy in once. Even when the crowd began the rhythmic cheer of *Kroo-lur, Krool-lur, Krool-lur,* he turned a deaf ear.

Thundering play after thundering play rolled down the field. Pads and helmets smacked, cracked, and snapped, but Krueller was blacklisted from the explosive action. Even when the team's alternate wide receiver was injured, Derrick was kept on the bench when Hominy sent in a freshman as replacement.

After the game, Derrick looked at the coach and said, "Why?" A cold stare was the only reply. Hominy pursed his lips, ignored the boy, walked over to a referee standing at the edge of the field, shook hands and asked about the family.

The following week, when he was given playing time during the last two minutes of the game, a real slap to anyone's ego, Derrick stopped the coach on the way to the fieldhouse. "Why?" he asked, almost pleading for an answer.

"Because you ain't worth crap, boy." The coach had just fed his own internal insidious beast a morsel.

That night, after a long struggle with the bottle he took from his apartment, combined with some Vicodin the coach had given him once for pain, Derrick Thomas Krueller ceased to exist. They found him the next morning out near the old stone quarry slumped over the steering wheel of his new cherry red Ford Mustang. The football his father gave him after his first touchdown in high school was beside him on the front seat.

Chapter 22

17 January 2010

Expecting a lunchtime delivery, Joel opened the door of his dorm room to find Roger Honeycutt with a pleasant smile on his face. It took him a second to process the fact that the pepperoni and mushrooms on a stuffed crust pizza was on hold for a moment.

"Sorry about not calling first, but…"

"Sure. C'mon in. Wassup?"

Roger sat on the edge of the bed, and Joel grabbed the chair from the computer desk to sit on. Both scratched their necks absent-mindedly for a moment to get relief.

"Neck hurt?" Roger asked.

"It itches. Looks like I have a crusty rash there from time to time for some reason. Maybe I should go to student health. Started around the beginning of December. Dreamed someone touched it with their fingers. Weird, huh?"

Roger scratched his own neck again and replied, "Yeah. Seems that sort of thing goes around. Forget student health. They'll just take up your time, grab their 10 bucks, and tell you to come back if it doesn't clear up!" He gave a little chuckle as though he had just thought of something rather amusing that he didn't wish to share. "Uh, you know those pictures that you were showing around, the one of Tyler Pettigrew that looks like me? I was wonderin' if I could have it to play a joke on somebody with."

"A joke?" Joel asked.

"Just a crazy idea I got, that's all."

"Sure, but I'd like it back. I come down from Tyler Pettigrew, you know. He's blood."

"Is this your only copy?" Roger asked.

Joel replied, "Yeah. The original is in the boxes at the library."

"Look. Could I have that other one, the one that looks like Tommy the cop? I could do some goofy things to that one after I scan it through Photoshop."

"You can keep the one that looks like Tommy, but I have to have Tyler's picture back. It's important for my family history project for Mr. Docket."

"Does he have a copy?" Roger asked.

"No, but he has seen it. I want to put the picture into my paper." Joel went on to explain the scope and sequence of the paper, but Roger only feigned interest this time. "As far as we know, this might be the only picture of Tyler Pettigrew there is, and although it's only a copy, it'd be a hassle to have to go make another copy. I would like to have met him and found out what kind of a guy he really was."

"I hear he was a pretty nice guy. Confident. Good looking. Smooooooth with the ladies! Well, with some of the ladies."

"I'm not so smooth. I guess I missed out on that gene!" Joel said.

They talked about the Crewe and some of the coming events that had been sent by e-mail from Paul Docket. Joel had been working on some of the induction rituals, memorizing what he could. The whole ceremony was daunting, and his memory for exact wording often escaped him. That frustrated him. When he was inducted, the ritual was perfect, and he had to make sure that each time he performed his part, it was perfect for the new members, too.

"Got a quick question. In the Crewe, do you know what is missing?" Joel asked.

"Missing?"

"Yeah. What we are to be *vigilant* about. I don't understand that part of the ceremony."

"The Alpha is missing," Roger replied. "Our Crewe has a leader, the Alpha. He's a direct descendant of a former Alpha. At least that was the original rule. After Tyler Pettigrew's father died, Tyler would have become the next one, but, as far as anyone knows, Beauregard never passed on his leadership to a direct descendant."

"So our branch of the Crewe is seeking what has been missing, the Alpha. I thought Mr. Docket was the Alpha," Joel said.

"Correct. He is. . .of the local Crewe. He is the provisional Alpha. He holds the office because of his age. If you are the direct descendant of Tyler Pettigrew as you claim, you could be what we have been seeking since he became a member in the 1880s!"

"It's over my head for now. Too much to process," Joel said.

"Gotta bounce for now. Ah, the picture. Thanks, bud. I'll get it back to you," Roger said. "Yeah. Maybe we could have a séance some night and see if ol' Pettigrew appears to pass down the Alpha degree. Woooooooooooooo!"

They both laughed and Roger thought that the kid had his sense of innocence that he had once had before meeting

Sarah Garret. Joel closed the door, rubbed his neck that was still burning a bit, and set up the ironing board to press a backlog of shirts.

Chapter 23

20 January 2010

Inspector Vasilovich pulled out three files and tossed them onto his desk before pouring himself a cup of black coffee from his battered thermos. He looked around for the sugar, but someone had taken the entire dispenser back to a desk in another office. It wouldn't have mattered much anyway. The spoon was missing, too.

He laid out the files horizontally according to the date each incident involving the Academy had been committed. Somewhere in the files a hint, a clue, as to what had really transpired had to be buried. Wall after wall. Stone wall after stone wall. Cement several stories high surrounded each file, figuratively, of course, and the more he tried to break through, the higher and thicker the cement became. He finally admitted to himself that he wasn't as sharp as he used to be.

After short deliberation, he put Jared "Grits" Hominy's file aside. It was pretty obvious to him what had happened. Mrs. Hominy and Roger Honeycutt both corroborated the story about Grits drinking himself into a stupor that night. The autopsy showed that he was inebriated beyond the legal limit. Foul play was ruled out. Still, Greenlawn seemed to becoming the strange death capital of the county, even the state.

As far as Steve's and Tim's deaths were concerned, the common link seemed to be the football team and the triangle that marked them. A sign of what? The Crewe of Adelphos? They weren't going to talk. But even things that are secret will often be shouted from the rooftops.

* * * * * *

Troy was cleaning up his room for the first time in about three weeks, maybe longer. Old socks and wrinkled shirts littered the floor where he had discarded them before jumping into the sack each night.

Five or six pizza boxes, some with crusty remnants of the treasure they once held inside, obscured his desk and recliner. A dozen or more old cola and beer cans, dented in the middle by his head during a macho moment, provided an obstacle course leading to the bathroom.

Roger Honeycutt knocked twice and opened the door on his own. "Thought I could hear you scampering around in here," he said. "Alone?" Roger was taken aback by the untidy condition of the room. The air smelled like old, sweaty sneakers.

"Yeah, alone. Alone with my mess. If I could push it all out the window and start over again, I would."

"You go on doin'. We need some chat time."

"What about?"

"Grits," Roger answered.

"Dead, gone, forgotten," Troy said after he plunked some cans into a garbage bag.

"The two of you were pretty chummy. From what I hear, you spent more time there than here in your own room."

Troy became defensive. "You were the apple of his twisted eye. Not me."

Roger grabbed him by the neck of his T-shirt and went nose to nose. "At least this apple ain't filled with venom," Roger said in a whisper before pushing him back. "Sorry, man." He stepped back from Troy to allow them both to have space. "How did you do it? How did you make a grown man go over the edge?"

"He was always over the edge. Ever since I first met him, he was over the edge. He self-destructed after he killed Steve and Tim. I watched him go downhill. There was no stopping the plunge. Excuse the pun." Troy packed up the pizza boxes and avoided eye contact.

"He didn't kill nobody. You know that. And the yell that would bring about immortality while jumping off a quarry cliff; well, who did he learn that from?" Roger asked.

"From me. Dumb is as dumb does! Can you believe someone so stupid?!"

"You got him. All because of your father," Roger said. *Blindside and go for the jugular,* he thought.

"My father? How do you know about..."

"A little snooping around here and there. Revenge, and you didn't have to lift a finger."

"No one knows the story except for...," Troy began.

"Except for your mother? Grits knew, and like you said, I was the apple of his twisted eye. He talked about those days at Easterling Glen Junior College to me. Get him boozed up, and he talked for hours. I think he took you under his wing to make up for what happened. Guilt. He never let on that he knew who you were to your face. How many Kruellers do you think he has had in his career? Two. That's how many. He certainly knew who you were from the first time he met you. I think he even tried to be a surrogate to you."

Troy's biggest fear was that he would be linked directly to Grits's death, a death he never regretted. In his mind, his father was pushed to suicide, and the *lex talionis,* the law of an eye for an eye, made perfect sense to him. Karma. Yin-yang. Full circle. What goes around…

As long as Troy kept making himself into Grits's image, he, not Grits, had the power. Troy was the creator. He had the power to replace the coach with a younger, more dynamic icon of who he once was. Like a vampire that sucks the blood out of its victim to remain young and alive forever, Troy sucked the imagination of who Grits had been back in the prime of his life right out of him and created a living representation of that icon right in front of his coach. Grits drank, so Troy drank. Troy smoked, so Grits smoked. Grits loathed his wife. Troy loathed anyone who tried to rule him. They complemented each other. They complimented each other. Mirror and image. Image and mirror. Each feeding off the other, but Troy was draining off Grits's energy. Troy sopped up and absorbed the coach's vitality.

Grits became mentally weaker as his power was transferred into a new idol for him to adulate, another god of fall, a September athlete, made in his own image and likeness. The only thing that Grits wanted more was to be able to observe that image forever, to live vicariously through his own likeness. Maybe that's what the Pride was all about, the coach constantly trying to create a reflection of what used to be.

At some point in their mutually manipulative relationship, Krueller instinctively knew to implant the idea of immortality into Hominy's mind. The irony of the entire ploy was that Troy thought he had made up the concept of immortality himself. But he didn't. He had brought it up out of his subconscious where the idea had lodged for quite a while. Maybe he overheard someone talking about the gods of fall, and he made a leap of faith; maybe he was just stretching his imagination to its limits. Still, he had to make Grits think he, Grits, had come up with the idea himself, and through an alcohol-clouded brain, the coach was receptive to the concept that Gruder supposedly had first mentioned it in the locker room, but Gruder was loyal to the Crewe and would never have betrayed any confidence. Gruder had been elevated and anointed during the August before his demise. He had seen the stars descend. Krueller had no conception about stars or water or the infusion of life, and Krueller's made up story was just fiction on his part. It wasn't fiction, however.

Troy continued to clean out the junk that had accumulated under his bed, but he was hoping to send a mental signal to Roger that it was time for Roger to leave things alone.

"McDougal says Docket told him that you were in Tim's room at the hospital the night he died," Roger said.

Troy knotted the top of the garbage bag. "Yeah," he replied.

"Were you in Docket's classroom when Tim got so sick?"

"Yeah," Troy replied. "But I didn't harm him."

"Harm him! He almost died there!" Roger shouted. "What were the two of you doing down there anyway?"

"We're talkin' Crewe business now, ain't it? I mean, well, you ain't gonna tell, are you?"

"No. Official business. Yadda, yadda, boy. Just continue," Roger said.

"I was told that there was a special initiation rite within the Crewe. Passing through this ritual made you more loyal, more respected," Troy explained.

"And this ritual was what?"

"It was printed out," Troy began, "on regular copy paper."

"I mean, What was the ritual? How did you know about it?" Roger asked.

"Got an invitation,"

"And who sent the invitation?"

"Dunno. Linebacker was on the e-mail. It just said something about advancing from the delta level to the gamma level in the Crewe. I didn't even know I was *on* the delta level, whatever that is," Troy said.

"Go on," Roger said.

"I was told to go to Mr. Docket's room on the middle level of Osolin Hall the night of the dance. Some red candles and some special tea representing symbolic elixir would be there and waiting. I could find the text for the ritual on Docket's desk."

"Did you attend the dance first?"

"Yeah. Orchestra was bad; DJ was worse. The whole thing sucked, actually. I checked my phone for the correct time, went downstairs, and saw Tim roamin' about. He explained what had happened to his shirt. He got an invitation, too, and would have come down earlier, but that girl spilled her drink on him, and he had to wash the stain out over in the janitor's area."

"Go on," Roger said.

"Everything was laid out. A couple of red candles, a T-shirt with a red stain on it, a cup with something in it, just as foretold. We scanned over the typed sheets and set things up the way it said to do. We lit the two candles and placed them on Mr. Docket's credenza. We read the script, placing our hands on each other's heads to call down blessings. We uttered oaths of loyalty and secrecy to the Crewe and sealed it all by drinking from the cup. The liquid was sweet, a cool tea."

"And the T-shirt? Why was it there?"

"The script said for Tim to put it on. The red represented loyalty, spirit, and that one would be willing to give up one's life for the Crewe to protect it from the enemy. It mentioned something about the enemy several times," Troy explained.

"And this enemy is who?" Roger asked.

"I don't know. The script didn't say."

"Then Tim got sick?"

Troy thought for a moment. "As instructed, I tore up the script. We then blew out the candles, and I tossed them in the trash. Tim joked and asked me what I wished for. I told him that I wanted a girl who wouldn't dump me first! Then he tried to swallow. It was obvious he was having trouble breathing."

"And you did nothing?" Roger asked.

"I was hoofin' it to the reception hall to get help. I could hear two security guards yelling back down the hallway about something. I saw them enter the room right after I left. I knew they'd take care of the situation."

"And?"

"And I got my coat and took off. I didn't want to be linked to something that wasn't my fault," Troy explained. "And you went to Tim's hospital room later," Roger said.

"Yeah," Troy said. "I didn't know what had happened. It was so harmless. I wanted to check on him. I felt guilty in a way. We had become Brothers of the Gamma. I stuck my head in his hospital room, but he was asleep."

"And you never told anyone about this gamma degree or going to the hospital?"

"No. We took an oath of secrecy. According to the script, vile things would happen to us or to our friends. I know it's all symbolic, but our word to each other was paramount. No reason to mention the hospital. I didn't want to get entangled in it all."

"There is no Brother of the Gamma! No ritual. No bonding."

"How do you know?" Troy asked.

"Trust me on this one. I know more about the Crewe than anyone around here," Roger replied.

"Ah, the errant Grand Wolf, I assume!!" Troy laughed and then howled with his face toward the ceiling.

Roger had to inwardly flinch at the thought that Troy had been taken in by a bogus ritual that ended in death as much as Grits had been taken in by Troy about a bogus ritual that ended in death, too. Life is often a series of parallels, but when you're engrossed in day-to-day existence, you can't decipher what is going on around you.

"You've broken just about every ideal of the Crewe, but you didn't kill Tim. You were manipulated just the way you manipulated Grits," Roger pointed out. Troy set about making his bed, but he remembered that he hadn't changed the sheets in a month or more, and it was time to do such. He pretended to listen to Honeycutt, but he really wanted him to leave.

"Look, I may have broken this and broken that, but Grits destroyed my whole life before I was even born. Isn't there a payback due on that loan?" Troy asked.

"That's between you and your conscience. Revenge is not something that we practice. Revenge operates at a lower level, a lower vibration. You do understand that we'll have to meet to decide if you can still be part of us. I'm sure, in time, that something can be worked out. But until that day, you'll have to be on fraternal probation."

"Do what you have to do. If I'm out, I'm out. I didn't harm Tim. That is someone else's doin'. Never did understand the whole crewe-thing anyway," Troy said. He plumped up the pillow and smoothed out the comforter.

"I'll get back to you on whatever we decide. Immortal. And Grits fell for it. You should major in persuasive speaking. Now that you've made you bed, you'll have to lie in it," Roger said and headed off to lunch.

CHAPTER 24

Greenlawn
11 August 1896

Trinity Academy had only one building, a long building with a bell and cupola in the center, set up for academics that first year. Living quarters were on the second floor for those who had to board. On the southern end of the property, a small barn near the dusty road that led up to Culver City kept watch over a few cows and two horses, a roan and a pinto. Tyler Pettigrew didn't have the vision that could turn the school into an agricultural magnet. Its location was perfect for animal husbandry, but he envisioned the Academy becoming a lone beacon, a solitary light, drawing only topnotch students to his land. His goal was to add a new building every year or two to attract a diverse base of students, eclectic in character. Whether one wanted to become a teacher, a doctor, or a lawyer, Trinity, as it grew, would prepare to offer the seeker of knowledge a modern training ground, complete with the best instructors and the foremost methods of instruction. He knew it was a formidable undertaking.

On the day marking his tenth anniversary of the Perseid meteor showers over Kennepointe, Maine, he awoke and took breakfast in his chamber as usual. The sun was starting to lose its strength in the afternoons, and he reflected on those afternoons in Maine where he found the waning summer, along with the memory of Miss Ginger, a sign that new things were on the horizon. He wondered if she had married and thought about the children she might have. Perhaps they might enter his academy to study someday. He often wished that he had met her other places in other times. They could have made a life for themselves, but his fate was irreversible at this point. And although they had had only a few brief encounters along the coast, in the park, and in her summer residence, he felt that their souls were somehow united.

He reminisced about home. He hadn't been to Louisiana in years. His mother passed away from what Dr. Buford Knight had called *swamp fever* in 1891, but Tyler believed that she had just given up. He was building his life up North, and she was wallowing in self-pity because no one ever came for a visit after she had taken ill and couldn't traipse about as much. She hadn't had a Sunday caller in perhaps two years or more, but when Tyler wrote her asking if she ever went calling on Sundays, she replied that she shouldn't have to. One calls on the widowed and the ill, not the other way around.

He didn't make it home for her funeral because winter held its claw-like grip on the area, and the roads leading to the railway junction outside of Culver City were impassable. At Easter, two weeks right after her passing, he was able to secure passage, take care of legal affairs, and sell the estate with his father's attorney being magnanimously compensated for his time. Tyler Pettigrew kicked the dust of New Orleans from his shoes forever.

By lunch on that eleventh day of August, he began to feel somewhat weak. He told the cook that he wanted to rest and would not be dining in his study. In the middle of the afternoon, he awoke from his nap. Chills racked his body and perspiration covered his brow. His tongue felt somewhat swollen, and although he had a great desire to drink, the thought of taking in liquids nauseated him.

Tyler drifted in and out of consciousness. Coldness began to creep its way up his body from his feet through his legs into his torso. No pain caused him to suffer---only a peculiar numbness relaxed him as his breathing became shallow. He fell deeper into sleep.

In the heat of the August afternoon, he slipped effortlessly away outside of his body and spiraled through a long, cylindrical object. It wasn't a tunnel per se, but it reminded him of a gigantic sea nautilus. As he twisted through its inner chambers, he became aware of water splashing faintly in the distance. A cove surrounded by high cliffs and wind-beaten rocks came into view. He had gone through the change for the first time. Tyler took a deep, satisfying breath that stung at first. He coughed. The scene around him startled him for an instant. His body, at first spiritual, ethereal, became materialized; the flesh then firmed. He was still clothed in his dressing room attire. His mind tried to comprehend all that had just transpired, but he knew there was no explanation to his satisfaction that could ever detail what his father and he had experienced at the moment that most people dread the most.

He sat upon the rocks and watched darkness swallow the Aegean Sea. The stars were magnificent that night. A small sliver of the moon, an arc among the stars, shed its faint crescent light over the bay. From the pathway leading up to the pasture land that stopped at the cliffs, a procession of men, young and old, some chanting remnants from the

Kuhduush, found their way along the stony path in their descent to the sea.

"Greetings be to thee, our brother!" the old leader of the procession said. "What is the hour?"

"It is the hour to convene," Tyler replied.

"By which name shalt thou be addressed? Your change is complete."

"By the name thou shalt give me based on tradition and custom," Tyler replied.

"This is Greece. The ancient place of wisdom and learning. During this present transition, thou shalt be known as Haralambos to me and to our brothers. Please join us on thy journey here."

Tyler nodded and accepted his new name for this portion of his eternal passage, and he soon joined in as three brothers united themselves to the ranks of the Immortali that night on the shores of the Aegean, where brotherhood was forged under the title of the Crewe of Adelphos. The coming forth from the bayous of Louisiana or from the parade in New Orleans seemed to be the material of myth. It was here upon the joining of the blue waters of infinity that the Crewe had first assembled. Lucas Granville had been right. Their spiritual home was Greece.

In Greenlawn, the housekeeper had just found his body lying peacefully and serenely in bed. Before night fell, the villages nearby heard of the tragedy that befell one so young. Rev. LeBoeuf led the funeral rites according to the Episcopalian Church, and he personally led the coffin two days later to the cemetery where Tyler Pettigrew, Founder and Academician, found his place of rest, at least from the life he had just passed through.

During his funeral oration for Tyler Pettigrew about the eternal nature of man, the reverend remembered his own passing from his estate of being Lucas Granville to becoming the Rev. LeBoeuf, when his boat crashed against the rocks one summer off the coast of Massachusetts within sight of his summer home. He awoke along the Mississippi shore not far from New Orleans. There he worked in the fields until it was time for him to study theology, a subject he used to gain the trust of others.

The night after Tyler Pettigrew's funeral, the fourteenth of August, Rev. LeBoeuf was called to the barn. The constable had found a member of the academy dead at the bottom of the old stone quarry after students informed him that one of their friends had been missing for a couple of days.

Friends on campus remembered seeing him down in that area near the water below the cliffs on the night of the twelfth. They had departed early, leaving their friend behind for a few final dives. Apparently, according to the constable, the boy dove into the water from up on the ridge and hit his head against a submerged rock. His neck was broken. Rev. LeBoeuf had to prepare another sermon to assuage the grief of the local community once again. The Crewe of Adelphos remembered the deceased lad in solemn assembly. His carelessness had suddenly catapulted him forever changed into a new place.

At the end of August, Rev. LeBoeuf summoned the staff to pack up Tyler's personal belongings and to bind the boxes with heavy string. The revered had the records placed in the library's cellar, hoping that Tyler would someday return for the records of his first life. He later thought about the *Kuhduush,* but it was too late. Someone, most likely, had already wrapped it up. He wanted to touch it, to read it, but that blessing was not to be his. He was not of the same lineage as Tyler; his roots were buried elsewhere.

After the Board of Regents convened within a month of Tyler's passing, Rev. LeBoeuf became president of the Academy. His insight and vision as a man of the cloth pushed the Academy into the 20th century with vim and vigor, attracting students from as far away as Berlin and, one year, from Peking. He was able to make a good living, but soon it was time for him to move on lest others would discover he was not what he appeared to be.

CHAPTER 25

22 March 2010

The day at the police station in Culver City had been overrun by crazies. Jude Martin had been dragged in again because he threatened his neighbor's dog for the third time in two weeks. Sally Dunfrey was caught drinking in her car during her break at the Sausage House by her manager. Sally claimed she had a bad cold and was taking something to drive out the sinus demons she was prone to and didn't like the idea that she wasn't free to choose her own medicine. It didn't matter to her that her manager didn't want her waiting on customers with the smell of alcohol on her breath, so she threatened to dump hot grease on his lap after she slapped him with a wet cloth he had used to wipe up spills over by the floor drain. Finally, Dieter Koontz had to spend the day in solitary confinement until after dinner because his wife said he was trying to exorcise Satan out of their thirteen year old son because Dieter found him looking at the lingerie ads in the Penny's catalogue.

When Milo Vasilovich heard that Billy was waiting to see him, he felt that at least one sane person still existed on the planet.

"Ah, c'mon in," Inspector Vasilovich said. "Billy, isn't it?"

"Billy, sir."

"You're the lad who found Gruder that rainy morning back in October. I remember you well." He pointed to an empty chair near the desk that contained the file folders that led to nowhere.

"I'm the one," Billy replied. He hadn't shaved in over a week. He sported a blue bandana tied around his forehead like a sweatband. His brown hair was bushy but clean. He smiled. Billy always smiled.

"And how can I be of help to you today?"

"Is it true that you once worked for the CIA or the KGB? How cool is that, Mr. Vilovich?"

"Vasilovich. It's pronounced *Va-sil-o-vich.* That rumor is still flying around out there, is it? No. I didn't work for anyone like that at all."

Billy scratched his head. "They say that's why you're such a good detective."

"If I'm such a good detective, I would have solved these cases a long time ago. Now, I'm sure you didn't come here to check out my credentials."

"No. I don't suppose I did."

"Well?" the inspector asked.

"Well what?" Billy answered.

"Why did you come here?"

"Oh. Yes. I have some information. Is there a reward or somethin'?"

"One has never been posted, son. But if you have something, I need to hear it," Milo Vasilovich said. Billy shifted in his seat. He scratched his ear and looked around the room trying to focus on something familiar, but he had never been in that office before. He was confused. "I'm waiting, boy. I have work to do today," Vasilovich said. When he was in a hurry, his eyes would often narrow and pierce a felon straight through. An eagle or a hawk or a predatory forest creature could take lessons from Vasilovich. He stared at the boy until their eyes locked. Like two wolves circling and trying to jockey for position, Billy wasn't going to look away first. Milo Vasilovich did, and he subconsciously signaled to Billy that the boy was in charge of the conversation.

"I was *sitting* in the steam room, not *going* into the steam room," Billy said.

"I don't follow."

"I originally told the police back in October that I found the body when I was on the way to the steam room. I didn't. I found Steve *after* I left the steam room."

Vasilovich busily took down some notes, leafing through one of the files at the same time trying to find the original report. "Why didn't you tell the truth?"

Billy pulled up his socks, smoothed out his jeans, and made sure his headband was in place. "If you knew that I was in the fieldhouse *when* he died and not right *after* he died, then you might think that I did it," he explained.

"So why are you here today? To set the record straight?" Milo asked.

"Yes, sir."

"I'll make a note of it. Is that all?"

"No, Inspector. I saw someone goin' into the shower."

Billy claimed he had seen someone entering the shower area that day because the window in the steam room door hadn't become clouded over from moisture yet. He explained that he had just turned the steam system on before he entered, hoping to relax the strained traps in his upper back, first in the steam room and then in the hot tub. They had been causing him agony for a couple of years, and just when he got the pain under control, there was always another sporting event that pulled and twisted the muscles even more. Young Dr. Matt Frain, the best chiropractor in the area, was always helping the guys with their strained, inflamed muscles, but Billy's injuries at that time would require at least two months of rest between training to get things back the way they should be, and he didn't have the time to sit out. He had to push himself if he wanted to be noticed. His dream was to play pro-ball, but that was every Trinity boy's dream.

"It was definitely a man," Billy stated. "He was fully clothed as I remember it. I thought it kinda odd, yuh know, but thought he might be going to fix a problem with one of the showerheads. One had been leakin' a lot earlier in the week."

"Height. Hair?" Vasilovich asked.

"Dunno. Normal height. Couldn't tell about the hair. He had hair. Wasn't bald."

"And he left when?"

"Didn't see him leave. The window steamed over from the inside by then," Billy replied.

* * * * * *

Cyberspace is an "unreal reality." It exists; it occupies a spot of sorts. But it is not a place you can go visit and spend some time sitting around enjoying the scenery. Blogs and WebPages posted to cyberspace, for example, can be forgotten and stay in that nebulous realm forever, or at least until the one who controls the domain chooses to click modify/delete.

Vasilovich was watching TV one evening when he noticed that the crime lab had confiscated some criminal's computer immediately after the arrest. He wondered if Gruder's computer contained any information; he was embarrassed that he hadn't thought of it sooner.

Steve Gruder had lived on campus, but his home was just outside of Greenlawn. Inspector Vasilovich paid a visit to Steve's mother the following morning. Mrs. Gruder had come to terms with her grief, at least the external expression of her loss. Inside, she was still fragile and vulnerable, and the inspector didn't want to rip open any of the smaller wounds that had healed.

She carried a small cloth hanky with her at all times, embroidered with lace, always ready to comfort her when she let her mind wander. "Would you mind if I took his computer with me? There might be something on there. It's worth the chance."

"Take what you want. Don't see how his computer will tell you anything. It was robbery, wasn't it? Isn't that what you said it was?"

"Most likely," Milo answered.

* * * * * *

Vasilovich sat at his desk trying to turn on Gruder's laptop without much success. The Inspector wasn't born into the computer-savvy generation, yet he had a fairly basic command of how to type up a document and find a few things on the Internet. Itch Schutte, his younger assistant with a degree from Alderson-Broaddus, surveyed the situation.

"Brought back your sugar and spoon. Walked off with it," Schutte said.

"Back in my day, if you had done that to your boss, you'd be walking the beat at three o'clock in the morning!"

"Back in your day, I'd be riding horseback through the countryside chasing criminals escaping on a buckboard!"

"Yeah…haha…Schutte. I can't get this thing to turn on. Too many buttons and they all look alike." Itch picked up the laptop, cradled it in his arms, and pushed a button. A soft whirring sound came from the computer. "I'm going through some of Gruder's files. Don't know why we didn't think of this before."

"While you're at it, you might want to Google him," Itch added.

"Oogle him?"

"No. Google him. Let me show you."

Itch hooked the laptop up to a DSL and went straight to the Google site. It didn't take him long before a variety of pages appeared with Gruder's name on them for perusal.

"We don't know if each Steve Gruder is our Steve Gruder, but it might be worth your while to sift through the information," Itch said. "He might even have some blogs."

"Google, blogs, and you expect me to figure this all out?" Milo asked.

"Yeah. Even old dogs can be taught to fetch a stick," Itch said, but he realized that the expression wasn't exactly right.

"You mean that old dogs can learn new blogs!"

There weren't many hits that matched the criteria that Vasilovich was looking for, but he did begin to concentrate on the first few. One was a blog that looked promising: *September 4: Had the usual run today. Did you ever wonder why there is a drive to run, to excel? By now, it's not light at 6 AM, but there's a light that keeps me focused. There's a light that urges me onward to success.* Vasilovich began to scroll down the blog slowly, looking for something that would definitely let him know that he had found Gruder, his Gruder. *September 5: A cold start. The first football game against McDonaldsport is on the horizon. Have to win this one. Team is showing low morale. How do I boost morale? Quarterback's job, isn't it? Somewhat down today. Got another note. In a bind about what to do.*

Vasilovich sat up and re-read the last two sentences in the blog. He then called for Schutte to return.

"Wonder what he meant by *another note*?" Milo asked.

"Don't know. Maybe he has files on the computer that contain that stuff," Schutte pointed out. He picked up Milo's spoon and stirred his own coffee, licked off the spoon, and put it back on the desk. Milo glanced up over his glasses, shook his head, but refrained from making a comment.

The final blog of any importance was just two days before Steve's death: *The shadows are closing in. The light is vanishing. I've given my ultimatum. But the Crewe that tapped me gives me hope once again. To stand alone against those who want to destroy is no longer a choice for me.*

Gruder kept his whole academic story on the computer in fewer than a hundred files. Most were for college courses he was taking, but even so, it would take a few days to sort through it all. And that's when Itch Schutte discovered the cached e-mail on Gruder's computer.

"We can access e-mail that goes back quite awhile. Looks like he never cleaned out the cache," Schutte explained.

"And then?" Milo asked.

"And then we can see who sent any e-mails to him."

Once they determined who had sent the e-mails, the sender could be traced right back to the exact computer that sent the mail. It would require help from the boys outside of Culver City, but those checks could be run rather quickly once the questionable e-mails were pulled. Milo was lost in all the technology once again, but he believed that the police would quickly arrest the sender of the e-mails, and the case itself would be immediately solved. He wanted to close the books on this case, embarrassed that he hadn't been as aggressive as he could have been. Milo assumed that the sender of the e-mails had done Gruder in. Milo's philosophy, molded in those days in the Soviet Union, was that one is always guilty until proven otherwise.

CHAPTER 26

A Peek into the Past
Observations from August and September 2009

When Steve Gruder was a freshman in high school, his dream was to go to college and play football on Friday nights and Saturday afternoons. He wanted to ease himself slowly into the adult world, and taking his time to find out who he was and what he wanted would be played out in the campus classroom and on the athletic field. He had his life outlined, at least as much as a young man could outline his life. Soon he realized total control is beyond one's grasp.

One day in August, sometime after the 11th, several weeks before his demise, he was re-evaluating his post-Perseid period. Everything was new. As far as his future was concerned, the time between each weekend was future enough. Controlling his expectations and all the possibilities was not within his options. The decisions and choices he would have to make had been unknown to him when in his innocent world of athletics and academics. Things of such importance, such as the change he had gone through, began to weigh him down. He had endured, of course, the confusing Crewe ritual down near the lake the night the stars fell and died although he didn't remember all of it clearly. That's when the e-mails began.

When he read those enigmatic e-mails at first, he thought they were from a brother in the Crewe who was present on the night of the Perseid rite of passage. His neck twitched from time to time, and it often burned when the e-mails arrived. He didn't know how to interpret those feelings.

When he replied to the unknown sender called *Linebacker,* it seemed to be just a friendly sort of thing. And although he didn't know who was sending the messages, he was happy that someone cared about how he approached life, cared for the team, and worked hard on academics. He believed he was being helped during his transitory stage. That was his theory.

About three times a week at first, he and the Linebacker bantered back and forth about school and hopes for the coming season. Steve asked for the Linebacker's identity on several occasions, but he was told that the revelation as to who he was would not be forthcoming at the moment. The Coach, according to Linebacker, was trying out a confidential Big Brother program to help the players form good sport and academic habits even before the school year began, but who one's Big Brother was had to remain anonymous. That added to the aura of mystery, and Gruder liked a good mystery.

When September bells called the students of Trinity Academy back to school, there was a sudden change in the tenor of the Linebacker's notes. It was subtle at first, and Steve wasn't sure what was being said. There were some innuendos, but nothing that would toss up a flag on the play. In the pit of his stomach, however, he had a nervous feeling about the in-coming messages. Often things were mentioned that were not general knowledge. No one on campus knew, for example, that he had driven to his grandparents' house for Labor Day, but Linebacker asked how his trip went. When Steve ended his romantic moments in the summer sun with Kara, Linebacker seemed to send condolences before others were aware. It wasn't that they couldn't have known that the two had broken up, but it was obvious that the anonymous Big Brother seemed to be watching out too much.

After a grueling evening of practice with pads in the stifling heat a week after Labor Day, Steve sat and sipped a glass of iced tea and caught up on his e-mails. The Linebacker told him how great he had been at practice that night, and if he continued to progress the way he had, he could lead the team to victory each week of the season. He was the *glue that held all the glitter on the paper.*

The first inkling that something was really abnormal was when Linebacker asked about how long Steve had worked in the campus records office as a student on work-study. Actually, it wasn't abnormal at first glance, but when Linebacker said that the Crewe needed a good, trustworthy man on the inside to help the team with keeping up grade point averages, it was self-evident that he was being asked to change grades on the permanent records in order to make sure that team members secured better scholarship money.

Steve's first reply was very innocent, yet to the point: *Are you asking me to change people's averages?* Linebacker assured him that that was exactly what he wanted him to do, and as a member of the Crewe, he had certain oaths and obligations that had to be obeyed.

Steve had ethics, but he often didn't have common sense in tight situations. He debated going directly to his boss, but he didn't have a name. He was sure, at first, that this was a joke, a test of his own value system set up by a Crewe member to see if he was made of the right stuff. Honesty was the first quality that held the Crewe together. His oath of honesty was something that he would not break. He responded to Linebacker that he did not intend to assist in any manner. The topic should be dropped.

Linebacker replied: *Have it your way, but what would your friends and relatives say if they knew you are having a chummy little relationship with Coach Hominy himself. You have been to his house several times, and ain't the two of you shared your curiosity of drink and drugs? Speculation? I don't think so. Why do you think you get all the playing time you do? It's not because you're that great. How would that all sit with the Board of Directors here? How about the Academy having an* ad hoc *review as to whether you are in violation of your scholarship grant?*

Gruder, stunned and shaking inside, couldn't believe that he was being accused of something that had never happened. He had been to Hominy's house once, maybe twice, but nothing happened that would besmirch his reputation. Lots of the guys went over to celebrate a victory, and he never used anything questionable at the coach's house. Steve fired back an e-mail threatening that if the attempt at blackmail didn't stop, he would take what he had to Sterrett Hamilton.

Days went by, almost a week, before he heard from Linebacker again. This time a quick note promised that even if Steve were not guilty of any impropriety, just putting the rumor out there would be enough to put doubt into the minds of the faculty, staff, student body, and his own family. *"Just remember, Gruder, you'll do what I tell you do, or the oaths you took in the Crewe will come back to haunt you."*

CHAPTER 27

24 March 2010

Itch Schutte removed the iPod headphones from his ears and finished typing up the interview between Inspector Vasilovich and Billy. From time to time, he walked over to the window and stared out at the parking lot. He didn't expect anyone to drop by for a friendly visit, but he always stared out into the parking lot when his mind was too wound up for him to concentrate.

Back at his computer, he turned Vasilovich's report into a well-organized piece of prose, a skill he had always thanked Paul Docket for after he had had him as a teacher in composition class. Most of Schutte's clerical duties were dull to him, but he wrote well and filed well. He was looking to be noticed. A nice promotion is always a pleasant surprise, but Itch knew that promotions were not always forthcoming where the budget was concerned. He stared at the computer screen and sipped on come coffee that he had overdosed with sugar and cream.

When he read the part of the interview where Billy recanted the original story, Itch sat upright and began to take notice of the change of events. According to Billy, he wasn't *on* his way to the steam room; he was *in* it when he saw someone entering the shower. A nagging feeling made him realize that something wasn't right. He wondered why Billy had returned to correct a mistake that had no bearing on the outcome of the case. For someone to come along several months later and deliberately change a story didn't make much sense. Was Billy a guilt-ridden kid?

He picked up his desk phone and dialed. "Hey, Barks. This is Itch. Yeah, up in Culver City. Listen. Get me any fieldhouse repair requisitions you have. Yeah. Ah, from the fourth week of September until the twenty-first of October. That ought to do it. Somethin' just hit me about the Gruder boy and the fieldhouse back then. Just fax 'em," he explained.

Barks was in charge of fieldhouse maintenance, and he took care of the building better than he did his own house. Nothing could be out of place when it came to the Academy because his reputation was on the line. He demanded a clean, efficient facility, and except for that one October morning, that is what he got.

* * * * * *

Itch heard the fax machine turn on, and after a few beeps, the sheets he requested from Barks over at the fieldhouse had arrived in proper order, slowly dropping into the receiving basket.

Milo Vasilovich was walking by when the transmitted files arrived, and he sat down his coffee to quickly observe what Schutte was shuffling through.

"That's it. We got him," Schutte said.

"Got who?" Vasilovich asked.

"The guy who probably killed Gruder," Itch said before passing on the information to Vasilovich.

* * * * * *

Billy sat in his convertible smoking a $12.00 cigar he received from a wealthy alumnus he had run into outside Abercrombie's at the mall. The taste wasn't great, not as smooth as it should be for the price, but it made him feel empowered. He wasn't sure what he should be empowered about, but when his uncles from out of town and the coaches from school got together on the weekends to watch a game, cigars seemed to be where all the strength lay. While the women made sure the beer was cold and the cheese and crackers kept flowing, the stench of about a dozen cigars marked the territory around the TV as being in male hands. The same territorial rules applied just as well to the area around the barbeque pit in the summer.

Billy watched people walking past his car. Some noticed him and nodded. Others apparently were unaware that he was sitting behind the steering wheel at all. He began playing a mental game with each passer-by. He wondered what secrets each one was harboring. Although he was young, he had come to realize that everyone played a game, and a gridiron wasn't necessary for some of the more challenging games at all. A friend of his jogged by and waved. Billy knew the boy was cheating on his girlfriend with her best friend. *Some BFF,* he thought. Secrets. Secrets everywhere. An old man with a cane appeared over near the park. *Bank robber from the 1940s.* A lady in a smart suit with a Gucci briefcase adjusted her belt for a second before moving onward. *Spy.* A swarthy man looked around before he dropped a letter into the mailbox. *Terrorist.* Billy's game was entertaining to him, but he had some secrets, too, and he wasn't about to share them with anyone.

About half way through his cigar, Billy decided that it wasn't what he wanted, and he tossed at least $6.00's worth of a good smoke onto the asphalt outside his convertible before he backed out of the parking lot and headed out to Gresslauer Park to meet up with some friends.

Before he got to Marge Street, Inspector Vasilovich, sitting in the back seat of his own cruiser driven by one of the new recruits, Stan from up Middle Run, had Billy pull over.

"Was I speeding, officer? Ah, hi, Inspector," Billy said as politely as he could when he saw Vasilovich approaching behind the patrolman.

"Good day, son. Could you follow us to the station? There is a new development in the Gruder case, and I think you can be of some help."

"Wow! A new development. That's been a long time coming, hasn't it?"

"Sure has," Vasilovich replied, looking over the top of his glasses. "Sure has."

Inside the second interrogation room, the one with the big mirror on the wall and the wobbly table with chipped Formica and coffee stains, Billy sat and fiddled with his baseball cap on his lap. Vasilovich rifled through some files he had on his desk, and Stan brought the coffee, cream, and sugar to the improvised summit.

"Let's get right to the point," Vasilovich said.

"That's called *cutting to the chase*. Yes, sir. That's what Mr. Docket taught us in class once," Billy added.

"Uh, yes. To the chase. The morning that Gruder died, you said that you were seated in the steam room and saw a man enter the showers. You couldn't see him when he left because the steam room door's window was wet with moisture. Is that correct, or did I take down the information incorrectly?"

"Nope. That's the way it happened."

"Now I have here a maintenance request from Barks, the custodian. You do know Barks, don't you?"

"Yeah. He's like a mentor to the whole team. He keeps a clean house, and we try to keep it that way, too" Billy said.

"You see, the steam room wasn't working that morning. Officer Schutte remembered because he often goes over there to use the steam room on his way to work here, but that week he couldn't go. They were waiting for a part to arrive so it could be fixed," the Inspector said. Billy picked up his baseball hat and put it on backwards. He shifted in his seat. He scratched his nose with his index finger. "So your story isn't right, son." When Vasilovich used the word *son,* he was trying to bond quickly, hoping that the boy's instincts for trusting a paternal figure would kick in.

"Maybe I got it confused," Billy said. "I know. I went into the steam room and sat and waited, but the steam wasn't working. That's it."

"I'm afraid that that isn't *it* exactly. Why did you kill him, Billy? I'm not looking for a long convoluted answer. Just keep it simple."

"I didn't." Billy removed his hat, spun it around on the table nervously and scratched his thigh as hard as he could.

"You were there, that much I know."

Stan stuck his head inside the door for a moment and motioned for the Inspector to come out into the hallway. Vasilovich's demeanor let Stan know that this was not the time for a tête-à-tête. Whatever he had to say was going to interrupt the flow of the confession, but he was obstinate.

He wasn't going to leave until the Inspector followed him outside.

"Inspector," Stan began, "I've been watching on the other side of the mirror. His body language says he's the *perp*. Body language is the dead give-away that he's guilty. See how he scratched and shifted. See how he twirled his cap around. You've got your man right there. Young Billy is guilty."

"You dragged me out here to tell me this, you nit-wit! Djou just take a course in body language at the local community college to keep up your license? Don't you think I know about body language?" His pitch rose with each word until his final sentence was a barely audible high whisper, something like a tea kettle a split second before it lets loose its shrill scream. "Then read my body language!" the Inspector spewed forth before turning on his heel, leaving the new recruit standing in front of the two-way mirror finally understanding why the old salt had no time for the young recruits.

"Now, Billy, let's cut to the chase, son, as Mr. Docket would say. You got yourself caught up in a mess, didn't you? Right now, I could have you locked up. Would you like that?" Vasilovich asked.

"No, sir," Billy replied.

"Just be straight with me, boy. Why did you kill Steve Gruder?"

"I didn't. That's all I can say," Billy answered. He shifted in his seat; his eyes scanned the mirror on the wall.

"You're covering something, aren't you, son?"

Billy didn't answer directly, but he looked Milo Vasilovich straight into his eyes and nodded his head in the affirmative.

"Who are you protecting? You're safe here. No one can harm you."

"I can't tell you what you want. I can't tell you very much," Billy said, tears filling his eyes. He hadn't felt this sad and confused since the neighbor's puppy he had been playing with ran out onto the highway and met its fate.

"Then what can you tell me?"

"I think he wore a badge," Billy whispered.

In the quiet of the interrogation room, Billy spoke in a barely audible voice, hoping that no one behind the mirror observing him was involved in what had happened in the fieldhouse.

"I went to take a steam bath, but there was some problem with it. It wasn't working. I went to the coach's office to view some football films on his DVD. Coach had left the door open a crack, so I went in. I took my jacket off and looked through some of the films in his bookcase. I heard someone in the locker area." He explained that he opened the door wider and saw Steve getting ready for his shower. Billy returned to look for the film from the first game in September. He wanted to study why he had made so many mistakes.

"What happened next?" Milo asked.

"I heard Steve turn on the water. Just after I found the right disc, I went to close the door to the coach's office for privacy. And it was then that I saw someone walking into the shower area." A blue uniform and the flash of the badge that reflected the shower lights for a second when the intruder turned the corner into the open stall area made Billy wonder why someone from the law was heading into the shower fully dressed.

"I thought maybe Steve had parked in the reserved spaces. Some kids do that when they arrive early. It looked like he might be getting a ticket. I watched the film for about fifteen minutes. I had to hurry to print out a report at the library.

The shower was still running when I left. No one ever stays in that long. I looked in. That's when I found Steve," Billy said.

"Why didn't you tell the authorities?" Milo Vasilovich asked.

"I was afraid. I saw someone from the law in there. After all, Greenlawn only has one cop, you know. Who else could it have been?"

"For now, this will between us. You don't know who was there, and neither do I. Understand?" Milo Vasilovich said.

"Hear yuh loud and clear."

"As long as he thinks you didn't see anything, you're safe," Milo said before dismissing Billy.

"There's something else, too," Billy said.

He didn't want to cut to the chase so quickly this time, but since he was in a penitential mood, he felt it was time to continue on with the confession. He didn't trust Vasilovich so much because of his gruffness, but he did respect the office he held. Billy fidgeted a bit and said, "One day last August before school started, I was out by the creek at Gresslauer Park dangling my feet in the cold water and drinking a beer after a hot, intensive practice, see. Grits decided to have a scrimmage although the temperature was so high in the evening that all sorts of health warnings had been posted for the athletes in the county by the health officers. I was seeking relief from the severe heat and humidity. Was guzzling down some harmless suds, that's all. Tommy the cop sneaked up behind me and almost scared my bladder empty!"

Tommy was known to appear and disappear at a moment's notice. He usually startled people with his sudden comings and goings. But this time, Billy knew he had been caught with contraband. His biggest fear was that he would be arrested and lose all that he had acquired through hard work and mountains of effort.

Tommy, on the other hand, didn't seem to care what he caught people doing. A good scare would sometimes straighten out a young man more than being hauled into the station for a deposition. That day, Tommy had something else on his agenda other than the rehabilitation of a college boy enjoying a cold drink down at the creek.

"Boy! Whatja got there?" Tommy asked. Billy dropped the blue can into the creek, but it was too little too late. The rest of the six pack was still sitting beside him on the rock. "Now don't go tellin' me that you're twenty-one. You know how many times I hear that line of jive? Let's look at your ID," Tommy said. Billy pulled his wallet out of his left front pocket and handed it over to Tommy, who was wearing his blue uniform and aviator sunglasses. "I've seen you play some pretty good ball. No need to worry about things yet, boy. I think you and I can make a good team. Yes, indeed," Tommy said followed by a smirk.

"Team?" Billy asked.

"See, son, it's like this. There's this little cocky quarterback on your squad. Gruder. Steve Gruder. I call him *Stevie.* He hates that. He's draggin' the whole thing down. Yes, sir. We gotta make some changes," Tommy explained without explaining much.

"Changes? What kind of changes?" Billy asked.

"Glad you asked, boy. Now as I see it, you wouldn't want to be run in for alcohol abuse, now wouldja? Naw. That could ruin your athletic record havin' an arrest on file and all. What would happen to all that scholarship money? How would your coach feel? Your momma and daddy wouldn't be none too proud, would they? You do see where this is all headin', don't you?"

"Not really," Billy said.

"Gawd, you are flippin' dumb, son. Flippin' with two *p's* dumb. We are going to solve the Gruder problem. Either he gets dumped off the team or you do. Is the light goin' on? Has the elevator reached the top floor? Look. You, me, and Roger---we're in the Crewe, and we take care of our own."

Billy thought for a second and replied, "So's Steve."

"Don't matter. He hasn't been in as long. Roger and I go way back. I mean waaaaay back. Roger is my buddy, see. I've got his back. He's got mine. His time has come. Time to rearrange the roster, boy!"

The best way to implement the plan, according to Tommy, would be to set Gruder up. Billy became the e-mail *Linebacker,* under Tommy's direction, of course, and was trying to blackmail Gruder into changing some team grades after the new school year started. Gruder would be set up, caught, and disgraced after Tommy pretended to get some inside information about the grade changes; he would launch an investigation himself. With Gruder out of the way, his friend, Roger Honeycutt, could get all the glory out on the field.

Billy began the process, but Steve wouldn't take the bait. Tommy promised Billy that if Steve didn't manipulate the grade files, then Billy's career might come to an end before homecoming. If Gruder or anyone else discovered that Billy was the Linebacker, then Billy would be finished as an athlete. It was Gruder's obstinacy that caused his demise. He remained honest to a fault. He portrayed the Crewe's ideals of integrity, virtue, and courage. Tommy pushed. Billy pushed. Steve dragged his feet. Then came the Orionid meteor showers in October, and Steve was gone within twenty-four hours.

Chapter 28

01 April 2010

The county crime lab returned Gruder's computer within ten days as promised, but the attached report didn't add any news about who could have committed the crime. In fact, the print-out didn't show anything that would raise an eyebrow.

The e-mails from the Linebacker had been traced to computers in the library, and the e-mail service he used required no identification. The only way to trace a visual image of the Linebacker back to a specific computer would be through video-cams, but they were on a two-week loop and had long ago self-erased. Even the computers themselves yielded no clues. The ones used by Linebacker were the "general" computers for use by guests and townspeople, and they didn't require a specific log-in code to be activated. But this information didn't bother Milo Vasilovich; he already knew who the Linebacker was before the crime lab returned their report. Billy's information lifted the veil surrounding the mysterious e-mail texts. The trap was ready to spring.

Vasilovich called Itch and Stan together and explained the precarious situation they were in at this point. If Tommy was a *cop gone bad,* he was also armed and dangerous. To move too quickly might make him suspicious, so Milo planned that there would be some surveillance and observations made. Nothing was to make him aware that he was under observation. The e-mail scam by Billy the Linebacker and orchestrated by Tommy the cop, coupled with Gruder's death in the showers, could be two separate crimes by two separate perpetrators. It was obvious that Tommy was guilty of blackmail. But murders committed by people impersonating cops, however, have been documented. Vasilovich began to wonder if someone hadn't tried to set up Tommy. After all, everyone liked him, but there was always the chance that someone didn't. And Milo had to be sure not to use haste.

* * * * * *

14 April 2010

Paul Docket had kept a low profile since Christmas. He pushed Tim out of his mind as often as possible, and he focused on his family history course that was gearing up for the final presentations. He was always amazed at the work that the students produced as they brought an ancestor or relative back to life, placing that person into history and giving him or her a new face in the present.

In the cafeteria at lunch one day, he ran into Roger Honeycutt, who was debating whether to have the pizza with pepperoni or the chicken sandwich with coleslaw. "Won't be long until you have another year under your belt here at the Academy," Docket said, picking up some cherry pie.

"Goes fast, doesn't it?" Roger replied.

Normally, little snippets of conversation between teacher and student drift off into space, barely remembered. The noise of the world intrudes. People smile and move on.

"Any plans for the summer?" Paul asked. The lunch lady plopped a big scoop of vanilla ice cream onto the pie without being asked to. The weight felt just about right to Paul. He eyed the ice cream and realized he was more infatuated with the cold blob than with the pie itself.

"Not sure. Maybe I'll work at the pizza place. Can always use the dough!"

"Good wordplay!" Paul laughed at Roger's wit.

"No pun intended."

They both walked together to a table near the windows that overlooked the small golf course. Neither had planned to sit with the other, but neither seemed to want to separate. Both noticed the grass slowly starting to turn from brown to light green, but it would still be a few weeks until the well-manicured links would be open for business.

Conversation didn't come easy. Both wanted to avoid certain topics of discussion, and after the mundane queries about the weather had run out, there was an awkward silence that made both of them feel rather uncomfortable.

"It always comes back to last October, doesn't it?" Paul said.

"Around here, everything seems to focus on it. The more we try to forget, the more it looms over us."

Paul said, "There are still those rumors that Hominy did both of them in. Any insights into that?"

"He didn't. Tommy, the local cop, told me that Grits was with him during and after the Christmas dance, and Grits and Tommy had breakfast together the morning Steve died. That ought to put any rumors to rest," Roger said.

Paul sat and processed the information. He nodded his head, cut the pie with a fork, taking up the succulent cherry filling into his mouth. Some birds were gathering on one of the trees near the sixth hole. Both stared at the arrival of more sparrows and remained silent.

"My source was at the hospital the night Tim died, and that shoots holes in your alibi story for Grits. Grits was there that night. He was seen outside the lobby," Paul said.

Roger replied, "I have it that he wasn't."

Although he did find it hard to believe that the coach could be wrapping up presents for the orphans up in Culver City, Roger had no reason to doubt what Tommy had told him.

"And," Paul continued, "Hominy *was* on campus when Steve died. That I know for sure. I was in the library annex at 6:00 that morning trying to find out if I could use a particular writing lab. I hadn't reserved it, and I wanted to make sure it was available. I was talking to Racine Woodburn about reserving a room in the Library Annex when Hominy walked through. The only reason I remember it was because Racine mentioned something about never seeing him move so quickly that early in the morning...or something to that effect."

"But Tommy said he was having breakfast with him at Denny's that morning," Roger replied. "Maybe you have your times wrong."

"Don't see how. I saw him. Racine saw him. I remember he muttered something to her about someone telling him to be at the fieldhouse for a meeting at 6:45, and if he didn't do something he'd be late. I forget what he said he had to do first. He was still puttering around at 6:30. I remember thinking later how strange it ended up for him. He had a meeting there and then all hell had broken loose by the time he arrived."

Roger focused on the tree with the sparrows, but they had all dispersed, and he wondered if he had even seen them at all. Paul stared at Roger's identification tag around his neck with his picture and signature. It was the ornate *H* in Honeycutt that caught Paul's attention. He had seen the script before in 19th century documents he used for family history research. *Where would Roger have learned to write that way?* he wondered.

* * * * * *

It wasn't that Paul Docket had been persuasive in his assertion that Grits could have been near the murders; it was just that Roger began to doubt Tommy's story about what had happened. A seed had been planted. He had that little gnawing feeling. Out at Gresslauer Park, he waited for Tommy to arrive after he called him on his cell. Tommy always looked like he had it together, but he appeared to be on the outside of things lately. Vasilovich didn't seem to want to involve him in any part of the investigation for some reason, and Tommy began to wonder what was really going on.

When Tommy arrived, he parked his patrol car under one of the naked apple trees whose buds were just starting to show. He approached Roger almost cautiously this time. No bag of doughnuts. No spring in his step.

Roger quickly explained the story that Paul had told him, and Tommy, his head down and his eyes focused on some trash a visitor had left beside the picnic table, listened to what Roger had to say.

"So, did you lie or what?" Roger asked.

"That's a strong accusation," Tommy replied. He scratched his chest. Roger touched his own neck and felt a rapid pulse.

"Well," Roger said.

"I wanted to cover for him, that's all."

"I know that Grits couldn't have done both those boys in. So do you. Why cover for someone you barely knew?"

"Because, by covering for him, I covered for me. Grits is gone now, so no one can discount my testimony about what I said. There's no double checking my story. I protected myself. I've been doing that for years, for decades. Don't you see? I did it," Tommy said.

"You did what?"

"I offed those two," Tommy said matter-of-factly. "One in the shower and one in the hospital. Snapped the ol' neck both times. The hospital incident was tricky to stage. I almost got caught. Didn't plan that one out as well as I usually do. Getting sloppy in my old age! You think I'm like you, but I'm not, see." He was emotionless during his confession. His voice or demeanor showed no remorse. His eyes locked in on Roger's for the longest time. Roger didn't give in and stared him down.

"What do you mean by I think you're like me, but you're not?" Roger asked.

"Haven't you figured it out yet?"

"Figured what out?" Roger asked.

"We have the same roots, but the tree is different, man. Same forest, different trees," Tommy explained.

"Roots? Trees? I don't follow," Roger said.

Tommy sat quietly. He observed some people running in the park trying to enjoy the warmer weather. It had been a long time since he enjoyed anything. When the time was right, he replied, "The Krewe of Orestus. That's me. That's my heritage. The Krewe your father warned you about in his letter once."

"That Krewe died out years ago, over a century ago. Had to. No one's heard of them in at least that long," Roger said.

"We have never died out entirely. I'm afraid I'm the last. Listen up. We mirror you. We imitate you. We can do everything but *become* you. We become *like* you, in a way. Like your face in the looking glass mirrors your image, so we reflect you. Therein is our deception. How we become similar to you is irrelevant," Tommy said.

"But...," Roger interjected.

"But...how do we keep on going without giving life as you do? We take it. We constantly take it. We're the hunters. We have to feed. Often the hunger is unbearable, insatiable. I don't know how else to explain it," Tommy said.

Roger remained silent. His eyes pierced through Tommy's trying to see what was inside of him. There was only an emptiness that he couldn't explain. "What do you feed upon?"

"Without you, we can't survive. Without us, well, without us you would have no natural predators," Tommy explained. "Do what you must. Perhaps you can end this cycle we talked about. I've grown tired and weary."

Not knowing what else to say, both shook their heads. After Tommy walked away slowly to the patrol car and pulled out of the small parking lot without looking back, Roger headed into the woods. A wolf crouched behind a tree and silently observed him passing by.

Later that night, after Roger thought about what had transpired out at Gresslauer Park, Tommy and he met on campus in one of the library's study rooms where they conversed until the library closed. Tommy bared his soul, and Roger began to understand. He asked Tommy if he had ever tried to end his, Roger's, progression as he had done to others. Tommy explained that he hadn't tried. Roger always led him to where the Crewe was, and where the Crewe was, there was always an unending supply of what he needed to survive. Tommy begged for release before the two parted that night. The solution to Tommy's dilemma had to be found before the first night of the Lyrid meteor showers ended one week away.

CHAPTER 29

16 April 2010

Usually, one had to give Racine Woodburn a long, convoluted reason for wanting to go into the archives, but this time, she was busy on her cell phone. She handed Paul the key and smiled. Paul Docket put the key to the archival room into his plaid shirt pocket and headed down the stairs to the lower level of the library.

He unlocked the first security door and used the same key to unlock the second. It struck him as being rather daft to have the same key open up two doors that were supposed to be protecting some dragon's hoard that the library had accumulated since it was first built.

Most of the shelves were collecting dust, and only a few bound copies of anything worthwhile occupied places of prominence. It wasn't as though he were looking for a rare volume of Dickens. It wouldn't have mattered; the library didn't own a rare volume of anything, just some old books with obscure titles that people donated from family estates because they thought the "library would have need of such things." The Academy always accepted such collections with the hope that the present donors, patronized by gracious librarians who chucked most of the donated books into the dumpster the following morning, would give some "serious" money to the college in their own wills instead of useless books. *Butter them up with honey and then collect the money* could have been the motto for the Office for Development and Financial Resources.

Paul had wanted to visit the archives for several days, but he got waylaid with meetings, student conferences, and a myriad of other things that kept him hopping from one project to the other.

Inside the archival unit, he spotted the wooden box on the bottom shelf that Joel had searched through when he had to document his report. Other boxes from that era marked "Founder's Files" filled some of the side shelves, but Paul was only interested in the one that he had seen before. Joel had previously wiped the dust off the top, and that made Paul's search easier. He switched on the light above one of the study tables and opened the lid. Joel had put everything back neatly; Docket could search through the artifacts with relative ease.

The chance encounter with Roger Honeycutt in the cafeteria two days before had brought Paul to this point. When he checked on the progress of Joel's family history project after eating with Roger, Joel said that the project was finished, but Roger hadn't returned the pictures of Tyler Pettigrew yet. Still, Docket couldn't get the resemblance between Honeycutt and Pettigrew out of his mind. After noticing the cursive *H* in 19th century style on Roger's campus ID, something clicked in Paul's mind. He just didn't know exactly what that *click* was. Family historians are born sleuths, and it is very common that they follow hunches even if the hunches themselves are vague.

He removed the pictures of Tyler Pettigrew and Lucas Granville and placed them to the side. Next, he found some short notations that Tyler had written over the years. Paul placed them on top of the photos for the moment. Nothing else looked interesting to him.

Over in the corner, he turned on the copier in order to make duplicates of the pictures and of Tyler's handwritten documents in the late 1800s. His gut instinct was working well. Suddenly, he felt the room fall out from under him as he stood by the copier waiting for it to warm up. It was the same feeling he had when he was in Tim's bathroom at the hospital. In his hand, he felt the picture he was holding turn very warm. He held on to the copier, but his legs buckled.

He saw water, a cave, the stars falling from the heavens, and a young man in a robe who looked somewhat familiar to him. Light surrounded the vision, and he saw the scene go dark. Then, as though time had passed on for a while, he watched as someone was pushed from the cliff above the water, but the body didn't radiate any light. It was already dead.

Paul let his vision run its course before he realized that the picture he had in his hand was that of a person who resembled Tommy Masheck.

He regained his strength once again, made his copies, and returned the key to Mrs. Woodburn. She appeared surprised that he even had it.

"You were on the phone when you gave it to me," he announced.

"Glad you're honest!" she replied.

Back in his academic office, he found a rough draft to a story that Roger Honeycutt had written by hand in English class the year before that Paul liked and kept. Tommy

Masheck's image kept coming to mind, and he remembered that in another stack he had placed some directions to a park in the southern part of the state that Tommy hastily scrawled down when Paul asked for the quickest route at the end of the preceding summer. He needed a place to relax for a few days before the new school year began, and Tommy was more than willing to give him a secluded spot where only the foxes say good night.

Paul methodically placed the picture of Tyler Pettigrew beside a picture of Roger from a pizza ad showing him tossing up some dough, visually inviting customers to come on in and watch the real magic of the pizza take place.

He systematically placed papers written by Tyler and Roger beside the pictures. He quickly looked through the documents, and even though not all the cursive letters matched, many of them did. Why would a college kid in the 21st century write in the cursive style of the 19th century… or even in a modified style of that period? He was surprised he hadn't noticed it before. Paul studied the picture of Lucas Granville from Kennepointe, Maine, in the 1880s, but he didn't have any documents in young Lucas Granville's handwriting to compare with Tommy's script.

Paul returned to the box of artifacts in the library later in the afternoon and searched through some more loose papers, spying some old letters written by Reverend LeBoeuf to Tyler Pettigrew when they traveled about trying to recruit for the Academy. It was the funny squiggle on the *g* in LeBoeuf's writing that caught his attention. Paul noticed the use of the final *t* script on some of the words in LeBoeuf's text that no one in the present generation would ever use.

Roger's handwriting matched Tyler's, and Tommy's matched LeBoeuf's. There were some modifications, of course, but the similarities were definitely present.

He made some more copies to take back to the office to study in greater depth. *What's the connection*? he wondered.

A picture of LeBoeuf in an old school annual in Paul's office sealed the final observation. Paul had studied that image once with the hope of having a student paint a picture of the Revered to be placed in one of the first halls the Academy had opened. Now he knew that Lucas Granville, Rev. LeBoeuf, and Tommy Masheck were the same, at least in looks and, to some degree, LeBoeuf and Tommy were the same in cursive. He also knew that Tyler Pettigrew and Roger Honeycutt were also the same. His mind then hit a brick wall. What's to be done with information that makes no logical sense?

* * * * * *

From the student parking lot on the south side of campus, Roger ran to the library annex faster than he ever did on any football play. Out of breath, he asked Racine Woodburn for the key to the archival area.

"That place is sure busy. You're the second person to ask to go down there today. Well, the third if you count Paul Docket's double visit. Do me a favor. Tidy up anything that looks out of place. I don't get a chance to go down there much, and I like my areas to look nice. You're so special. You're all so special," she said and scurried off to see why the student copier had jammed in the computer room.

The archival room was dark, and it took Roger a second to locate the switch. The light fixtures that hadn't been changed since the 1920s reminded him of a place he had visited in the South of France for some reason. Maybe it was the art deco style. He didn't remember the place exactly; he just had a feeling of déjà vu for a moment. He sneezed twice. Dust was in the air. He saw it floating around the lights.

On the bottom shelf, he recognized his old wooden box that housed some of his written expressions in life. He found it rather amusing to see what Rev. LeBoeuf had squirreled away. *Is this how I was to be remembered?* He removed his picture and that of Lukas taken during the final days of summer in 1886 and put them into a folder. Sifting through some more material, he tried to remember what he wanted to find, other than the two pictures that could raise some questions.

The search was frustrating to him. He unpacked the entire box. He arranged the material in chronological order. Standing back, he inspected it all once again. The *Kuhduush*! He was sure that it would have been put there. Lukas-LeBoeuf-Tommy would have placed his most honored treasure there unless he was afraid that someone would find it. He thought hard and focused. Those few librarians over time who wanted to sort and document the collection never took the time to archive what was there because, to be honest, no one had much interest in who the founder of the school was. After all, he left only a legacy that spanned a single year. Rev. LeBoeuf had taken over the school as much as he had taken over the boats and ships he sailed in Maine in a century past.

What happened to the *Kuhduush*? He had a theory. His neck pulsated and began to itch. In scratching it, he broke the skin and drew a few drops of blood. It had to have been removed recently.

Chapter 30

Noon
18 Apr 2010

Buck McDougal tried to salvage the steak he had just burned at his cabin. He was a good chef, a cautious chef, but the deer standing outside the kitchen window near the clearing, a possible future meal, had distracted him, and he was afraid that the charred Delmonico wouldn't even make his dog wag its tail.

Buck noticed the Mazda pulling up beside his truck. The small window above the sink was letting the smoke from the kitchen escape, and Roger stopped for a moment and wondered if something was on fire.

"C'mon in," Buck shouted through the window. "Just a little cooking incident."

Inside the living room, Roger sat down on the leather couch that Buck had covered with an Indian blanket from Arizona and listened to the noises coming from the kitchen area.

Buck put his culinary delights on hold and walked into the living room. "Here's some coffee to perk things up," Buck said. Roger took a sip, found it too hot, and set the cup down on the mahogany table that was littered with old fishing and hunting magazines, most of them previously stained by coffee mugs.

"I stopped to snoop through the old archives at the library," Roger said. "I got my picture and Tommy's out of the box and took care of them and some other documents, if you get my drift. I couldn't find one thing, though."

"That being..." Buck said, interrupting himself with a slurp of coffee.

"The *Kuhduush*. I know it should have been put there with my old effects."

"Check out the mantle over there," Buck said. Roger looked above the fireplace, noticing some old antiques that were used in cabins back in the late 1800s, things that still looked familiar to him, to both of them. He saw the small brown book tucked in between two other leather-bound editions that Buck had bought awhile back. One was a signed first edition of Jack London's *White Fang*, and the other was some obscure novel, *A Lantern to Light the Way*, about life in Manitoba during a blizzard of 1876.

"And how did you get this?" Roger asked.

"Docks brought it out to me on Christmas Eve."

"And you didn't tell me?" Roger asked. Buck sensed he was miffed at the thought someone had stolen from his collection.

"How did I know you or he would be digging around in those musty archives? It's safe here. Nobody's gonna touch it. Blends in, wouldn't you say? Would have told you, but we don't keep company very often."

"And Docket. Does he know what it is?"

"He was just happy to know that such a book existed. I was almost ready to further him into the Crewe, but we got waylaid Christmas Eve. I let it drop. Anyway, he got the book from that Joel kid who found it in your records. The *Kuhduush* gives credence to our degrees, after all," Buck explained.

"*Credence,* that's a mighty big word for an assistant football coach who teaches a little science from time to time!" Roger chided.

"I wasn't always just brawn, rugged looks, and being a good-time Charlie, yuh dipstick. Remember?"

Roger grabbed a pack of cigarettes off the mantle, toyed around with one for a while, and put it back into the pack. "Last time I had one of these was New Year's Eve 2006."

"Go ahead. It's not like it can kill yuh," Buck joked.

"Later. We've got some more problems than whether a smoke will do me in." He tossed the full pack onto the table in front of the leather couch.

Over cooling coffee, Roger explained the situation with Tommy and how he wanted to handle it. Even though he didn't know all the specific details, he also explained what Tommy had told him about the Orestians hunting and feeding on the members of the Crewe. Buck didn't seem to be surprised, but nothing ever seemed to surprise him. He had a good handle on people and their emotions, but he kept his ideas to himself. Nothing, however, prepared him for the story about why the Orestians are predators. McDougal's neck began to burn. Roger's started to itch and then burn. Roger picked up the *Kuhduush* and thumbed to a marked passage: *The Perseids can give life to the lifeless and hope to the hopeless, but the Lyrids can take away what was given falsely. He to whom the gift was passed must lay naked the betrayer.*

"The Lyrid meteor shower will peak on the 21st and 22nd this year, give or take," Buck said. "What else is there about it?"

"Says here in the Book of Pisho that *one so cursed as to have broken the trust of the brothers can be changed in the twinkling of an eye to the former self, and then vanish, void of all blessing and continuation. His contamination will, therefore, be naught. He shall find himself at peace. The night of the Lyrids giveth all and can take away all, not to usurp justice and retribution, but to sustain it,*" Roger read. "I'm not sure if it applies to the Orestians, but I think I know what must be done to tip the scales of justice in the right direction."

"I'll let you take the *Kuhduush* and finalize the ritual. It's all in there, but like a puzzle, it only makes sense when the parts are finally pieced together," Buck said.

Both drank their black coffee after a steaming refill.

* * * * * *

Vasilovich, moving from one room to the other at the station, had put together his plan. He was going to call Tommy in for questioning on the morning of the 22nd just after Tommy's daily departure from Denny's. That should give them all enough time to make sure the stakeouts and the paperwork are all in order. Itch and Stan had been paying close attention to every move that Tommy was making, but nothing looked suspicious at all.

CHAPTER 31

Afternoon
18 April 2010

The pictures and handwriting of people who should have been long dead made Paul Docket wonder if the Crewe was hiding something sinister or glorious. How was such a thing possible? Was it part of the onion that he kept trying to peel? And the more he peeled, the larger and more complex the onion became. It was like the Phoenix rising. Out of the ashes, out of nothing, rose the Phoenix gloriously into new life. That which should have been stripped down to nothing kept growing and blossoming. Instead of knowledge, he kept uncovering confusion.

He grabbed his materials he had copied in the library and drove recklessly in his Jeep out to Buck's cabin. The spring rains made the going slippery at best, and he found himself downshifting constantly to negotiate the curves and the rain-slicked conditions. Ruts in the road splashed mud and goop onto the windshield. Slamming on his brakes just before the dirt drive ended near Buck's cabin caused the Jeep to spray up a few clumps of black earth onto the side of the Dodge Ram. *Buck won't like that a bit,* he thought. He saw Roger's Mazda and wanted to break out into a chorus of

"Hail, Hail, the Gang's All Here," but that would have been too sarcastic. . .even for him.

He knocked twice and walked in uninvited. Roger and Buck both looked over at the door in tandem.

"Sorry for the intrusion," Paul said. "I was doin' a little research and thought maybe someone around here could give me some answers."

Buck and Roger shifted on the couch a bit, but they didn't make eye contact with themselves or with Paul, who plopped himself down between his friends without being invited to do so.

"So what brings you here?" Roger asked to be polite.

Buck grabbed a smoke from the table in front of the couch. Roger helped himself to one, too. The ride was just going to get bumpier. "Help yourself to the top-shelf-brandy over there by the bar," Buck said. Paul smiled but did nothing to indulge Buck.

"Take a look at this," Paul said, and handed Roger and Buck copies of the pictures and documents. "Any comments?"

"Comments?" Buck asked. "What should we comment about?"

"Why do you and Tyler look so much alike, Roger? And study the photo of Tommy and Lucas Granville, our mystery man from 1886. Another coincidence? Now shift to the handwriting samples. Roger's and Tyler's are very similar, and so are Tommy's and Rev. LeBoeuf's. Don't have a sample for Lucas, but Lucas's photo looks like LeBoeuf and Tommy. So, if it looks like a duck and writes like a duck. . .you know the rest."

"What's all this have to do with ducks?" Buck asked after walking to the bar and pouring himself some Courvoisier.

He took a substantial gulp and invited the others to do so. Even if Paul couldn't stomach the rot-gut stock that Buck usually served, he had acquired a taste for good brandy. All three cordially sipped in silence.

Roger was the first to break the quiet of the short meditative moment. "There's not much to tell. What you see is what it is," he said casually.

"That's right," Buck began. "Why is it so hard to understand?"

"You want me to believe that Tyler is you, Roger, and that Lucas and Rev. LeBoeuf are Tommy the cop? That's what I'm supposed to conclude?"

"Isn't it what you want to conclude?" Roger asked. He poured himself another small glass of Courvoisier and downed it straight.

Buck said, "We told you that the Crewe was like an onion once. You keep peeling it and discarding each layer. Didn't you ever wonder what the final layer would be like?"

"I always felt that there was something more, something much deeper, but I couldn't grasp how to find it. The more I peeled, though, the bigger the onion got! Now you're telling me that the onion should be down to its last layer," Paul said.

Roger added, "It was always around you, yet you were blind to what was, is, and shall be. Before my father died in 1885 in Louisiana...yes, 1885...he gave me his *Kuhduush,* perhaps the only copy there is, and there I began to search for the answers. I am grateful that you brought it here. I was never sure what they did with it when I passed on to Greece. I should have asked Tommy, but I didn't think he knew. He never brought it up. I digress. Unfortunately, others from the Krewe of Orestus, our archfiends of yore, have often infiltrated and tried to destroy us from within,"

"No one has destroyed anything. I'm the Alpha of our den. Nothing happened on my watch," Paul said. "I would have known!"

Buck and Roger left Paul sitting on the couch and conferred silently by the fireplace.

"Paul," Buck said, "it's just that things are not always what they seem to be. One branch of the Crewe is purely social. That's the branch you're in. You meet, have nice rituals and rites, a handshake or two, and then you split up and go home until another day. Most members of the Crewe enjoy such a social pastime. You were tapped. The mailmen did their job. Finally, there was a nice induction ceremony, and you moved up several degrees over time. But for you there was nothing more. For most, there is nothing more. Roger and I were tapped here at the Academy this time around, but Roger and I had been through the ritual before...actually, again and again over time. In many places.

"The branch Roger and I are in is made up of a different group of brothers. As Immortali, the Inner Circle, we protect the organization over the decades in various places. Over centuries for some members. From time to time, the Orestian betrayers, infiltrators, who seek to destroy us, often gain access to our dens. Complex? Yes."

"I still don't get it," Paul said.

Buck replied, "You're not supposed to get it all. It's not your problem yet. It may never be your problem. You are not so advanced. I can't be plainer. Under the promise of your obedience and by the virtue of your office, you are required not to reveal what has been made known to you. I am very clear about that. You can do nothing that would jeopardize us or our work."

"And what is your work?" Paul asked.

Roger responded, "To heal and to help the downtrodden and those in pain with their mortal existence. We give dignity to those lost in the throes of humanity."

Paul sat and thought. He believed that this was the first time he had ever heard Buck and Roger wax almost eloquently. It was difficult to understand that perhaps the personas of one Buck McDougal and one Roger Honeycutt were nothing more than an act, a cover-up as to who they were.

Buck took the pictures and documents that Paul had brought along, studied them for a moment, and with one quick snap of his wrist, he tossed the papers into the blazing hearth, destroying the evidence that Paul could use to give up the faithfully guarded secrets. Without the documental proof, whatever Paul said would be taken as a tale told by a lunatic at best. Roger had already taken care of the original pictures earlier, as well as the written documents, without Mrs. Woodburn being any wiser. No one would be able to trace him to the past except for Joel, and Joel's day was soon coming. Paul, realizing what Buck had just done, looked at the ashes disappearing up the chimney. He was a man of his word and would not break his promise of obedience, but he wasn't going to be left out of any further explanations. "So how does all of this tie into the death of the two boys?" he asked.

"Leave it alone. The night of the Lyrids will solve that problem," Buck said.

"The meteor showers? My vision had the showers, and then a body was thrown from a cliff near the sea, but I often never know if it is what was or what will be," Paul added almost out of breath.

"A great imagination you have, Docks," Buck said.

"Yeah. A great imagination? A marvelous imagination!" Roger echoed. "A wonderful English teacher, Mr. Collins, told me the exact same thing about myself in 1886 when I didn't understand, too. He was an excellent mentor I have come to respect."

"And I thank you for the compliment, Tyler, but you should have been more punctual to class. I always did hate tardiness," Buck replied and grinned. "Why *were* those people sitting on that bench?" He laughed out loud this time. Roger laughed back. Paul showed no emotion whatsoever at what was obviously a private joke. Being a third wheel wasn't his style. He knew when it was time to leave.

On his way to the Jeep, he felt that they had cut him off from the brothers he had grown to trust. They almost made it sound like he was not part of a real Crewe at all, and his position as Alpha of the den was nothing more than some type of illusion, a perfunctory office for a perfunctory branch. It wasn't the first time he had been kept in the dark about things, but this time he took it personally. After he got into his Jeep, he began to wonder if they hadn't just pulled a mean-spirited joke on him to see his reaction. Maybe the pictures and the documents were part of an elaborate hoax to test his loyalty. He shook his head and drove off through the woods.

Roger and Buck cleaned up the cabin quickly after Paul left because the Immortali in the area would be arriving shortly to prepare for the night of the 21st. Originally, that evening was just to be a special convocation, a council that meets every ten years, but circumstances had changed the character of the gathering this year. Most of the brothers arriving from so many places were unaware of the shift in plans. The weather had warmed up quite a bit over the past few days, and there were no showers in the forecast. The heavens would be open for viewing the rain of the meteors.

"Are you sure Tommy will come to this?" Buck asked after he went into the kitchen.

Roger thought for a moment and replied, "Yes. I sent him a text message, and he promised to show up. He knows what has to be done. I think he's tired of always having to live a lie. He wants to find some sense of peace this time. If we fail to succeed, one of our members will not make it very long. We gain our energy on the night of the meteor showers, and he knows that. He feeds off our energy. His deceit always lay in the fact that we believed that he was one of us," Roger explained.

"I often noticed that he never touched his neck at times when we were all together. It's so common for us that I don't pay much attention to it in others, but when I think back…," Buck pointed out.

"Even at our rituals, he was often over on the fringe of the group. He never was directly involved. On the night of the Lyrids, however, he will be."

Buck said, "Have you wondered why we are all here now? Me, you, Tommy, and the rest. This is the first time that we have come back to a particular place all together after being scattered when our tenure in Boston had run its course."

"It's strange, but this convocation might bring us the sense of justice that we have been seeking, perhaps unknowingly. Normally, we go to other bodies of water and never see each other again except on rare occasions. I often wondered why Lucas found me as LeBoeuf and then as Tommy. I think I know. By following me around at those times, he had access to the Crewe in order to still his hunger. Soon a new epoch in our history will begin. It is time for the cleansing process. With Joel, we will finally find that which was lost to us."

* * * * * *

The *Kuhduush* states that one who has betrayed, one who is the betrayer, shall never imitate the Immortali again after the discovery has been made. The ritual was not specific, but Roger and Buck found references in the text to stop the betrayal and the invasion by the self-confessed Orestian fraud. How these deceivers managed to infiltrate themselves as members of the Immortali was not clear. They do not give life but destroy it, yet their progress through life is akin to what happens to the Inner Circle of the Crewe of Adelphos, yet it is not exactly similar.

The Orestian intruders witness the night of the meteors, but their own force of life within them begins to deteriorate rapidly afterwards. In order to survive and pass themselves off as Immortali, they must find one of the Immortali alone, destroy the alignment of the neck to the body, and absorb the spirit as it passes to a new existence. They do not become the deceased, but they utilize that person's life force as their own. That is what Tyler Pettigrew's father meant when he wrote: *Often, they try to hide within our dens, sometimes with success. They'll suck the life directly out of you.*

Roger remembered back at the end of the 1890s when Bram Stoker's *Dracula* became such a novelty in Europe. He often surmised that Bram was, perhaps, an Immortali himself or knew about them and how they infused life into those who are worthy. Only the Orestians bastardized the process.

Roger wondered if the Orestians were the true vampires of Stoker's novel in the first place, and through his written work, he hid the spiritual realities of good versus evil behind fantastic fiction.

Roger thought about how Tommy, then known as Lucas Granville, appeared at the cove that August night in 1886. Lucas knew what was about to transpire even though Tyler didn't. But by participating in the ritual, Lucas was able to see who the new members were and could renew his bonds with the elders once again. He recognized them later in the world on the night of the falling stars in other places, too, and later attempted to stop their ability to help suffering humanity. Lucas was the Lone Wolf that was able to infiltrate, just as Tyler's father had once predicted. What Tyler didn't know at the time was that the Orestians had to destroy life every time the meteors streaked across the heavens to maintain their own false sense of immortality. Here one Immortali died. There another one. Nobody would notice the demise of the Immortali by such cleverly crafted means. For soon after the ritual, most of the Immortali left quickly to move on to new things, but a few tarried behind, and those who remained behind alone were as vulnerable as young deer when the wolves begin to circle.

Roger finally understood, therefore, that when each member of the Crewe's Immortali branch passed on under normal circumstances, he would appear in other places and have no more contact with previous friends. That was the perfect opportunity for the Orestians to work their evil. After the enemy had taken in the life of a member, the body of the deceased might be found, but the fully initiated Crewe members, if they became aware at all of the death of one of their own, assumed that the brother had just passed on and migrated elsewhere spiritually, much as they themselves had done over time. It wasn't until the triangles came into play that Roger began to wonder about what was going on. He made no connection between Steve's and Tim's death. To Roger, Steve was killed by an assailant for some unknown reason, and Tim died of shock due to a nut allergy. He just thought that a Crewe member had marked the bodies at death much like his mother had placed the golden triangle over his father's heart the day of his burial in New Orleans.

The Orestians, however, marked the victims of their sacrifices with the inverted triangle, the vertex pointing downward, sealing the victim's ability to materialize somewhere else. Even Coroner Schaffer and his assistant were confused as to why the triangles on the bodies were inverted, but they didn't say anything. Within the Crewe itself, there was no story that the soul of the loyal member would be blocked from making its appointed transition. The *Kuhduush,* long locked away, could not be searched for definitive answers.

The concept that one had to die alone for the soul to disperse was well known to the members of the Inner Circle, but the real reason had been veiled over time. In reality, the end had to happen in quiet solitude to prevent the presence of an Orestian from taking the soul and the soul's energy into himself. Brothers had lost that important piece of the puzzle. It didn't matter, really, if other mortals were present, so long as one of the Orestians wasn't present at that "dreaded" moment. But the brothers didn't know that. That is why many, knowing that their passing was near, sought seclusion, but they didn't know the true purpose behind seeking out seclusion. They thought if they passed alone, no one would see the soul exit and migrate. The convocation was sorely needed this decade to separate fact from fiction. The brothers would have much to digest.

Buck and Roger commiserated about the loss of so many people over the years. Every time there were the meteor showers, someone's passing on had been unknowingly hastened. It was now evident to them that these wretched vipers, the Orestians, had always been as close as the ceremonies themselves. Seven showers each year and seven times members of the Immortali would be taken in various dens all over the world, but no one seemed to notice until now. Perhaps now was the time to stop the evil that lurked in the dark. For the first time, the opening ritual about the Lone Wolf they all had taken as just some type of hidden allegory now had such an obvious meaning that they wondered why no one had been able to detect it before.

CHAPTER 32

The Night of the Lyrid Meteor Showers
21-22 April 2010

Evening was fast approaching, but the sun still hadn't run its diurnal course. Paul had pulled his Jeep over along the road opposite the lake to see if he could view any of the happenings that he, apparently, wasn't worthy to attend. He didn't know what was to become of his branch of the Crewe, the Crewe he had shepherded and nourished for all those years. He was too old, too long in the tooth, he came to realize, to be involved in esoteric groups in the first place. He came to understand that these societies were for the young who had bonds to strengthen and brotherhood to forge. He was long past those days of secret grips and ambiguous passwords. He was angry with himself for being suckered into something that he now held in contempt. The hours that he had spent in guiding the youth of the Crewe to live life by higher standards were all for naught. The Immortali hid behind his group like chameleons in the woods, and after all he had done, he was not found to be worthy to join their side.

When he left the cabin a few days ago after his encounter with Buck and Roger, he entertained the idea that he was the brunt of some terrible joke, a hoax perpetuated for some unknown reason. Why was he the object of such ridicule? When he analyzed it more, what had he ever done to cause Buck, his best friend, to not want to confide in him?

Buck's final comment was about the promise of obedience to the Crewe. In the light of what he had learned and in light of how he felt, obedience was an empty word for broken trust. He could promise nothing any longer.

He had just turned on the motor when he looked up and saw a police car slow down and park behind him. The feeling was somewhat eerie, and that sensation of déjà vu started to rise. Tommy approached the driver's side window and asked if everything was all right. Paul shook his head in the affirmative, but his body language said otherwise.

"Not going to the Crewe function tonight on the other side of the lake? Big doin's I hear. Convocation night. Happens only every ten years," Tommy said.

"Wasn't invited. Guess I'm not as 'advanced' as some of the others."

"Mind if I see your license?" Tommy asked.

"Why. I'm not doing anything illegal, am I?"

"No, but we're expected to check every time we interact. New law from up in Culver City. Keeps things on the up and up. If we ask everyone for their license, then we can't be called out for profiling. Homeland security and all that," Tommy said.

"For heaven's sakes, Tommy. I'm not some kind of terrorist casing the lake. We've been in the Crewe for how long together?" Paul asked.

"Guess you're right. I know who you are anyways."

"Going over to the Buck's cabin for the shindig tonight yourself? Paul asked.

"Yeah. Promised I'd show up for the festivities. You might say that I have a special invitation."

"I figured you would. Yeah, I know about you. I know about Paul and Buck. You're not what you all seem to be. Maybe nobody's what they seem to be. Don't worry. Your secret is safe," Paul said.

"Let me ask you somethin'. Did you ever have the embrace?"

Paul remembered his dream after Tim's death. He remembered the terror that encroached after that question from the unknown officer. He was hoping his nightmare was not part of tonight's reality.

"Embrace. Sure. Haven't we all?" Paul said, lying because he thought it might change the outcome of his horrendous dream that had gnawed at him since December.

"Honesty is one of the Crewe's virtues. You should practice it more," Tommy warned.

Paul sat staring out the front window. His mind began to inject fear. This was worse than the dreams of the planes going down into swamps or crashing on runways in the rain. Through his peripheral vision, he noticed Tommy shift his weight. The young cop slowly removed his aviator glasses and put them into his pocket. Tommy waited. The viper in him sprang, and Tommy hastily reached through the window and grabbed Paul by the head, twisting it to Paul's left. Docket couldn't manipulate himself out of the vice-like grip. Tommy's hands felt cold. His breath smelled putrid in Paul's nostrils. Tommy angled himself to have a clear view of the right side of Paul's neck. Instinctually, he went in for the kill. Paul's worst fear had been realized.

The vice-like grip held his head firm. The sharp, gut-wrenching pain piercing through his neck into the muscles where the shoulder, neck, and jugular come together left him paralyzed; although Paul's mouth was open trying to make some sound that would attract attention, he was unable to scream. He had chosen an isolated spot out in the woods off the beaten path to sit and browbeat himself about not being within the confines of the Inner Circle. Nobody, not even those across the lake, were even aware that he was so close and in so much anguish.

Paul's head hung limply on his shoulder. Tommy backed slowly away and wiped his mouth. "I can't leave you the *Kuhduush* or anything like it to follow, but you will now be able to follow your instincts in order to survive. I'm the guest of honor on the other side of the lake tonight, but I couldn't let the tradition of the Krewe of Orestus just pass along with me. You will be its only member once I'm gone. But if you don't want to be as lonely as I've been, you can 'make' friends easily. I've been alone for over a century and a half fighting off who I am. Ashamed of my very existence. My daddy's legacy to me. The others were caught and dispatched, for lack of a better word, over time by other branches. You truly are the Lone Wolf. See, it wasn't just an old metaphor after all. The hunger is the worst. The deceit, well, you'll learn to live with deceit."

Tommy sped off to the cabin with his lights flashing and his siren wailing to add to the drama. Paul sat looking into the mirror, but he was unable to see his reflection at first until he mentally focused on who he had become. His tongue felt swollen. He drooled onto his shirt. It took over an hour of sitting in the quiet to regain his ability to speak, to think. He heard a wolf howling in the forest, and he knew what he had to do.

* * * * * *

The brothers had all congregated along the banks of the lake that stretched and meandered from Buck's cabin for three miles to its eastern shore. A small hut had been erected the previous summer to represent the Cave of Elijah, and although the area around the lake was bucolic, it was not as dramatic as what one could experience along the untamed shores of Maine or areas of California where the ritual was more spectacular at night. Still, the serene beauty of the pristine woods gave the brothers time to reflect about the grandeur of the world that they had so long been a part of.

For this particular night, many had arrived from distant places, Sacramento being the farthest away, for the special convocation. The Crewe always enjoyed the particular bonding that these nights could bring each decade. True, they met seven times annually throughout the world in their various branches, but the convocation was always a time for personal feelings to develop and friendships to grow. The rush of the modern world meant that so many were scattered to the farthest places upon the land and the sea, but no matter where the brothers found themselves, they always seemed to return to a spot where the Immortali, the Inner Circle, could gather unnoticed once again.

This particular meteor shower was not as impressive as the one in August, and although only ten to twenty meteors were expected per hour, some years often witnessed many more. Shortly after midnight, the first meteor was sighted. The Brother-of-the-Lance quickly called all to order and the ritual so familiar began.

At the appointed time the familiar *What is the hour?* was asked once again. The brothers, recognizing the cue, slowly moved to their places near the water's edge. As silence began to pervade the area, even the woods behind the cabin became hushed in anticipation. The last of the brothers took their places near the ceremonial podium, and a few stragglers looked up toward the heavens to notice if the stars had, indeed, begun to fall.

The Keeper-of-the-Lance spied a meteor shooting through the sky, and others, heads upraised and eyes sharply focused, agreed that the hour had indeed arrived. They could now convene.

The brothers formed the double triangle with the newer Immortali creating the innermost one, protected from the world by those who have witnessed years of earthly experience.

Brother-of-the-Lance:	*Form your lines and guard your rank! An imposter here among us goes!*

Normally, this is how the ritual began from decade to decade and century to century, but the imposter was only playing a part. Tonight, the imposter was real. He knew what awaited.

Brother-of-the-Code:	*Hold him firm; present him here!*
First Guard:	*Let us call the roll to see if any are tarrying away from us this eve. Whose place has he taken? Wherein lies his deceit?*

(A call of names is performed by the Knight-of-the-Registry standing at the podium.)

The brother selected to be the Lone Wolf always goes to a couple of the brothers and tries to pass himself off as a valid member. When his mistake is caught, he admits that he has given the signs and tokens in error, corrects his handshake, and moves on with the ritual. This night, the night of the Lyrids, Tommy Masheck waited to portray the Lone Wolf.

Knight-of-the-Registry:	*Your name, Brother Wolf, is not here. You are not listed. Your deceit has been flushed out!*
Lone Wolf:	*I have given the pass in error; my rank escaped me for a moment.*
First Guard:	*It is well that you admit your error. Pass your rank grip to me slowly, so that no more confusion can come herein to our den.*
Lone Wolf:	*I shall pass the rank grip one more time. There is no confusion in the den.*

Try as he might, he was unable to give the correct rank grip. The Brother-of-the-Lance took his spear and forced the imposter to the center of the inner triangle. The brothers began to break rank, slowing forming two concentric circles around the deceiver. First, the inner circle moved clockwise. At the same time, the outer circle began to move counter-clockwise. Tommy had never seen this part of the ritual. In fact, no one had witnessed this particular ceremony before, but some of the older masters had learned it long ago thinking it to be symbolic. He stood in the center watching the movement begin to pick up its tempo. He tried to maintain his bearings, but the incessant turning around him caused him to become a little disoriented. A slight twinge of nausea began to rise in his stomach. He closed his eyes, but in the blackness of his mind, he felt himself spinning, much like an inebriate who lies down and stares at the revolving ceiling after a night of debauchery.

The brothers, circling slightly faster, began the "Song of the Bond." Those in the inner circle put their arms around the waists of the brothers next to them; those in the outer circle placed their arms around the shoulders of the brothers next to them. Their feet moved faster and faster as the tempo of the song increased. Each foot crossed over the other, similar to a Greek dance. In the inner circle, the right foot crossed over the left; in the outer circle, the left crossed over the right. The movement repeated itself; the rhythm accelerated.

Tommy opened his eyes, but all was a blur to him as the brothers moved and twirled around. He began to feel his strength weakening. Looking up toward the sky, he noticed a meteor streak its way into oblivion. He couldn't help feeling that he was that meteor. Numbness took away his ability to think, and the lack of sensation spread down his body. He freely wanted to depart this world for he had been a part of it too long. His fear was beginning to dissipate.

Somewhere outside the circle, a voice began the incantation from the Book of Kanduúr within the *Kuhduush*: *True he never was; loyalty was foreign to him. A Son of Orestus, an Orestian fraud, had infiltrated and soiled the noble brothers. He has sapped us of our dignity and sapped us of our strength. Many lie discarded along the shores of time. Woe unto him who deceiveth. Woe unto him who passed as the Lone Wolf. His deceit will be discovered and his guilt will be uncovered until his foul deeds have been expunged from his and our memories alike.*

The brothers stopped encircling the traitor. They paused and gazed upwards awaiting the next meteor. Several minutes had to pass before their wish was fulfilled. Lances were pointed at Tommy's heart. He could hear his own blood slowing. His pulse, always audible to his senses before, was weak. He was in a state of complete submission.

The brothers formed two parallel lines, one to his left and one to his right. The Brother-of-the-Lance escorted the Brother-of-the-Veil from the Cave and placed him at Tommy's feet. "Raise him up," he commanded. Several brothers lifted Tommy up, and although he could barely stand, the helping hands of the others steadied him. He hung his head in shame. He hung his head not fearing his end. It was the release he had wanted for such a long time. "Tommy, you who forged his way into our den as Lucas so long ago, I bid you listen. From the swamps of old you belong to a lineage most ignoble, most dastardly. Through no fault of your own have you been placed on the errant way. Another made you the way you are. You had no choice. Of that you are not guilty, yet you have drained us over time. You have caused us to fear the unknown assailant in the light and in the dark."

The Brother-of-the-Veil approached. Two of the assistants raised his veil, and that Brother-of-the-Veil made a triangle with his index fingers and his thumbs joined. Tommy felt a pinch and a bite of sorts, and the Brother-of-the-Veil withdrew the curse, siphoned out the counterfeit life that had dwelt within the bodily shell and dispersed the spirits his tainted soul had absorbed into the cold night air. Tommy, now limp and relaxed, was placed upon the ground, upon the symbolic place of burial where one rests from earthly cares.

From out over the lake, the earth gave a slight shudder. Three meteors crisscrossed directly above the congregants.

Tommy sprang up from the ground on his own volition, devoid of the souls of others. He was thirsty to replace them. With the next meteor, his face contorted; his lips parted and retracted in a mocking smile. His teeth, sharp teeth, irregular teeth, glistened in the light of a torch. His last desire at trying to absorb life was now foiled. His eyes opened wide and stared in revulsion at those around him. Tommy could not reach their souls. He could not feast upon their spiritual food. The brothers present were aligned. Bodies and necks were aligned. They all felt a flutter in their veins, but he had no power to take what was not his. Their moral strength was his mortal demise.

The brothers looked on as he nodded his head, recognizing his fate. He looked into Roger's eyes, his friend whom he had betrayed over and over. After a profound shriek that came from deep within his own being, his body vanished from their midst as though it were trying to catch up with the expelled souls that had just left in a sudden flash of light. The strange smell of scorched earth remained behind. The Brother-of-the-Purification came out and swept away the dirt upon which Tommy had vanished, and with that rite of purification, three splashes of the frigid lake water upon the spot of separation, he verified that Tommy had disappeared into the ages of ages, never to drain them of their strength again.

* * * * * *

Roger and Buck slowly walked back to their posts near the make-shift cave to await the next part of the evening. Their eyes reflected the sadness and the loss of Lucas-LeBoeuf-Tommy, someone whom they had known for twelve decades.

Tommy's transformation brought the last verse of the Book of Kanduúr into focus: *That which is false must vanish like unto the morning dew that is burned off by the incandescent rays of the iridescent sun. If the flash of stars crosses forever at the moment of his demise, the soul of the unjust one disperseth into realms forgotten, to remain unknown, never to be recalled.* Tommy was gone. The unknown assailant would be silenced forever.

The brothers lighted the twelve torches, and from the cave, dressed in white and gold, processed the embraced brothers; those who had been hidden from the grueling cleansing rite would become tonight what had been promised to them from of old. Roger and Buck escorted Joel, Billy, and the Coyote to their place on the shore. Adam and Troy chose to remain in mortality for a little while longer although they had been so embraced privately at the cabin during the Wolf Moon in January. Now, unlike in earlier days, the ritual of the meteors was explained to each. It was only fitting that they had their own free agency to chose. Their trustworthiness was sacrosanct even if they chose to remain in their present state. They would not tell the uninitiated. When the time was right, they could proceed.

The water that night in the lake near the cabin was bitter cold, but being uncomfortable during the three immersions was of short duration. The Coyote caught the chills the most, but as soon as he fell into his blessèd sleep, he was quickly wrapped up in a blanket and taken inside to lie beside the warmth of the fire.

Billy smiled when the meteor that signaled his entrance into the Inner Circle passed overhead. He had to wait a little over two minutes for the next one to pass, but he did not chill or complain about the water temperature. After the third pass of the celestial messenger, he put on the rose and silver robe that marked him as a true brother forever. He could heal and he could comfort those in dire need of a human's caring touch.

Joel was last. After his immersions, the Brother-of-the-Veil approached. When the veil was removed, the boy looked up and beheld Roger. "Thou art flesh of my flesh," he began, "bone of my bone, blood of my blood, and sinew of my sinew. Thou art that which was lost but now is found. Thou art the Alpha, restored unto our generation. For that purpose we have been driven here from lands beyond the veil, and from lands beyond the seas of time. As you complete me, so I complete you."

Stepping forth from the brethren appeared Beauregard Pettigrew and his father, Harland Pettigrew. The three surrounded Joel. Roger placed his index fingers and thumbs together to form a triangle on the right side of Joel's neck. Beauregard did the same on Joel's left side. Harland made the sacred triangle over the top vertebrae. All three gave the breath of infusion. He raised his head and observed the thousands of stars above him. The heavens were now quiet, and he sensed for the first time that he had purpose and being. He became aware of what felt like a molten fluid sluggishly moving through his veins, cleansing him and renewing his life. Joel did not fall into slumber, nor did he swoon away as others had before. He raised his arms in jubilation and banished the iniquity that the Crewe of Orestus had perpetrated on his band of brothers. He blessed Paul Docket for having led him to his family once again. He rejoiced in returning to his lineage that for so long had been absent.

Steve Gruder and Tim observed silently from the water's edge. They had been freed from the tyrant's grasp. They were now material once again. Others long forgotten came forward as renewed beings that once had been lost along the sands of time to the Orestian deceiver, and they all renewed their bonds, never to fear the unknown assailant again.

* * * * * *

On the other side of the shore, Paul Docket watched through binoculars as each of the twelve torches was cast into the lake. Clouds rolled in and sealed the sky. The festivities had ended. He heard shouts of joy and songs of praise arriving through the night on wings of melodies that his ears were never meant to hear.

He walked around the perimeter of the lake for a while and waited on the other side camouflaged by the tall grass until morning. Paul was biding his time until his first hunt. He felt weak. He was hungry. He was in the state of physical and emotional collapse. Paul approached the cabin through the woods before the new day dawned not wanting to be seen, so violated did he feel, so vile was his heart. His muscles ached, yet they appeared to be larger and much stronger than before. He couldn't explain the dichotomy between being so weak, yet feeling so strong.

All was quiet. The sun was poised to rise within moments. Searching, scanning for prey, he stalked as silently as possible. Tommy was right; natural instincts had taken over. Two birds flew from the thicket to the trees, but they would not satisfy his appetite. He paused and crouched once more. He listened. He heard the blood passing quickly through his veins.

The back side of the cabin wasn't so impressive, but he saw logs for splitting and bird feeders to keep the wild flocks alive until nature conquered the wildness again. Nothing interested him back there. He once thought the cabin had been a bastion of strength and beauty; he now detested what it stood for.

The sound of splashing water echoed in his ears. He experienced a shiver, an arousal that the morning oblation was near. From the side of the cabin, he watched Buck McDougal dive off the short pier several times into the frigid water of the mountain lake that morning before resting on the dock's edge near the canoe. The water invigorated him. Buck dangled his feet a few inches above the cold, murky water. The meteors had renewed him the night before. Paul crept quietly up behind him, as silently as a wolf stalks lightly on padded feet. The prey was in sight. His teeth began to ache. His muscles flexed and hardened. It was time to feed.

Made in the USA
Middletown, DE
15 October 2021